Stilett
For Me, Please!

E.V. HEWITT

Interior format by IndieDesignz.com

For my father—

a shoemaker, my teacher and introducer to women shoes.

"The stiletto is a feminine weapon that men just don't have."
Christian Louboutin

Chapter One

The sound of breaking glass stirred me from my sleep and I sat up quickly. Not moving an inch, I held my breath in anticipation of more noises. I slowly exhaled, counting the seconds. The second bang made me reach without thinking for the aluminum bat I kept under the bed. Someone was trying to break into the apartment! My heart was beating a hundred miles a minute as I tried to open my eyes but couldn't. They felt heavy, as if something was preventing me from opening them. In the darkness, I leant over again, my fingers searching around for the bat. I lost my balance, falling forward onto the floor with a loud thump.

Groaning, I turned over onto my back and reached up to touch my face, my fingers feeling for what was impairing my vision. Slowly, my brain registered what it was I'd forgotten: I had gone to sleep wearing an eye mask. Another crash echoed from downstairs. I forgot the bat. Pushing the eye mask over my head, I searched around the floor for something else to use as a weapon. Finally, my fingers came into contact with a long, sharp object. A stiletto. Perfect! I grabbed the shoe, clutching it as if my life depended on it.

"Kate!" I heard my name being called out from downstairs.

It didn't make sense. What kind of robber would break in and call out your name? Either I was still asleep and this was all an odd dream or it was some screwed up hallucination. Feeling fuzzy and slightly disoriented, I looked at the alarm clock on the dresser. 8:30am. I had only landed a handful of hours ago after a long flight and crossing who knows how many time zones. The building had to be on fire: why else would anyone try to break in?

"Kate, are you up there?"

Recognizing my friend Olivia's voice, I sighed heavily. Lying back down, I closed my eyes and hugged the stiletto to my chest.

"Good, she's here, there's her suitcase."

"Check upstairs, Emma."

Emma? What was she doing here? Scratch that, what were *they* doing here? At this point, I didn't care. I couldn't formulate a coherent thought. All I wanted was to go back to sleep. I didn't even have the energy to climb back into bed. Painfully, I pulled the comforter down from the bed and covered myself with it. Whatever those two were up to, I couldn't be bothered.

"What if she has someone up there with her?" I heard Emma say as they got closer.

"*Please,* who is going to be up there with her?" But for a moment, Olivia paused. "Catherine Seeley," she called out, sounding a bit unsure. "We are coming up. If there is anyone up there with you, they have exactly five seconds to get dressed!"

If I had any energy, I would have actually laughed. She was right. No one would be up here with me, but it was nice that she had given some warning. The bedroom door slammed open, startling me for a second time. I screamed. Emma screamed. Olivia switched the lights on and I squinted as my eyes tried to adjust.

"What the hell are you doing?!" Olivia demanded.

Clutching the stiletto, I stared at them. Emma held her hands over her chest. "You scared the shit out of me," she said. "What are you doing on the floor? And what's with the shoe?"

"I thought you were robbers! I was looking for my bat but I could only find this," I said.

"Really, Kate," Olivia said. "'Death by stiletto', I can see the headlines now. Put it down before you hurt yourself or, worse, break the shoe." She took it from my hand and dropped it on the ground.

"What were you going to do with a bat?" Emma asked.

I shrugged. "I'm still a New Yorker," I said, as if that answered everything.

Olivia looked down at me, shaking her head. "I can't believe this. How can you still be in bed? You agreed to meet us at my flat over an hour ago. Emma came in from the country," she said. I looked at Emma. She gave me an apologetic shrug. I really doubted poor Emma wanted to be here this early; but Olivia was a force to be reckoned with. Seizing the opportunity, I climbed back into bed, taking the comforter with me.

"Oh no you don't!" Olivia tugged at my arm but all she managed to do was push me further into my cocoon. "Let's go, up you get!" She pulled the comforter off me.

"Jesus, Olivia!" I sat up angrily and gave her a death stare, but it didn't faze her. I loved Olivia, but right now I was contemplating killing her.

She didn't back off. "You were supposed to call us when you landed. I offered to pick you up from the airport, we could have gone straight from there."

"Cut me some slack!" I begged. "My flight was delayed. And I'm sorry if I didn't think about calling you when I landed, I barely even remember how I got home. I got no sleep on the plane because a baby cried for the whole flight and the kid behind me was kicking my chair all the way from LAX to Heathrow."

"Olivia, look at her, she's in no shape to come with us. Maybe we should let her rest, she can meet us later," Emma suggested, handing me back the comforter. But Olivia grabbed it from her and threw it on the floor.

"No, I need all hands on deck," she said.

I shook my head in disbelief. Resisting the urge to stick my tongue out at her, I pulled the bed sheet over me and lay back down.

"You know what you need?" Olivia said.

"My comforter back and for you to go away?" I moaned.

"Coffee," she said, pulling the sheet from me. I shivered and curled up in the fetal position.

"Leave me alone," I whined. Although, a cup of coffee sounded very tempting.

"Coffee sounds like an excellent idea; I'll make you a cup while you get ready," Emma said. I sighed. I wasn't going to win this one. I had no choice but to get up.

"Thank you, Emma," I managed, and swung my legs off the bed. "You're mental, you know that?" I said to Olivia.

"You say that like it's an insult… We have less than an hour. Go to the bathroom, throw some cold water on your face and let's get going," Olivia instructed.

"How did you get in?" I asked, still a bit dazed.

"I used the spare keys you gave me."

"Remind me to ask you for my keys back. Those are emergency purposes only, Olivia," I reminded her. But I could see it was going in one ear and out the other. It was coming back to me why she was here…

Olivia looked at me with piercing blue eyes. "This is an emergency."

"*Please,* this is so not an emergency –"

"Let's agree to disagree, shall we? We don't have all day. You could come in your pajamas, or you have exactly five minutes to throw on some clothes. Take your pick."

I laughed. "All right then, calm down…" The look on her face was enough to make me rethink lying back down. I grabbed the clothes that I had taken off at the foot of the bed a few hours before and headed to the bathroom, quickly shuffling out of my pajamas and into my jeans and sweater.

"Hurry up, it is critical that we get there ASAP! Olivia yelled. "Doors open at 10am. If we don't get there soon there will be nothing left!"

I paused, my hands on the zipper of my jeans. "The store hasn't even opened yet?" I said.

"Are you crazy? No one is going to be out there! Only the three of us will be there when the doors open the day after Christmas because we are insane!" I zipped up my jeans, quickly brushed my teeth and threw cold water on my face to wake myself up a bit. Looking in the mirror, I cringed. My eyes were bloodshot; my hair was in knots. I needed a good combing and perhaps a bit of makeup to help me not look so horrid. I picked up my hairbrush in one hand and opened my makeup case with the other.

Olivia pushed her way into the bathroom and took the hairbrush from my hand. "Are you kidding? We have no time for all that!" She walked out and I picked up the brush again, trying to pass it through my hair to no avail.

"Here," Olivia said, marching back in and handing me a pair of sunglasses. "You can fix your face later. Tie your hair up in a bun and put a hat on. Let's go."

I stared at her, shocked. Who was this woman? And where was my friend? Olivia never left the house without makeup unless it was an emergency, and even then she managed to put on mascara and lip gloss.

"Are you all right? I've never seen you like this. You weren't even like this for your wedding. I don't understand why we have to go so early. You know what would get me going? Breakfast! Let's go eat first," I said, giving her a soft smile.

Olivia grabbed my shoulders, almost hysterical. "Listen to what I'm about to say very carefully," she said slowly. "My wedding was not the biggest sale Harrods has. I've waited all year for this; they have nearly every major designer at a discount." She stared at me, her hands still on my shoulders, waiting for me to react as if what she had just revealed was enough to convince me to run out of there like a mad woman. I vaguely remembered agreeing to this lunacy right before I left for the holidays. I figured she would have forgotten. At this moment, I wasn't sure who was the crazy one: Olivia for coming up with the stupid idea of going to the sale, or me for having agreed to come back early to go with her. She was this worked up over clothes? I mean, I loved designer anything on sale but, right now, sleep was more important. And let's not forget that she had practically broken into my apartment. I was in no mood at all.

"Really, Olivia, I think I should stay here. I don't feel well, I can't think straight…"

"What is there to think about?" she asked. "There are Christian Louboutins on sale, for God's sake."

I shrugged. "I've seen them on sale before. What's the big deal?"

"Have you got them at seventy percent off before?" she asked.

My eyes widened, finally realizing why Olivia was in such a frenzy. She nodded with a smile, knowing that I had at last grasped the importance of this sale. I immediately began to calculate how much money I could save and started to grin like a cat. My jet lag was magically disappearing.

"Emma!" I called out. "Please put the coffee in my travel mug to go!" I turned to Olivia."What are we still doing here? Chop chop, let's go!" I said, putting on my sunglasses as we headed downstairs.

Chapter Two

The three of us got in the elevator and I took a big gulp of coffee, burning my tongue in the process but not caring as the caffeine went through my system.

"Coffee making it better? Emma asked.

I nodded. "Keep them coming all day and I won't hurt anyone. What tube are we taking?" I asked, taking another sip.

"The tube! Oh, honey, it's Boxing Day, public transport is a nightmare. I've got a taxi waiting for us downstairs," Olivia said. She had left nothing to chance. She looked at her watch, frowning, as we stepped outside and climbed into the taxi.

I leaned in toward Emma. "I don't recall her ever having been like this over a sale before, have you?"

Emma shook her head inconspicuously. "It's a bit frightening, I must say," she whispered as Olivia gave instructions to the driver.

"Right, let's go over the plan," Olivia began once we were on the road. "Upon arrival, we immediately head to the shoe department and we don't stop to see what's happening on the ground floor, no matter how enticing the sales may seem—and, believe me, it will be very tempting. Do not get distracted. We have a mission. Once completed, we can go back and explore the store, but only after."

Emma gave me a worried look. Olivia sounding like a shopping drill sergeant was quite intimidating. I had never bothered to come back to London in time for the post-Christmas sales, but the prospect of walking out with a pair of Louboutins for seventy percent off was enough for me to let Olivia be a raging maniac if it got me the shoes.

This was a strength of hers: she always found the posh sales. And I knew that one of my weaknesses was shoes. It had taken me twenty-odd years to discover my strengths and weaknesses. Ask any woman and she could tell you hers with absolute certainty. If I asked Emma, she would say her strengths lay in the arts, Olivia would say fashion, and as for me, I was certain about three things. The first was I had a shoe obsession and I was not ashamed to admit it. What woman didn't? I loved all types. But my weakness, my absolute weakness, was designer shoes. Not just any designer shoes; on sale, steeply discounted ones. The rush that I got when I could say I had bought them at fifty percent off or more was unparalleled. Place me in the Sahara desert: if shoes were water, I would find them. Place me in a store and I could find the best pair of shoes at the best price. It was a gift. I had managed to acquire an exquisite collection (none at retail price) that I was extremely proud of. I still silently squealed sometimes going through my closet.

Shoes made me happy, and I certainly deserved happiness. I had always done what was expected of me. I was a good girl who had gone to college and carved out a very nice career for herself. I was moving up the ladder and, for the past five years, I had been living in London, a city that I'd longed to reside in since I was a child. And no, I do not speak with a British accent, though my friends back home say I sound more and more like a Brit every time they hear me. My friends here, however, can't believe how strong my American accent is after having lived in London for so long.

Olivia sighed at the traffic. "Ridiculous! I did not sneak out of the house, leaving Brandon in bed, to be faced with the crap…" She leaned in towards the driver. "Excuse me, can you take Sloane Street?"

I lifted my shades and whispered to Emma. "Did she just say she snuck out?"

Emma nodded. "Snuck out on Brandon and his family," she whispered back.

Olivia turned to face us, making Emma jump. "At this rate, there'll be nothing left but the Collinses!"

I smiled at Olivia's use of the term Collinses, because the second thing I knew about myself was that I loved *Pride And Prejudice.* My love for *Pride And Prejudice* was eternal. I had read the book countless times, watched every cinema and television version ever made. I was so obsessed that I had concluded that there were four types of shoes every woman owned (and, in my opinion, the description fitted the men they dated, too): the Collinses, the Bingleys, the Wickhams and the Darcys. Yes, I had named them after the lead male characters of the book. We all had these shoes in our closets, under our beds, wherever we were able to store them.

Stop for a moment and think… How are these shoes similar to the men in our lives? Who doesn't remember Mr Collins? Plain, boring, a tad ridiculous Mr Collins. Jane Austen described him as sensible and cautious. He was reliable; he wouldn't give you any surprises, he was very predictable. Now, think of a pair of shoes that fit that description. Plain, no sparkle, no color outside of the basics… We all had a pair or two like this. There was nothing wrong with this type of shoe, it was reliable but boring—just like the men who were Collinses.

The Bingleys, now, these were the kitten heels, the shoes you would wear to feel prim and proper. When we wanted to feel good about ourselves, they did the job. Mr Bingley was "excessively handsome, extremely agreeable". This man, you were proud to be seen with. We took care of these shoes and would wear them quite often.

The Wickhams were naughty and sinful shoes. "His appearance was greatly in his favor; he had all the best part of beauty, a fine countenance, a good figure, and a pleasing address… Mr Wickham was the happy man towards whom almost every female eye was turned." Just like the men, women lusted after these. They hurt like hell after a couple of hours but you endured the pain for the compliments. These shoes, I loved, and were the type I had the most of in my closet. And thinking about the men I had dated, this was the one I knew the most about. What I really sought, however, was something altogether different—the Darcys.

For me, The Darcys were the crème de la crème: classic, elegant and almost annoyingly perfect. Even in the book, the ladies declared he was better than Mr Bingley. Austen described his "fine, tall person, handsome features, noble mien" and you could say the same of the shoes—you knew they were something special. These were the designer shoes I got on sale. "I only wear Darcys," is what I wanted to say. I immediately thought of my Jimmy Choos, my colorful Christian Louboutins, but I desired one kind above all else—they were harder to acquire because they never went on sale: the classic black Louboutins. My ultimate Darcy's. No matter how I tried to justify it, I couldn't commit to paying retail price. I would start to think about all that could go wrong; the heel would break or they would get scuffed. All sorts of scenarios ran through my head. I passed them in stores, longing to try them, afraid to do so.

Then, one day, somehow, I got lucky—or so I thought—and met my own real Mr Darcy. Only it turned out he was a cross between Mr Wickham and the devil; though, if I had to choose the lesser of the evils, the devil would probably be the winner.

Which led to the third thing I knew about myself: I had horrible taste in men. If a man was a shoe, I might as well walk barefoot!

Chapter Three

I'm sorry, miss, but the streets have been closed off," said the driver. "I'll have to turn around and head—"

Olivia cut him off. "We can get out here. Cheers!"

"We can what?" Emma asked as Olivia paid the taxi driver.

"Come on, ladies, let's go," she scooted us out. The moment she got out of the cab, she began to run. We started running after her for no other reason than that she was running, and I stopped as my coffee began to spill out. Olivia turned around, reached for my travel mug and, in the same motion, chucked it in the trash can.

"Oh my God! I liked that mug. I can't believe you just did that!" I cried as I raced after her.

"I'll buy you another! It's a casualty of war," she called back.

I turned to Emma, grabbing her hand as I stopped running. "Is she for real?" I yelled. "What war? We are going to a freaking department store." This was ridiculous. We had plenty of time to get there.

As we turned the corner towards the store, we come to an abrupt stop. My eyes widened in shock as I stared at the largest crowd I've ever seen trying to get into Harrods. The only time I'd seen this much shopping chaos was in the States on Black Friday. After we've spent time with our loving family and friends, giving thanks for what we have, we're off like vultures, greedily shopping in the sales, fighting off the crowds. This was the British version of that. The city was still decorated in holiday cheer, only no one was happy being pushed and shoved like cattle through the doors.

"This is exactly what I was trying to avoid. But no matter, stay close, if we separate, head to the fifth floor!" Olivia yelled. Everyone was practically on top of each other and my feet didn't even touch the ground as I was carried through the doors. This was why I steered clear of these types of sales. The crowd was already making me anxious, and the headache I had wasn't helping. Grunting, I tried to move, but I was being shoved in all directions. Emma grabbed my hand and pushed me through.

"I can't believe I agreed to this. How did she manage to convince us to do this?" I asked, biting my lip as I got elbowed.

"I have no idea!" Emma said as we maneuvered our way towards the escalators. Olivia was already near the top, taking the last of the steps two at a time.

The moment we stepped into the Shoe Heaven, my complaining ceased. The chaos was forgotten and my heart began to race. It was like stepping into a candy land of shoes: Prada, Chanel, Jimmy Choo, Alexander McQueen, Stella McCartney… the list went on and on. There were flats, boots, stilettos, all lined up for my choosing, and my fingers were itching to pick them up.

People talked about meeting *the one*—when your eyes would lock across the room, the crowds would part and time would stand still. Well, I had never experienced that with a man.

Shoes, however, were another matter. In the middle of the melee, through all the noise and excitement, it caught my attention… *the shoe.* My eyes focused on a pair of jeweled black Jimmy Choo stilettos. In my opinion, love at first sight existed with shoes, not with men. I felt myself being pulled towards them like a magnet until I was a few feet away from touching them.

"Excuse me, you must get in the queue." A well-dressed salesman broke my connection with the shoes. Five angry looking women were nearly, practically hissing as they gave me dirty looks.

"Oh," I said in surprise, finally seeing the ropes that were blocking the entrance. I looked behind me; there must have been at least twenty women in front of us. I had never seen anything like it.

Olivia grabbed my hand. "We'll come back!" she said.

"But I want to check those out," I said, looking back at the shoes.

"Trust me on this one," she said, pulling me towards the back of the store, arriving at yet another line. My mouth opened, ready to protest, and I saw it. The Mecca. Louboutins arranged from one end of the wall to the next: pinks, yellows, reds… all the colors of the rainbow. I began to drool.

"I can't believe there are queues to look at the shoes. You would think they're giving the shoes away for free," Emma said loudly as we made our way to the end of the line.

Olivia pushed her blonde hair back. "They practically are," she said. "And I intend to leave with a pair of shoes or there will be blood." She smiled deviously.

"And you thought she was bridezilla at the wedding," I noted to Emma. "This is a totally different person."

I had to admit, it was a bit ridiculous to be standing inside a store in line as if you were queueing for a club with two bouncers waiting to let you in. For the prices we were about to pay, they should have been serving us champagne. Olivia was stretching her neck, trying to look over everybody's heads.

"Look at that!" Olivia hit my arm hard and groaned as she watched a woman trying on a pair of scorching sandals. "Those are gorgeous. I could wear them to the gala…" she murmured to herself.

"I swear she has a pair just like those… really, how much of a discount are we talking about?" Emma asked. She hated spending money on things she deemed unnecessary. But that was Emma: the practical one.

Emma Whitman and I had met when I first moved to London from New York City. It was a random encounter at the National Gallery. I went for a guided tour, and Emma was placed on tour duty. She was an assistant curator at the time. I had been eagerly anticipating my first visit to the museum, and in came Emma: tall and slim and proper. She looked as if she had been crying. Red hair pulled back in a tidy bun, glasses hanging perfectly on a chain, tweed skirt, black businesslike pumps, holding her hanky in her hand as she discussed the paintings with a soft, shaky voice. It was depressing and, one by one, the group wandered off until only I was left. She apologized profusely and ended up telling me her problem, which we discussed all the way around the museum. We've been friends ever since. Emma tended to date the Collinses. One thing none of us could understand was how an intelligent, beautiful woman could be stuck on the simple shoes of life. In turn, she didn't understand our fascination with shoes.

"Emma, remember: size 36, 37 and 38; just grab, grab, grab, I'll sort it out once we sit," Olivia instructed as the line finally began to move. When we were let in, Olivia, who had taken off her coat, jetted straight to her size. I walked a little slower towards the rack and picked up a shoe, turning it over. Hmm… regular price seven hundred pounds, on sale for four hundred and fifty. Not bad, but it had to be less than that; it wasn't getting my heart pumping. I looked up and saw Olivia running from one end of the rack to the other, grabbing shoes like a crazy woman. All you could see was her blonde hair bouncing up and down.

I chuckled, looking away as my iPhone began to vibrate. I looked at the screen, scrolling down. Only one name could make me come to a halt in the middle of the biggest shoe sale… Jackson Barnes. The ex, whom I now affectionately called evil spawn. I hadn't heard from or seen him since the horrible break-up several months back. Of course, when I first met him, I didn't think he would turn out to be the devil incarnate. On paper, Jack was a real catch: great family, fantastic job, had never been married and had a proper posh British accent (which I had loved ever since I watched Colin Firth playing Mr Darcy). After dating more than my share of Wickhams, I thought I had found Mr Darcy at last. He was perfect, or at least appeared to be. Jack was what I had envisioned the man I wanted to be with: tall, dark and handsome. The man was brilliant and had a Cambridge degree to prove it. He was known in the City for being the man who made deals happen. Spoke three languages, could practically create a budget for the country if required. He was almost flawless… almost. Except he had one tiny flaw that Mr Darcy did not possess—he cheated. Jack didn't understand the meaning of the word "faithful". For him, it meant "go shag other women while being in a relationship". Jack had turned out to be Mr Wickham, and even though I wore Wickhams on my feet, that was not the type of man I wanted to end up with.

Taking a deep breath, I read the email again. I couldn't decline going to the meeting my boss had scheduled even if it meant seeing Jack. I had known this day would come. Actually, I was surprised it hadn't happened sooner—my suspicions were that Jack had something to do with that. I felt myself getting angry at the thought of seeing him again after all this time. The first few weeks after it ended, I cried, I repeatedly called, emailed and texted him. If this had been a few months ago, I would have run to this meeting, taking the opportunity to see him. Now, I sought what every woman wanted when wronged… revenge. I needed him to regret the day he broke my heart. I wanted blood. Well, I wanted him to see what he had lost, anyway. But a week to prepare? Was that possible?

"Kate, put the phone away!" Olivia called out anxiously. When I looked up to tell her to give me a moment, I stopped, my mouth open in amazement. Her arms were stretched out like she was holding a beach ball, only she was holding about fifteen shoes. "These are your size, regular price is eight hundred pounds!"

I gave her a nod, turned my attention back to my phone and began typing a response. "You know my rule, Olivia," I said.

"Of course I know your silly rule. But these are heavily discounted."

I smiled. "Heavily discounted" to Olivia could mean about twenty-five pounds off. I continued to type without looking up.

"The first number is a one," she said.

Immediately, I stopped typing. My eyes shot up and took in the shoe that she was barely managing to keep hold of. A fuchsia-pink suede stiletto, peep-toe. My mouth began to dry up and I felt my heart start to race. Had I heard her correctly? She was wrong; it wasn't possible that the price of that beauty began with a one. Those shoes were last season at most.

"Excuse me, are you done with those?" a woman asked, approaching Olivia, eyeing *my* shoe.

"NO!" I said, making my way to Olivia's side and grabbing it. "She's holding it for me," I said in my boldest voice. There was no way she was going to put one finger on it.

"But you have others like it in your hand," The woman protested to Olivia.

"We're trying *all* of them," Olivia interrupted, clutching the shoes closer to her chest. The woman gave us a nasty look and, muttering to herself, walked away. Olivia handed Emma some of the shoes. “Be careful, I don’t trust her,” she warned, her eyebrows lifting. “Mind where you put the shoes, someone might nick them.”

“You do realize that you only have *one* of each, right?” Emma pointed out. “What exactly is she going to do with one shoe?”

She was right, of course. It was silly to think the woman was going to steal a single shoe, but at this moment, I didn’t care that Olivia was behaving like a mad woman. The only thing I cared about was verifying the price. I held my breath as I turned the shoe over. There it was. The sale tag. One hundred and thirty-five pounds! I wanted to cry, scream and shout. I had never seen a pair Christian Louboutins at that price. I sat down, removed my boot and sock and said a little prayer, my fashion life passing before my eyes. *Please, please, let these fit.* I was not getting this close for these shoes not to fit me. Closing my eyes, I pushed my foot in. They fit! They fit!

I looked at Olivia and Emma with the biggest grin. “They’re perfect!” I said.

And I knew exactly what I would wear them with and when.

Chapter Four

Today was the day. I had been up an hour before I needed to. I hadn't been able to sleep with anticipation. My mind was running a mile a minute imagining all the different scenarios that could take place when Jack finally saw me. Each involved his jaw dropping to the floor when he laid eyes on me. I had strategically planned the ultimate makeover all week. Diet… check. Haircut… check. Mani and pedi… check, check. I planned like a general heading for battle. The only thing that was capable of ruining my choice was Mother Nature; she did not care what your plans were, or what shoes you wanted to wear. It had been raining all week leading up to the meeting. So much so, I had a backup outfit in case the rain didn't let up. I had gone to bed praying the weather would change by some miracle. I needed this day to be perfect.

The moment I looked out the window, I smiled. No rain! The sky was clear and, on the horizon, the sun was rising. I jumped up and down and began the process of getting ready. I put in my hot rollers and inspected my outfit and, most importantly, the shoes. Opening the box, I grinned: Jack wasn't going to know what had hit him!

Two hours later, I still felt joyful as I walked down Canary Wharf in the four-inch stilettos—not an easy task. A true stiletto wearer becomes an expert in avoiding the puddles and cracks, especially on the streets of London. I hummed my way to the office, catching a few guys giving me *the look.* I felt and looked great, like a strong, independent woman. After all, I was from the Bridget Jones and Carrie Bradshaw generation. After everything they went through, they got their man. I just needed to teach mine a lesson. I was ready to kick his British arse!

My heels clicked on the marble floor as I walked into the lobby and made my way through security. I stopped near the elevator banks, took out my lip gloss and sprayed a bit more perfume. My stomach was in knots as the elevator made its way up to the offices. When the doors opened, I paused for a brief second and took a deep breath. It was now or never.

I had been to this office countless times, but, for some reason, today, I felt out of place as I made my way to the reception desk.

"Kate Seeley to see Jackson Barnes," I told the receptionist with a smile. I grabbed the handle of my handbag tightly.

"Someone will be right with you," she said, eyeing me up and down, her nose wrinkling a little. The looks she was giving me were starting to make me feel a little self-conscious. There was nothing wrong with my outfit, I thought, as I tugged down my skirt.

"Ms Seeley?" A woman wearing Collinses came out to greet me.

"Yes," I said, my heart beating quickly.

"I'm sorry but Mr Barnes will not be joining you today. Unfortunately, his earlier meeting is running behind schedule and he asked that this one commence without him." She looked at me, her glasses falling to the bridge of her nose, and rolled her eyes as she looked at my shoes. Suddenly, I felt ridiculous, inappropriately dressed, as I took in my surroundings; the women were dressed in smart, safe suits, not in black and fuchsia dresses.

He wasn't going to be here?! I didn't know whether to start laughing or crying. All the planning, the rehearsed speech, everything had been for nothing! I felt ridiculous. The dress was wrong, I knew it, and now I had to walk in there looking like I belonged at a wedding rather than in an office.

Without a word, I followed her towards the conference room. Eyes looked up at me and I tried not to meet anyone's gaze as I glanced around for an empty chair. Quickly spotting one at the end of the table, I made my way towards it. I just needed to get through this meeting. The day was ruined, it couldn't get any worse. Suddenly, I became aware of a pair of familiar cornflower blue eyes staring at me. My blood ran cold and I realized the day was just about to get worse... much, much worse.

The eyes that were giving me the most disapproving look of all belonged to none other than my archenemy, Philip Spencer. Yes, Spencer from Spencer & Lockhart, my firm. His family had been founders and owners of the company for over two hundred years. Philip was arrogant, rude and always behaved with a sense of entitlement

The first time I met him was at a polo tournament sponsored by Spencer & Lockhart. It was actually where I also first met Jack. Now that I think of it, Philip was the reason Jack began speaking to me at the event—another thing to add to my list of reasons to hate Philip Spencer.

I had been so excited to attend something so British, I had gone a tad overboard with the hat, the dress and the shoes. To mark the occasion, I had purchased my first pair of Jimmy Choos: beautiful beige and white stilettos. What I hadn't considered was that I would be walking on grass all day, and my heels kept sinking into the ground. When I stepped into a pile of horse manure, I completely lost it; they were my first expensive pair of shoes and I freaked out (rightfully so). Perhaps yelling, "Fuck! Is this horse shit?!" at the top of my lungs was not the appropriate way to behave, but I was literally having a nervous breakdown.

That is where Philip came to what I thought was my rescue. At first, he actually looked quite handsome, almost like Colin Firth's moment coming out of the pond as Mr Darcy in his white and blue polo uniform. Instead, he looked at me quite crossly and said, "You must refrain from using such profanity on the grounds, this is a civilized sport. I don't know how sports are conducted in America but such language is not appropriate here." I tuned him out, staring at him, my lips trembling in shock and embarrassment as I stood in dung while he lectured me.

I was ready to start crying, when Jack (who was playing on the opposing team) came to my rescue. He made Philip go away, apologized for his rude behavior and turned to me with the most captivating smile I had ever seen. And when he offered to clean my shoes, I knew I had found my knight in shining armor. He had saved me from embarrassing myself further in front of Philip and, most importantly, he had saved my shoes.

Since then, I had detested Philip. I never forgot how he made me feel like a foreigner who didn't belong. I would run into him here and there in the corridors, but I would avoid him, only speaking to him directly if necessary. The girls in the office loved him. He was successful and, on top of it, handsome. I wished he had warts on his face but sadly he didn't. Luckily for me, he was sent to New York not long after, and I barely saw him these days.

But of course, on the day I already felt like my stomach had been kicked in, I had to deal with him. I quickly sat down, pretending he wasn't there.

"Kate, what are you wearing? Did you forget you had a meeting today?" he leaned in, startling me.

"It's called a dress," I hissed at him, placing my documents on the table and giving him the dirtiest look I could manage. He looked back at me, holding my gaze equally.

The meeting began and we both looked away from each other. For the first time in ages, I questioned what I was doing here, three thousand miles away from home. The meeting dragged on for a couple of hours, and as it was coming to an end, the clouds rolled in to match my mood. It was going to rain.

"Shit!" I said, biting my lip. I had completely lost my mind this morning and had not packed a pair of Collinses. What had I been thinking? I wasn't some tourist. I knew better than to think it wouldn't rain in London at some point during the day.

"What's the matter?" Philip asked.

"I forgot my umbrella," I said, shoving the papers tightly into the smallest bag I owned. Stupid, stupid... I looked out again.

"Hm," was all he said as he walked away. Sighing in relief, I picked up my trench coat. The last thing I wanted to do was get into an argument with him.

"Kate," he called out as I turned to leave. He was holding a gentleman's umbrella.

"Here," he said. He looked me over, his eyes resting on my shoes, and shook his head. I pressed my lips together angrily. Once again, he was judging me. If he'd had the last umbrella on earth which, in my desperate moment, he did, I wasn't going to take it.

"No, thank you, I'm sure the rain will hold off," I said.

He smirked. "Doubtful, but suit yourself." He lowered it to his side. It was taking all my will power not to take off my shoe and hit him over the head with it. Calling him a few names silently in my head, I left the conference room in search of something that I could use as an emergency shield from the rain. Spotting the stack of newspapers on the coffee table in the waiting room, I grabbed one quickly.

Making my way outside, I knew what I desperately needed

was a taxi and pronto. As the first few drops fell on my face, I saw a newsstand selling umbrellas out of the corner of my eye. *Please, please, hold on.* I silently pleaded with the sky. I took out some money and handed it to the man, and opened the tiny excuse for an umbrella. It barely covered my head; it would definitely not shield the shoes.

How could I have been so careless? If a million-dollar company needed refinancing, I was your girl. Make a guy jealous, I was useless. I had failed miserably! Somehow, without even trying, Jack had got the upper hand. He had won this round without even being there! How was that even possible?

The drops came down a bit faster and I walked quicker, searching for a taxi. It was a race against the downpour that was threatening to start. This was going to be nearly impossible at the beginning of rush hour, when everyone wanted one. And, once again, as if Mother Nature had a bone to pick with me, the skies opened and the rain began to pour down. People began scrambling for cover, and I stood on the corner, spotting the only available taxi. I quickly hailed it and attempted to run, tricky on slippery wet pavement, as cold water was already seeping through the peep-toe into the soles of my shoes. I stretched out my hand to open the taxi door when I was pushed aside. I stared at the man who had done the pushing in shock and we grabbed the door handle at the same time.

"Oh, come on! Are you serious?" I asked, looking up at him in a daring sort of way. He stared at me and almost backed off.

"Sorry, luv, I was here first," he had the audacity to say.

"No, you weren't. I was running for the taxi, you must have seen me. You were obviously behind me…" I sighed, seeing that I was losing the battle. He was not letting go of the door and neither was I. He looked tired and was getting wet, but so was I. There was only one solution.

"Could we at least share?" I asked politely, biting my

tongue. The longer he took to consider my suggestion, the more damage was befalling my shoes. I even cracked a tight smile, staring at his weary blue eyes. This was all he was going to get—flirting was not one of my strongest points. If I had been Olivia, he would probably be paying the fare.

"Where are you going?" he asked hesitantly, his hawk nose twisting from one side to the other.

"The West End."

He yanked the door, making me jump back. "Sorry, I'm not heading in that direction," he said. You're better off taking the tube. Good day."

I grabbed his arm without thinking. He looked taken aback and slightly afraid. The taxi driver looked at us, annoyed.

"Make up your minds," he grumbled.

"Give us a second!" I said.

I turned back to the man. "Right, listen, mate, give me a break here. You don't know the kind of day I've had." He clearly didn't care but I told him anyway. "I feel like I just got dumped all over again by my ex. Today was supposed to be my day of revenge and you know what? He didn't even show! Do you see my outfit? Take a look at my feet." I pointed to them like a crazy woman. He had no choice but to look at them. "Do you have any idea what these are?" I asked, startling him. "*Do you*?"

"Shoes?" he responded, unsure of what I was going to do.

Frankly, I knew I'd lost it. I laughed. "Of course, you're a man, what do you know? These are Christian Louboutins and they are getting ruined because I'm standing here having to explain myself to *you*." I looked down at them with pity.

He shook his head. "Crazy American. Good luck with that," he said, getting into the taxi and slamming the door. The taxi driver sped off.

"Whatever happened to chivalry, you twat?!" I yelled out. The umbrella lifted up with a gust of wind and I fought to get it back down. I couldn't believe him. The men in this city… and they wondered why so many women were still single? Perhaps I was going soft: what had happened to the New Yorker in me? I had been living here too long. I should have shoved him out of the way and taken control of the situation. I could have taken him down.

I scanned the street trying to figure out what to do next. The hotel across the road was my only chance of catching another taxi. As I begin to cross over, a taxi pulled in. An older man signaled it and waved me over. He looked like the quintessential English gentleman. I closed my crappy umbrella, feeling my hair was plastered to my head anyway. Chivalry wasn't dead after all. Not the kind of knight in shining armor I'd had in mind but, nevertheless, a gentleman.

He waved at something to my right and I realized he wasn't looking at me. From the corner of my eye, something caught my attention. Walking towards us, almost in slow motion, was a stunning woman, legs up to the sky and looking like Heidi Klum's twin sister. She had bouncy blonde hair, which the rain seemed to avoid unlike my soaked brown mop. I couldn't stop staring. Her tight beige dress looked like it had been painted on. And her shoes! I gasped as I looked at her feet, the flash of recognizable red soles. Dear God, those weren't just any pair of Louboutins, but the ones featured in this month's Vogue, listed as 'price per request'. For someone like me, that meant if you needed to ask, you couldn't afford them. Those did not go on sale, and if they did, they were never discounted enough. These were shoes that I could not possibly afford without giving up some basic necessities like shelter, food, possibly a kidney… minor things. She strutted with power. She was hot and she knew it. Better yet, she was paying no attention to the rain like I was. If her shoes got ruined, so what? She probably had three more pairs waiting for her at home. I pictured myself walking like her, with those marvelous shoes, my hair flowing behind me in the wind, the perfect song playing in the background like a movie. Men lining up with taxi doors opened, begging me to choose them.

"Excuse me."

My thoughts were broken as she brushed past me. The man was grinning like an idiot, helping her get into *my* taxi. I was left staring in shock for the second time in mere minutes. He got it for *her*, not for me! He hadn't even noticed me. I looked at my umbrella clutched in my hand, using all my willpower not to clobber him over the head with it. Our eyes met and he tilted his bowler hat at me. I rolled my eyes at him and made my way across the street. Not only was I useless at planning revenge, I was also not taxi-worthy for any man. My only chance now was to run back to the train station. Opening the umbrella, I dug for my mobile and texted Emma to say I was running late. I was soaked, and all because I had refused to swallow my pride and accept Philip's offer. But the thought of him looking down at me was enough to shake off any regret. The second I made it to Canary Wharf Station, the rain magically ceased. *Seriously?* I cursed under my breath and pushed through the crowd. I opened my purse, my fingers searching around for my Oyster card but I couldn't find it. I was being shoved in all directions as people tried to get through.

"Ouch!"

A man brushed past me. "Bloody tourist," he mumbled under his breath, slamming his wallet on the scanner. Ignoring him, I looked again, found the card and made my way through. With every step that I took, my shoes made a squishing sound that made me wince. I caught sight of my reflection and shook my head. I looked like a hot mess. Even my makeup was running. The most sensible thing to do would be to head home and change but I was already late. Suddenly, I began to feel the hairs on the back of my neck stand up. I turned and, for a moment, time stood still and I wished the earth would open up and swallow me. I stared at the dark, handsome man. *It couldn't be.* I bit my lip frantically, taking another look.

It was him! He hadn't spotted me yet. If I jetted out of here in the next thirty seconds, it was possible that I could escape unnoticed. "Shit, shit, shit!" I huffed under my breath. How could this be happening to me? I had been ready this morning, but not now, looking like a drowned rat. Fate couldn't be this cruel. I turned and bolted towards the escalator, not caring who I had to shove out of my way and ignoring the looks and comments I was getting. Stupidly, I made the same mistake as Lot's wife and looked back, knowing as I did that I shouldn't. This time, piercing brown eyes opened wide with recognition and surprise. At that moment, turning into a pillar of salt would have been preferable.

"Kate!"

Pretending not to hear him, I put my head down and began taking the escalator stairs two at a time. Please let there be a train at the platform. Please!

"Catherine!"

I pushed my way off and ran to the platform as the train doors were about to close. I practically jumped like Michael Jordan, squeezing myself into the crowded train cart. Now the question was had he managed to get on as well? My hands were shaking as I held on to the pole, not daring to look up. I didn't want to give him any eye contact. If he had happened to make it on, then I would pretend I'd only just seen him—easy enough. The doors closed and I finally looked up. He wasn't anywhere in sight. I sighed in relief and my heart started beating again. The chorus of *Alleluia! Alleluia!* seemed to play all around me, I wanted to clap and jump up and down. I was safe!

Chapter Five

No one on the train was any the wiser that I had dodged a major bullet. The carriage was silent of chatter: the only noise was the rattling of the train and music pumping loudly from the headphones of a guy who was practically on top of me. I shifted my weight from one soaked foot to the other, mentally cursing myself for not having worn my Collinses. I could have worn the black ballet slippers I got for twenty quid. Now look at me. I was supposed to be a smart, educated, sensible woman, not this sad-looking creature who had ruined a good pair of shoes. Where was my gumption? I had been so focused on making Jack jealous that I had lost all sense of logic and had left my tote bag at home because it didn't flatter my outfit.

If I had any sense, I wouldn't have cared to begin with whether he was going to be there or not. I should have acted like it was a normal meeting: no fuss, no planning, I should have just worn a smart business outfit. But I knew the real reason I was acting so irrationally… I was still in love with him. There, I had finally admitted it. Deep down, I still loved Jack, no matter what I said to my friends or the lies I told myself. Even though I knew I was better off without him and that I had done the right thing in breaking up with him, I still loved him and was still the fool.

Once again, I was making excuses, only this time, I was trying to convince myself that I no longer felt anything for him. There had been no joy when I found out that he'd been cheating on me. Even when the signs were so obvious, I tried to deny them. I sighed, thinking back to the excuses I had made then, when he said he was working late, and I ran into his colleagues who clearly were not at the office. I made excuses that he had to work harder to prove that he earned the right to be there. I didn't want to believe he was lying because I was in love with the illusion I had created. My friends told me to wake up when all the inconsistencies continued. He would conveniently not hear his mobile when I called, he was vague when he went out with the guys, and sometimes I thought I smelled perfume on him when he came home. But all I did was make more excuses instead of confronting him. He was so clever and his tactics were so calculated that I briefly thought it was possible I had imagined the whole thing… until the day I saw them together. Then I knew I had to end it. Even when we broke up, I still hoped he would apologize and swear never to do it again, but instead he ran like a coward.

Soon after breaking things off, I had a moment of panic and thought that perhaps I hadn't given us a fair chance. I called, left messages, but instead of apologizing, Jack turned it around, blamed me for breaking up with him. I had been a mess and had only recently been feeling better. My friends were there, helping me through it. Bless them, they told me that it was clearly his loss and that once I moved on and found another guy, Jack would come back, begging. But what happens when that doesn't occur? What do you do when you can't find the one after countless dates and girls' nights out? I was the good one in the relationship. How come he got to move on with someone else and I was left missing him, hoping to find someone to replace the void inside? It was brutal out there.

Like I said, with men, I sucked. This is why I stood by shoes. Have you ever seen a woman's face when she finds a pair she falls in love with? It's practically orgasmic. All is forgotten in that moment, and you are transported to a parallel universe where none of your problems exist. What else made you feel special and didn't care about how much you weighed, if you were single or married? The right pair of shoes cured the blues —cheaper than therapy.

I found that dating a man was like choosing a pair of shoes… women spotted, women tried, women acquired. Only with shoes, there were no politics, no games and no grey areas. You chose the shoes, they were yours, unlike most men who took forever to even admit they liked you. Shoes were quite upfront. If they were going to hurt you, the pain was instant. Every so often, there was a shoe that you instantly fell in love with and all was great until you tried them on and they broke your feet. However, the shoes gave you the option to either continue to wear them despite the pain and discomfort, or quit and never wear them again. So if you chose to try to break them in, you and only you were responsible for the pain.

A deceitful man, however, was more malicious than that. He didn't immediately reveal his false-heartedness. At first, he seemed like the perfect gentleman, waiting for you to slowly fall in love. He messed with your head, made you think that he cared about you. He whispered sweet nothings in your ear, and made you feel special. And then when you were head over heels, thinking that he was Mr Darcy, he went in for the kill.

The couple adjacent to me brought me back from my reverie. I watched as the guy leaned against the door and she leaned into him, looking up at him, lovingly—but instead of looking at her, he was staring at the pretty girl across from him. I frowned. Another reason why I stood by my shoes: they were completely loyal. They wouldn't flirt with another, nor get tired of you and feel the need to replace you. We women complicated things by making excuses, we created the drama in those complicated relationships. If the shoe hurt, and we loved the shoe, we suffered with our pinched toes, clenched our teeth and carried on. The pain would numb our feet at some point, right? We handled love the same way. In the end, all we were left with were ruined feet and a broken heart.

The train finally arrived at my station and I dashed out as quickly as I could. Luckily, the restaurant was near the station and I made it in record time. The moment I got inside, I spotted Emma.

"It's about time, I was about to call in the hounds." She kissed me on each cheek and took in my appearance. "Oh my God, what happened? I thought you were seeing Jack today."

"I had to take the tube. Didn't you get my text?" I asked.

She looked at her mobile. "No, I hate this shit phone. I get no reception anywhere!"

I smiled at her use of my expression. It had taken a while to get proper Emma to say that word; we were slowly working towards something stronger.

"Where's David?" I asked, looking around for him as I hung my trench coat on the back of the chair.

"Running even later than you, but for him, being late is making a grand entrance." She had a point. David was always the last to arrive, like the Queen.

"So what happened? You look like you've been through hell. Why didn't you take a taxi?" she asked.

"It seems I'm not taxi-worthy," I said. Emma lifted her eyebrow and I filled her in as I drank the wine she handed me. "The old guy was the worst. I wanted to assault him with my umbrella. The two things that made me hesitate were the fact that he could have possibly died from shock and the thought that he might actually enjoy it… A hundred years old, but his other head apparently still works just fine."

Emma laughed. "Seems to be the case these days."

"But the shoes the woman was wearing, they were to die for. I wanted to turn to him and say, 'She's not wearing those shoes for you, babes. She's wearing them to be the envy of other women such as myself who know the difference between designer shoes and trainers.'" I wiggled my toes, closing my eyes with regret. I watched as Emma sipped her wine a little too casually. Her face looked flushed, almost matching her hair. I knew that look: she had done something and was afraid to admit it. The only time she ever had that look was when she was dealing with Henry, the Collins of her life.

"Okay, spill it," I demanded, crossing my arms in front of me.

Emma took a couple of deep breaths. I waited, knowing what she was about to say, silently hoping his name didn't pass her lips.

"Henry called me today…"

"I knew it!" I practically jumped out of my seat. "Did you pick up?" I asked. A few customers turned to look at us, giving us annoyed glances. I lowered my voice. "Never mind, of course you did. What did he want?"

Emma looked down. I gulped down the rest of my wine. I was going to need strength for this. "Let me remind you why you shouldn't be talking to him. One…"—I held up my index finger—"you turned down your dream job in New York because he asked you to stay: a job, let me remind you, that you wanted more than anything in the world. He said 'don't go' and you didn't..." Emma was about to speak but I jumped in.

"Two..."—I held up a second finger—"he dumped you a few months after you turned down the dream job, saying the relationship was going too fast for him. Too fast! After he made all those promises and made you stay. So forgive me if I'm not happy to hear that Henry has decided to resurface," I said. I felt bad opening that wound again. But it had been painful to see her heartbroken when Henry dumped her.

"He apologized. Well, he sort of began to apologize, that is," she said, almost in a whisper. I sighed, knowing Emma was not used to standing up to people.

"He'll apologize all right if I ever run into him and kick him in the balls. *That* will make him ask for forgiveness," I said.

The ladies sitting at the table across from us started giggling. They were gawking at someone and I turned to see who. The handsome man approaching us was stylishly dressed in a well-tailored suit—Prada from the looks of it. His raincoat was neatly folded across his arm. I couldn't help but smile. Standing there, looking like he was about to walk down the red carpet, was David Cunningham, one of my best British friends. I had met him on an internship in New York. He was a successful lawyer, gorgeous and single. He smiled when he saw us, with perfect pearly white teeth. The hostess took his coat; I looked at mine in a heap over my chair. Emma got up to greet him, happy for the distraction.

"Hello, sit, sit. I think I'm being stalked," he said by way of greeting.

"Again..." I said. David was magnet for crazy stalkers. He gave me a look that could strip wallpaper.

"I don't look for this to happen to me you know—"

"Don't tell me it's that nut job Michael Priest..." I interrupted.

"He wasn't that bad..." David said.

"The man said to me over lunch that he wanted to take off your skin and wear it. You don't find that bad?" I asked.

"He was kidding. But no, not Michael. This one I found

on Grindr. We met, we shagged and now he's conveniently always around the area. I had to turn off the tracker."

I looked at the women, still staring. They didn't realize they were barking up the wrong tree. Though they may have hoped that David was just metrosexual, he was, in fact, gay.

"When you say tracker, what exactly does that mean?" Emma asked.

"Exactly what you think it means… I'll show you in a moment. But *you*," he said to me, "what is going on with all this?" He waved his hand indicating my disastrous appearance.

I groaned. In all the excitement of listening to Emma, I had forgotten to go the restroom and tidy up. David was notorious for criticizing my outfits. "Did you go to some emo party that you forgot to tell me about, or are you going for the morning-after look? Not cute."

"If you haven't noticed, it's raining cats and dogs out there —yet somehow the rain missed you," I noted.

He grinned. "It's called an umbrella. You've been living in London for how long now? And you haven't figured out that it rains here? We've spoken about your appearance hundreds of times. In particular, when you are meeting *me*…. I have a reputation to maintain here." He winked at me. "Besides, weren't you meeting Jack Stableboy?" he smirked.

"You know perfectly well his last name is Barnes," I pouted.

"Yes, well, I knew it had something to do with a stable. Was I wrong?"

I gave him a dirty look.

He sighed. "Don't hate me, I didn't name him. I'm the one who had to come across town in the rain to hear about this epic tale of revenge, and by the looks of you, I don't think I'm going to like the outcome. *Please* tell me you did not go to work looking like that. I didn't think we needed to discuss your outfit but now I'm regretting not having done so. I love you but, seriously, go and comb your hair." He smiled like he had just said the sweetest thing. That was David for you, no sugar-coating. I passed my hand over my hair, ignoring his glances.

"Forget about me. Emma, tell him what you just told me," I pressed, pushing my hair behind my ears as David motioned for me to fix the other side as well. Emma and I stayed quiet, looking at each other.

"Don't just stare at each other, what is it?"

"Henry called..." Emma began, biting her lip, her body becoming tense as she braced herself.

"*And* she picked up the phone! Can you believe that?" I interrupted, throwing up my hands frantically.

David rolled his eyes. "*Imagine that,* she picked up the phone, extraordinary. Who does that when it rings?" He smiled at her. Emma gratefully returned the smile. Well, when he put it that way, it seemed silly of me...

"Fine, *fine*, am I the only one who remembers what he's done?" I blurted out, exasperated.

David turned to me. "I didn't realize we were meeting for an intervention. If we're going to discuss Henry as well, we are going to have to get totally pissed. Better yet, why don't we discuss stable boy? What happened this morning? I didn't even get a call from you."

"No, let's not talk about either of them," Emma said, taking us both by surprise. "Let's talk about something else and not let them ruin our lovely evening... David, tell me about this tracker."

David took out his phone with a look of excitement and began scrolling through it. "I'll show you," he said. "Here's the latest conquest. It says he's about 300 yards away. If I want to see him, I hit 'available', and we meet up to do things that will make even me want to go to confession."

"Oh, for the love of God," I said, incredulously.

"Yes, we said that a lot," he said, amused.

"Okay, TMI, please spare us the details on this one, we're about to have dinner," I said.

"Nonsense, there is no such thing as too much information. You girls love it. How else would you get ideas about how to satisfy those straight boys if it wasn't for my escapades?" The lady next to us gasped, and David lifted his glass to her. "That's what happens when you eavesdrop on other people's conversations," he said through his teeth. I gave her an apologetic glance.

"It's quite simple and no strings attached, of course. Unfortunately, you do get the occasional stalker," he said to Emma, turning his phone off.

"Aren't you glad you asked?" I said to Emma. "And then you wonder why you get stuck with those types of people," I said to David.

"Don't knock it until you've tried it. I could set up an account for you in just a couple of minutes." He began messing with his phone again. I practically leapt up from the table and grabbed it from him.

"Don't you dare!"

He laughed. "Calm down, I was only teasing. Although, have a think, will you? It would probably help to relieve all that tension you clearly have."

"I hate you," I joked.

"You adore me and you know it. Sorry about this, Emma, but if I don't ask, she'll bring it up anyway. What did Henry want? Am I correct to assume he wants to meet?"

Emma nodded.

"The more important question is, do you want meet him?" David continued.

"Of course not," I answered.

David gave me a scolding look. "Is your name Emma?"

I frowned and topped up my glass of wine.

"What did he say, Emma?" David asked.

Emma looked like a deer caught in headlights. "He didn't exactly say much, he just asked if I could meet him in person to talk."

I made a sound of protest and David kicked me under the table. I flinched and gave him a dirty look, then kicked him back: we had resorted to acting like preschoolers.

David seemed unfazed by my poor excuse for a kick. "And did you agree to meet with him?"

"I said I needed time to think about it. I honestly did not know what to say!" She looked flustered. She gave me a pleading look. "There is a part of me that wants to meet with him. I can't explain why, I just do. But then, part of me also says don't be a fool, he humiliated you, and I don't think I can bear to be hurt by him again."

Emma looked like she was about to cry. My heart went out to her. I knew what that felt like. Wasn't I the one running around like a lunatic this morning and all for what? What exactly had I hoped to accomplish at the meeting if Jack had been there? Would I have talked to him like we were old pals or acquaintances politely discussing the weather? I was a fool, a fool that had ruined the best shoes I had acquired to date.

David held his glass carefully in his hand and swirled the wine around, pondering. "Men are bastards, with me being the exception, of course. Darlings, you're damned if you do and damned if you don't. My advice—and the only thing I will say on the matter—is make him work for it. Don't let him come back without having earned it. He needs to be taught a lesson and the only way men learn is when you inflict pain."

"*Really*?" I asked, not believing his explanation.

David stared at me. "All right, you, what bitter pill did you swallow today?" He gave me a *drop it or else* glance. "Moving on to more important matters, are we still going shopping tomorrow with the new Mrs Brandon Robertson and Elizabeth?" he asked, changing the subject.

David still loved calling Olivia Mrs Brandon Robertson. I had actually met her through David. When you first meet Olivia, it's hard not be intimidated. She's gorgeous, blonde, tall and looks like a model. On principal, you want to hate her on looks alone, but she's such a great person that you can't help but fall in love with her. Elizabeth De Verde was a fellow New Yorker. We had met at a random party here in London and had instantly bonded over that.

Our group of five did many things together, but the thing we enjoyed most was shopping.

"Yes, Harvey Nicks," I said, looking at my planner.

"Fantastic, I'm actually in need of a new pair of loafers. I threw out six pairs of shoes—the soles were worn out. And while we're at it, perhaps we can get you something from the twenty-first century in which to store your appointments," David commented.

I flipped through the pages, shrugging nonchalantly. "Firstly, I like writing things down, it makes me feel like I'm in control," I said. "And secondly, I don't trust gadgets."

"*Why not*?"

"What if I can't retrieve my data? What if the screen blanks out? What if –"

"Oh, forget I asked," he said, raised his hand to stop me. "Whatever, keep your dinosaur diary, all I care about is getting my loafers."

"Why did you throw away six pairs of shoes? You could have had them resoled," said Emma. David looked at her as though she had two heads. He looked confused.

"*You do know* that you can get shoes resoled for, like, twenty quid," Emma pointed out.

"Since when?" he asked, sounding unsure.

"Since the invention of shoes," I offered, sipping my wine.

"There is no need for sarcasm, Bitter Katie. I don't think about these things. If my shoes look worn, I get rid of them and buy a new pair… it's that simple. But if I could resole them, hmm…"

That was David: a shoe whore. If they bothered him or he got bored, out they went. Just like his relationships. With David, sometimes you didn't know if he was kidding or not. I wasn't sure if having shoes resoled was something he truly wasn't aware of.

"Oh, I almost forgot, Olivia isn't allowed to buy any shoes tomorrow. She is asking, more like demanding, that we make sure she does not walk out of the store with any type of shoe… not even a Collins," I informed them.

"Why?" David asked.

"They just bought a house, David. I'm sure she's on some sort of managed allowance." Emma said.

I grinned. Olivia didn't have an allowance, she worked. But Emma was certainly going in the right direction.

David seemed shocked. "Brandon gave her an *allowance*? Unbelievable. She needs to divorce him. I will file the divorce papers for her myself, pro bono. Didn't I tell you girls from the moment I saw him there was something dodgy about him?"

"Did you now?" I crossed my arms in front of me. "I recall you being all 'oh, isn't Brandon hot, he looks like Henry Cavill'," I said. In David's eyes, Brandon could do no wrong. That was, until he thought Brandon was cutting Olivia's shopping budget.

"Besides, it's not like that at all, it's her New Year's resolution. She wants to go a month without buying shoes," I said, watching their expressions turn to disbelief.

"Why would she do that to herself?" said Emma. "She'll be miserable and so will we for the entire month! She should have given up something else. Like exercising."

David looked at her thoughtfully. "Hmm, but that would include sex, wouldn't it?" He thought about it, then nodded. "Yes, that would definitely include sex and, as much as we love shoes, Brandon is pretty hot and I could not be celibate for a month with him around."

"The two of you, really! *Brandon* is the reason she's doing this. It was his idea," I said.

David shot me a look of disgust. "Then maybe she should have added exercise—that would serve him right," he said. No one got in the way of David's shopping. Emma and I looked at each other and burst out laughing.

Opening my front door a couple of glasses of wine later, slightly light-headed and feeling content, I kicked off my shoes and placed my keys on the table. Carefully, I bent down and picked up the shoes, inspecting them. They seemed three shades darker after being soaked. Perhaps if I dried them off, they would look better. Sighing, I went up to my bedroom, checking if I had any messages. I hit the play button and began to undress.

First message: "Catherine, it's Aunt Elena, are you there? Have I dialed this correctly? There are so many numbers… I was calling to say hello… Helloooo! I was thinking, remember how you wanted to get married on that island in the Caribbean when you were a little girl? Well, I thought, rather than wait for you to get married, why don't we have a family trip there instead? I'm not getting any younger, honey. Call me soon, love you!"

Leave it to her to throw in that little bit there. No matter what I did, Aunt Elena would always chuck the marriage card in; she was old-fashioned like that. Marriage, however, was the furthest thing from my mind. Why was it that the moment a woman hit twenty-five, people assumed marriage was next? Ridiculous. I made a mental note to call her and turned on the shower. The second message started, it was *his* voice. I ran back to the bedroom and stood over the machine.

"Kate, it's Jack… I'm sorry I didn't make it to the meeting today. I wasn't aware that you were actually going to be there, otherwise I would've wrapped up my meeting earlier. I got held up, you know how it is." He paused. I knew Jack well enough to know he was making small talk to get to the point that he really wanted to make. "I saw you at the tube station. You were dashing off and I thought you saw me, but I suppose I might have been *mistaken.* Call me. It's been too long, we should chat."

My heart raced uncontrollably upon hearing his voice. I had planned for over a week and he hadn't even had a clue that I was going to be there. I didn't know whether to laugh or cry. I replayed the message and sat at the foot of the bed feeling defeated as his voice filled the room again.

Chapter Six

Harvey Nicks on a weekend was a madhouse, full of locals and tourists. I began to search for the group and spotted Elizabeth the moment I got off the escalator. She was looking very studious with her black-rimmed glasses and her curly hair up in a bun. She was trying to pry a pair of shoes from Emma's hands and Emma was holding on like her life depended on it.

"Give those to me," Elizabeth demanded. "You're a single woman, why must you choose shoes that only my grandmother would wear? I take that back—even my grandmother has more style than this. Here, try these on."

That was Elizabeth: just like David, she had no censor. Whether it was appropriate or not, she said whatever was on her mind.

"'I'm not looking for fashion, Elizabeth, I'm looking for comfort," Emma said, but she took the rose-colored shoes Elizabeth had chosen for her and turned them over to look at the price. She cringed. "I'm buying shoes, not making a down payment on a flat. These are like the Manolos you and Kate insisted I buy. Remember that?" she asked contemptuously.

Elizabeth shrugged. "*Barely.*" But I could see from the look on her face that she did.

"They were beautiful, I'll admit. But they're in my closet because I can't walk in them. The first time I wore them, the heels got scuffed after I almost killed myself going down the stairs."

"But did you die?" Elizabeth asked. "*No*, you didn't. You know what that tells me?"

Emma took a deep breath. "That I need more practice?"

"Exactly!" She placed her arm around Emma's shoulder. "Don't let that one experience keep you from enhancing yourself. What's a little pain when the end result is pleasurable?"

"I'll break my neck," Emma insisted.

"Small price to pay to look fabulous," Elizabeth said.

"She's joking, Emma," I intervened.

Elizabeth squealed upon seeing me and gave me a hug, leaning in to whisper, "Well, of course I am, I don't want her killed. She just needs more practice *elsewhere,* if you know what I mean."

"Is that what they're teaching at Oxford these days?" Emma asked, smiling. "I can hear you, you know."

Elizabeth was currently in grad school for psychotherapy, sex therapy specifically. She liked to do things to shock us or, as she put it, to 'get us out of our shells'.

"Good for you, Emma, stand up for yourself and have some spunk," she said, taking back the shoe. "Fine, go with the ones you like, I give up. I will say, Emma, that there are some cute flats. Keep that in mind while you look. They don't have to look outdated!"

David approached us in his cool weekend outfit: jeans, a grey cashmere sweater and not a hair out of place. He had loads of shopping bags already. The fact that he was hanging around while we shopped for shoes was a red flag that he was up to something. And my suspicions were confirmed when I noticed the good-looking salesman eyeing him.

"It's about time you got here, lightweight. You only had two glasses of wine. Even Olivia got here before you did."

"Where is Olivia?" I asked. David pointed to the corner. Olivia was sitting on a couch, looking absolutely miserable. Her hair was in a perfect blonde bun, which, no matter how many times I attempted to duplicate, I could never accomplish. She was looking down, playing with her engagement ring. It was enormous. I could see it sparkling from where I was standing. She caught sight of me, smiled faintly and walked over.

"No, absolutely not," David scolded as he headed over to Emma, taking the odd-looking shoe she had in her hand and placing it back down on the table.

"*Oi*, I'm waiting for the other one," Emma protested, picking it back up. The salesman approached us and David mouthed *'no'* to him. Ignoring David, Emma thanked him and took the box.

Olivia took David's arm. "Let her be, she likes what she likes. At least she can buy those today. How did I think I could come here without buying anything?" Her hand went around her throat. "Is it me or is hot in here? I can't breathe. I think I'll wait for you guys over at the cafe."

I gave her a sympathetic smile. "Deep breaths, babes."

David placed his arm around her. "About that, Olivia... I've found a solution to your dilemma."

I crossed my arms in front of my chest and waited, knowing that whatever was going to come out of his mouth could potentially cause trouble for her. Who was I kidding, it would be guaranteed trouble. Olivia stared at him, her blue eyes full of hope.

"I can buy the shoes for you. Think of it like a shoe proxy. If you see something you like, tell me and I will buy them. You can pick them up after the month is over. Problem solved." David grinned.

Olivia squealed, hugging him. "That is brilliant, you are a genius!" She stepped away then hugged him again.

"I know," he said, matter of fact.

"That is so wrong," I said. "What are you going to do next, negotiate Lent?"

"If I had to! Where there's a will, there's a way. I'm a lawyer, it's what I do—and I do it quite well." He was glowing in Olivia's joy.

"You're so going to hell," Emma said, laughing.

David grinned. "Probably, but I'll have loads of company… all the cute ones anyway." He took Olivia's hand. "Look around, darling. Pick a shoe, any shoe!" He gave his best evil laugh.

"Now I see why he makes so much money. Very clever," Elizabeth said, watching them.

I agreed. David was a fox. There was nothing he couldn't talk his way out of. I was about to reply when my gaze landed on a pair of killer Brian Atwood black studded boots. Forgetting about David, I walked over and picked up the boot carefully in my hand like I was handling a newborn. "These are gorgeous!" I gushed.

Elizabeth took the other. "I think I just came in my panties."

"Liz!"

"*What?*" she asked innocently, and grinned. I gently stroked the leather. There was no way I could even consider buying these but there was no harm in trying them on. Stunning. Simply, stunning. There were no other words for them.

Elizabeth inspected the boot. "Your size. It's a sign." She handed the matching pair over.

I sat down, took off my shoes and slipped in my right foot first, moaning at how perfectly they accommodated my foot. She gave me a knowing look, watching me pull on the other boot.

"Oh my God, I love them!" I stood up. They looked incredible. I felt amazing and tall.

"Emma," Elizabeth called over. "Take a look at these." She pointed at the boots. "These are the pair you must buy. They say to a man, I want to dig these into your back, wearing these and only these."

Emma blushed. David stepped behind her and covered her ears.

"Elizabeth, censor yourself, you're scaring the child. Pumps first. We've discussed this, remember?" He smiled in a wicked way, a personal joke between the two of them.

She snapped her fingers. "That's right, screw-me shoes come later." The couple adjacent to us gave her a dirty look.

"Sorry, she's American, what can I say? Can't take her anywhere," David said. They left, making us laugh.

"Get them, Kate, I demand it," Elizabeth said.

I took them off and saw the price. "Yikes!" I put them back on the table quickly. They were not on sale. This was a major investment. I had a pair of shoes in mind for that price, and I couldn't even bring myself to try those on. As my Aunt Elena said—if God intended us to walk in shoes that high, we would have been given a pair at birth. I shook my head in disbelief. I was losing it; I was actually quoting Aunt Elena's quirky philosophies. My fingers touched the boots again. They were going to haunt me like a certain someone.

"You know you want them," Elizabeth said, the little devil voice on my shoulder.

"It's not practical, did you see the price?" I said.

"Aren't you getting a bonus?"

She had a point. I could charge them and pay later... *No*, I would not do this. I mustn't. "I wish I could, but I promised myself," I said. "Let's get out of here before I do something dangerous." But my hands wouldn't let go of the boots. They were perfect, I could wear them with so many outfits.

Let go, Kate. I told myself. *Step away… you can do it.* I looked up at Elizabeth with a sad face. As I stepped away from the boots, I knew my shopping mood was gone. No other shoe was going to compare to the Brian Atwoods.

We finally called it a day and headed to the Fifth Floor Bar. It was a brilliant concept: you shopped, took a break with a glass of champagne, and continued shopping. David joined us a few moments later with a bag containing Olivia's proxy shoes. She was dying to reach for it and could hardly stay still in her seat.

"I can't wait to wear them, David, you saved my life back there. Thank you so much!" she said, excited.

"What are friends for? I couldn't let you suffer while the rest of us ran around in bliss. What kind of person would I be if I allowed that to happen?" he asked.

Elizabeth laughed. "You're such a giver, honey."

"I live to serve. I can sacrifice with the best of them," he said with a smile, proud of himself.

"David, before you become a martyr, let's order, I'm starving," I griped.

He picked up the menu. "Bitter Katie joins us again." I stuck out my tongue at him. David looked around. "There's not one hot man here. All the good-looking men are probably playing football, which reminds me… how's the hubby, Olivia?"

"He's fine," she said quickly, picking up her glass of champagne. That was not the Olivia I knew. She gushed about Brandon almost as much as she gushed about a new pair of shoes. Now she looked like she just wanted to hide.

"Yes, he *is* fine," David added in a cheeky tone. We all laughed, except Olivia, who wasn't smiling.

"Are you in sinful bliss?" Elizabeth asked. When Olivia didn't respond, Elizabeth gave me a puzzled glance. Something was bothering her.

"I am—I mean, we are newlyweds and all," she finally said.

The four of us waited.

"But..." I prodded.

"It's been a slightly difficult adjustment." She took a deep breath. "All right, if you must know, we got into a fight," she threw out quickly.

We all stood quietly.

"Well, do you want to know what we fought about?" she asked.

We all nodded, waiting with anticipation.

"My cooking." She looked around as if one of us should take her side. The problem was Olivia was lucky if she boiled water correctly and Brandon was a chef who cooked delicious works of art. Yes, the kitchen was traditionally the woman's domain but, in this case, it was Brandon's. The fact that Olivia tried to cook was actually quite frightening. Any time she cooked, we ended up ordering takeaway.

"Why were you cooking?" Emma asked.

"I wanted to surprise him. He'd always been quite impressed with my cooking and would always eat everything, he'd even have seconds."

David was fighting not to laugh. We all knew Brandon did not like her cooking; the poor guy was in love and didn't want to hurt Olivia's feelings.

"So I decided to roast a chicken... But it was a busy day and I forgot to take the chicken out the freezer. I had less than an hour before Brandon got home so I turned the oven up and it ended up being cooked much sooner than the recipe said it would." She paused and took another gulp of champagne. "It looked amazing, my romantic dinner with my new husband... Everything was perfectly set. Brandon came home and was stunned, and all was great... until he cut into the chicken. It was raw!"

"Oh dear," Emma said, covering her mouth.

Olivia's eyes opened wide. "My chicken was undercooked!

Brandon started laughing and laughing. He said he loved me but to stay out of the kitchen. Can you believe that?"

"Honey, if a man told me to get out of the kitchen, I wouldn't argue!" Elizabeth said. I had to agree with her.

"That's not all," she added. "You know the bathroom upstairs? It's so old-fashioned—'antique', he calls it. It has one tiny shelf that barely fits a mirror. I don't have room for my makeup and creams." She looked at me with desperation and I nodded, sympathizing with her—any woman would.

"I hired someone to install more shelves and thought 'problem solved'! But the walls are so old that nothing holds up properly. This morning, one of the shelves fell on Brandon. He started yelling, and then I started yelling. He told me not to have any more work done in *his* house without discussing it with him first."

Ouch. I thought.

"He's territorial, men can be such buffoons," Emma offered, trying to reassure her.

David put down his drink. "Hey, what am I, chopped liver?"

Elizabeth smacked his shoulder lightly. "It isn't a pissing contest, David, and you know it. Emma's right, Olivia, I hope you put the shelf back up... don't let him win."

"Whatever," David rolled his eyes.

"I don't understand this. When we were dating and I stayed over, he didn't move any of my things out of the way. He didn't order me out of the kitchen. He was sweet and polite. What happened to the man I fell in love with?" Olivia asked desperately, looking at us for answers.

"Do you really want me to answer that?" David asked. Again, I knew whatever he was about to say would not be good.

"No," I said immediately. "It's an adjustment period, that's all," I added quickly. I looked at Elizabeth for reinforcement because Olivia looked like she was about to lose it.

"Everyone goes through it," Elizabeth said. "I mean, I have roommates, we're still learning to live around each other."

Emma nodded in agreement. They began to encourage Olivia. From the corner of my eye, I looked at the two women who had sat across from us. The tall, blonde, beautiful one placed her bags on the floor, laughing at whatever her friend was saying. Instantly, I recognized her and froze. After the ex, the next worst person to run into is his current girlfriend, especially when she was the one who took him away from you. I couldn't look at her and say she was a cow, because she was absolutely stunning. Would I have been happier if he had cheated on me with some unattractive woman? Yes! There was nothing worse than having your boyfriend leave you for someone more attractive. I got up quickly and excused myself, heading to the bathroom. I needed a moment—and I needed to make sure I looked decent!

Thanks to Olivia, I was well-dressed. But even in my stylish jeans, cool top and ankle boots, I felt inadequate. My savoir-faire style seemed childish next to hers. I quickly went into a stall, hiding like a scared creature. This was ridiculous, I had nothing to be ashamed of, nor did I need to hide. I wasn't the cheater. I was here with my friends, and I was not going to let her ruin my afternoon! Making up my mind, I washed my hands and refreshed my lip gloss. I pushed the door but someone was pushing it from the other side.

"Sorry," I said. Suddenly, there she was. Amanda Egerton… The succubus.

"Kate! I thought that was you," she said in one of those fake voices.

"Amanda," I said looking up at her 5'11" frame. Her sapphire-blue eyes looked back, taking in my appearance, eyeballing me like the evil creature she was. She smiled, as cool as a cat.

I looked at her feet. She was wearing flats, typical for someone of her height. However, these flats were not Collinses, not in the slightest. These were the Darcys of flats. Her type always had Darcys and she had taken mine.

She pushed her blond hair to one side. “Shopping?” she asked.

I gave her a look. “Well, this is a department store,” I said, taking a deep breath. At least I could console myself with the fact that it was possible the girl had no brain. This was about as much polite conversation as I could muster. I turned to leave without saying a word.

“I’ll tell Jack you said hello,” she added. Those words made me stop in my tracks, anger began to take over and I turned to face her. She was still smiling, as if she could sense what I was thinking. I wondered if she would continue smiling if I grabbed her by the hair and placed her head in the toilet. The idea was extremely tempting. Instead I turned and left.

Elizabeth was waiting for me outside against the wall. “Do you want me to go in there and beat her up?” she grinned, making me laugh.

“Don’t tempt me. She’s not worth it.” I was shaken. “This encounter was bound to happen sooner or later.”

“Well, it’s over now.” Elizabeth said. “So you’re done with the anticipation. But I can still go in there or wait for her here and trip her on the way out. Just say the word, my friend. Her ankle will probably snap in two if she hits the floor.”

“I can’t be angry at her: it’s Jack’s fault, not hers,” I said looking back at the bathroom door.

“Of course she bears some of the blame,” Elizabeth said, shaking her head. “She knew he had a girlfriend when she started seeing him. You know, back home, there’s a nice little word for her that rhymes with itch.”

“Not worth our time. Come on, let’s go. Besides, we don’t want to be the reason Americans are banned from here for violent behavior, do we?”

"No, I suppose not." She glanced at the door. "At least let me scare her?"

I laughed. "Come on," I said, pulling her by the arm and heading back to the group.

Chapter Seven

David and I were the only ones left after lunch. Since the sun had disappeared and the clouds had rolled in, we decided to head towards King's Road. I filled him in on what had happened in the bathroom.

"I was so stupid, I had no comeback line. I just left like a scared little girl."

David linked his arm through mine. "Why didn't you confront her? That was your opportunity. I'm all about behaving like Victoria Beckham but sometimes you need to be feisty like Cheryl," he said.

"I'm serious, David."

"So am I! I love Cheryl. She's a lady but she doesn't let people walk all over her. You could learn a lot from her. You could also dress more like Victoria; it got her *my* future ex-husband."

I laughed. "Keep dreaming, dear… and I dress just fine, thank you very much."

He gave me once-over and shrugged. "If you say so."

"You can be so mean," I said.

"And your point is?"

"I couldn't fight her even if I wanted to. I can't be like you and have rebellious impulses, I'd be kicked out of the country."

"My rebellious impulses are an unavoidable part of my life, but that's what makes it fun. Besides, you have indefinite leave. You'd probably be arrested at most, but I'd use my government connections and have your record erased," he offered.

"Oh, would you now?"

"But of course! I would have bailed you out and everything. I'll tell you this much, you would have felt much better having slugged her than you do now."

"How very generous of you, I'll remember that for the next time," I said. Sensing my discomfort, David pulled me to a stop.

"I know that look, Catherine Seeley. Trust me. You're better off without him. You do see that, don't you?"

"How do you know what I'm thinking?"

"I'm gifted."

I sighed, looking at him. "Why couldn't you be straight? You're perfect," I asked, repeating the cliché uttered by legions of women.

"Oh, sweetie, you're so cute. Why couldn't you be a boy?" he asked, laughing. "I sympathize with you, I really do."

I linked my arm back through his. "What would I do without you?" I asked, meaning it.

"For starters, dress like the pilgrims that founded your country," he answered.

"I don't dress like a pilgrim," I protested.

"You used to before I came along."

"And you wonder why I have a complex," I joked. I groaned. "Why am I feeling lost all over again?" I looked at him, defeated. "How can I move on when I haven't found anyone? I'm the one who's still single. Even on dates, I think about him, comparing them to him."

"Are you really having second thoughts?"

"No," I answered, unsure.

He gave me a look.

"Yes. Okay, you know what? I don't know." I stopped walking.

"Which one is it?"

"I'm still trying to figure things out, David."

"There is nothing to figure out; he's a loser who doesn't deserve a moment of your time. You know what he is?"

"What?"

"A sample sale Jimmy Choo shoe!" he exclaimed.

"I don't understand."

David looked disappointed. "If you don't understand, you're worse off than I thought. You have lots to learn."

"He cheated on me," I said. "I know I can't go back." There it was, I was unconvinced, and my voice said it all. Shocked at myself, I looked at David. "I hate when you do that! When you think you know what I'm feeling."

"That's because I do."

"I don't like you." I said, but of course I was teasing. He had the decency to look surprised. "You don't have to like me, darling. But I think someone is still hung up on a certain guy." He looked at me. "I'm not saying another word. Let's forget about it. The last thing I want is to get into a row with you over Jack."

"Yes, let's drop the subject. But you still have that look."

Grinning, he crossed his arms. "I can't help that I'm beautiful, Kate. You're going to need a blindfold if that's the case."

I laughed. "No, you can't help it, can you? So who's this guy you're going out with tonight?" I asked, changing the subject.

"Pablo, he's from Brazil. Why don't you join us?"

"Oh no, my days of being the third wheel are over. I'm actually looking forward to staying in and watching a movie," I admitted. I was tired. I just wanted to go home.

We continued walking towards my flat, discussing Pablo.

David stopped in front of my building. "If you change your mind, call me. Don't let today's little incident make you throw away all your hard work at the gym by eating a tub of ice cream. You'll regret it in the morning," he said, giving me a quick hug.

"Are you going to explain the sample sale Jimmy Choo thing?"

He shook his head. "No, you'll have to figure that out on your own."

"Am I supposed to thank you for the lesson, Master Yoda?"

"You love me. But I'm not joking. You'll look more like Yoda than I will if you eat that ice cream."

"Get going!" I dismissed him and ran inside.

A couple of hours later, I was on the sofa with a blanket over me, waiting for a takeaway and watching Joe Wright's version of *Pride And Prejudice.* When I needed a little comfort, this was the perfect remedy. No matter how many times I watched it, I continued to fall in love with that movie again and again. What was wrong with wanting an old-fashioned romance? It was possible I was born in the wrong era. I thought about how I would look, living in that century: my dress, my hair … I stopped at the shoes, wrinkling my nose. I preferred the shoes in this century. I turned my focus back to Mr Darcy.

Miss Elizabeth, I have struggled in vain and I can bear it no longer. These past months have been a torment. I came to Rosings with the single object of seeing you… I had to see you. I have fought against my better judgment, my family's expectations, the inferiority of your birth by rank and circumstances. All these things I am willing to put aside and ask you to end my agony.

I sighed. "End my agony." This was a man who wasn't

afraid to just lay it on the line. Could I be like Elizabeth Bennet and turn Jack away if he came to me and said those words?

The phone rang and I got up to answer it. "Hello?"

"Catherine, how are you? I hope I'm not interrupting."

"Hi, Aunt Elena. No, you're not interrupting." I paused the movie on Mr Darcy's face.

"I was thinking that I want to come visit you in London. You've been there for, what, three years now?

"Five," I corrected her. "Aunt Elena, you can visit whenever you like. You let me know when and I'll buy you the airline tickets. It will be fun, I promise."

"But you know my doctors are here…" She went on to list the reasons her doctors were better. "But you could come out here, couldn't you? You haven't visited us in a while. Did you get my message about the family trip?"

"I did, so sorry I haven't called back. I think that's a great idea. Why don't you talk to everyone and see what they have in mind."

"I wish we would be going for your wedding. It is such a beautiful island."

"I agree," I said, rolling my eyes. That was all one could do with Aunt Elena.

The doorbell rang. I was relieved to have an excuse to end the conversation. "Aunt Elena that's my food, I have to go, but let's talk this week. I'll call you. Love you."

That was a close one. If I allowed her, she would start talking about my past boyfriends and which she had liked best and how I shouldn't be alone in a foreign country. Grabbing my wallet, I took out some notes. Without looking, I opened the door, handing the money to the delivery guy. He wasn't taking it. I looked up, slightly annoyed. Jack was standing before me, looking devilishly handsome and holding my takeaway. I blinked quickly a few times, making sure I wasn't imagining him.

"Delivery," he smiled, lifting the bag.

I stood open-mouthed, unable to speak. I was makeup-free with my hair in a bun, wearing old grey sweatpants, my university sweatshirt and, to top it off, fluffy socks. His dark, almost black eyes stared at me and I feel my knees buckling. *Get it together, Kate!* I instructed myself, he's seen you like this plenty of times before. *He also cheated,* my inner voice said. *Channel Elizabeth Bennet, be poised, stand your ground... be confident.*

"You're not the delivery guy," I said, stating the obvious.

"Sorry to disappoint. I bumped into him on the way up."

"Here take this," I mumbled, giving him the money.

"No worries," he said, not taking it. "May I come in?"

"Thanks, yes, of course, sorry, come in." I opened the door further, letting him in. I closed my eyes, closed the door and placed my wallet on the foyer table. I quickly undid my bun and let my hair down. I should run upstairs and change. *Stop. Take control of the situation,* I said to myself.

"What are you doing here?"

He turned around to face me. "I've been asking myself the same question since I found myself walking in this direction. May I place this in the kitchen?"

"Sure," I said as politely as I could, watching him head toward the kitchen. He stopped in front of the television and smiled at the scene.

"Some things never change," he said, continuing to the kitchen. "The renovations turned out great," he called out.

"Hate you," I mumbled under my breath, not caring if he heard me. I clicked the television off.

"What was that?" he said.

"Nothing," I responded. This man knew everything about me, and even though it had been a few months since he had been here, I didn't want him to know I was still doing the same things.

I breathed in his scent. His cologne was something I had always found intoxicating, a citrus, lemon tone to it. I still had a sweater of his stowed away in my closet that faintly had that smell. I suddenly felt worried that he would somehow find out.

"I'm sorry Jack, I'm not following. Why you are here exactly?" I asked, walking into the kitchen. He was leaning against the counter, all six feet plus and staring at me, making me feel nervous. Not wanting to look at him, I began taking the food out of the bag.

"I left you a message last night."

My heart pounded against my chest. He was here, why was I questioning him? *Don't scare him off.* I placed the containers on the table. "I got the message. I meant to call, I just haven't gotten around to it," I said, hoping it was a good explanation. What I really wanted to say was *I was scared to call and say that I've missed you.*

"Of course, silly of me to think otherwise… you used to call me right away after I phoned."

I stopped. Had I been that pathetic? "Things change."

"Yes, they do," he said. I felt him walking towards me and when he touched my arm, I closed my eyes. He turned me to face him. "In the past, you wouldn't have ignored me at the tube station either."

I looked up at him, embarrassed, ignoring the comment. "Would you like a glass of wine? I was about to pour myself one." His eyes rested on my lips, making me lick them self-consciously. He smiled. "I need to get the wine…" I managed. Without a word, he turned and opened my cabinet, reaching for the wine glasses, remembering exactly where they were. This small gesture made me lose it, how he still felt right at home.

"Honestly, Jack. How could you be surprised that I haven't returned your call and it's only been twenty-four hours? What about all the messages and emails that I left for you months ago? I'm still waiting for your response," I grabbed the corkscrew and began trying to open the bottle of wine. The damn thing wasn't working. Jack took the bottle from me, his fingers wrapping around my hand. The feeling was the same—I was a fool to think it might have been otherwise. I let go of the bottle immediately and he opened it effortlessly and poured me a glass.

"You have every right to be angry at me. I apologize. I shouldn't have said that... I've been a coward and seeing you yesterday made me realize that. I've been ignoring the obvious. We didn't exactly leave things with any kind of civility. You left so abruptly and didn't give me a chance to explain."

I stared at him in disbelief and snorted. The fuzzy feeling from a few seconds ago was quickly evaporating. He had to be delusional. I placed my glass down on the counter.

"Unbelievable. I left abruptly? Let me refresh your memory, *Jackson*. I didn't leave abruptly. I was begging you to talk things through, remember? And all you did was brush me off. If anyone lost any kind of civility, it was you."

"It wasn't like that," he protested.

I laughed. "Really? Then please enlighten me as to how you saw it. Or are you confusing me with Amanda, who I ran into today, by the way." I watched as his face paled. "Remember her? She was the reason. So let's not twist this around—you cheated on me. *That* is why I left."

Jack put his glass down next to mine. "I'm not proud of what I've done to you, Kate. I am very sorry about that, I really am."

Of everything I'd expected to hear from him, that wasn't it. I'd thought that if he came and apologized, I would feel validated. Only now, having him here, looking almost boyish, was making me melt. I didn't want to feel sorry for him! He deserved for me to be angry with him and never forgive him.

"I think you should go," I said in almost a whisper, afraid that if I didn't say it, I would actually accept his apology. Jack hesitated, passing his hand over his face.

"All right," he sighed. "When you are ready to talk, call me. I would really like..."

"Don't say it," I interrupted, shaking my head. I did not want to hear the 'let's be friends' speech. He looked at me with regret written all over his face.

"Goodnight, Catherine." He bent his head, kissing my cheek softly, and walked out. I heard the door shutting and realized I was shaking and not breathing. I wanted to run after him to tell him that I loved him once and that he threw it away. Once? Now I was the one who was delusional. I lowered my head, mad at myself for letting him go. I knew I had made a mistake. I was still in love with him. The only thing keeping me from running after him was my pride.

Chapter Eight

"We're going to be late, Emma," I called out to an empty room. Emma lived in a gorgeous little upscale flat in Chelsea, a gift from her parents. Her closet alone was to die for, which she did not take full advantage of. Emma's wardrobe consisted of grey and black, with a splash of white. But since she'd been hanging out with us, she was finally becoming more adventurous, adding a colored handbag here and there.

"How about this?" she asked, coming into the room wearing a black dress that looked exactly like the other three she had tried on. I had nothing against the little black dress, every woman should own at least one, but the ruffles on this one were not flattering. I wrinkled my nose, trying to spot the difference between this dress and the other two.

Taking her hand, I pulled her into the bedroom. "You must have something with some color in here," I said, opening up her closet. I stared at a lonely pale pink dress that had been pushed all the way to the back and pulled it out. "Voila!"

"It's a little too revealing for the opera, don't you think?" she asked, unsure.

"Not at all!" I said placing it against her. "This is perfect. Try it on."

She took the dress from my hand and began to change.

"I'm glad you're going out with Greg tonight. I think you'll like him," I said. Greg was a friend of Mark, a guy I'd gone on a few dates with after Jack. Mark and I had met at a work seminar when Jack and I first broke up. Nice guy, there was something sweet about him. But I didn't feel that spark I felt with Jack. When he'd suggested that we do a double date with one of his old college buddies, I immediately thought of Emma.

I began to look through her shoes: black, grey, charcoal… black, black and black. Round-toed loafers and clogs. *Quite a variety,* I thought, taking a deep breath. She needed help. If I was Elizabeth from Jane Austen's world, Emma was Charlotte, the loyal and complaisant friend. It was time to get her an upgrade from her Collins to a suitable Bingley. Luckily for her, we were the same size in most shoes. I took out the gold strappy Giuseppe Zanottis I'd brought along with me, knowing this would happen.

"Are you sure this isn't too short?" she asked. I turned around. Emma looked beautiful. The soft pink complemented her hair perfectly.

"Absolutely not. Try these." I handed her the shoes. She took them with shaking hands.

"Kate, I can't, what if I snap the heel?" Her scared face made me hesitate, almost wanting to take them back from her and hold them tightly against my chest.

"I trust you," I lied. She looked unsure and I was frightened, but I tried to look encouraging. She needed support. I smiled. "Come on, Cinderella, try them on."

"Can't you call them and cancel? Say I've fallen ill, and then we can head to the cinema or something."

"No. Besides, you're not going to be alone; I'm going to be there with Mark. Greg is fun, it will be fun," I said, trying to convince us both. I needed to go out, move on from Jack. Ever since he had walked into my safe bubble, I'd been having a hard time not picking up that phone and calling him.

"Are you sure? Remember Olivia set me up the last time and it turned out to be a disaster. The guy only spoke about himself the entire night, I hardly said a word. Remind me why I'm doing this again?"

"Because he's a great guy *and* he hardly speaks," I insist.

"If he's that great, why is he still single?"

Why was it everyone kept asking that? What did that say about us single people? Sometimes you just didn't meet the right person. Did that throw me into the 'what's wrong with her?' category? I worked long hours and it was hard to meet anyone. Some people were just busy and had no time. That did not necessarily mean there was something wrong with us.

I was stuck on Jack. Emma was stuck on Henry. I didn't want to believe it meant the end for either of us. Look how many shoes there were in the world. Not all were pretty or useful, but there were some amazing ones out there, you just had to keep on looking until, one day, without warning, you found the perfect pair that made your heart stop and your breath catch and—your knees wobble. I wanted to be swept off my feet. All women did, whether they admitted it or not. If I couldn't find my Darcy, I might as well wear Collinses for the rest of my life!

Emma checked herself out in the long mirror.

"Have you called Henry back? Is that what this is all about?" I asked her.

She paused. "No, I haven't. I wanted to but I've given it some thought. What you said is true—what would be the point now?"

I sighed in relief. She was finally starting to get it. "You're going to do so much better, Emma. Keep ignoring him, it's the best thing you can do for yourself. Men are replaceable; a good shoe, however," I looked down at her feet, "is not."

Emma laughed. "I worry about you and shoes. You're obsessed."

"And you just figured that out now?" I laughed. "I'll tell you this: I would be a happy woman if you just placed me in a shoe store for the rest of my life."

Dinner at The Wolseley turned out to be predictable but not as boring as I'd thought it was going to be. Emma seemed to be enjoying herself with Greg and they were currently discussing a new collection at the Tate Britain.

Mark smiled at them. "They seem to be getting along well," he said. I had to agree with him. Emma looked quite happy.

"They are totally engrossed in the conversation," I said with a soft laugh.

"Clearly. It's like we don't exist."

"I suppose we can talk about government regulations if you like," I joked.

Mark laughed, looking at his watch. "Luckily for us, it's time to go."

As we headed to the Royal Opera House, I leaned in to Emma. "Isn't this better than the cinema?" I asked. She nodded in agreement. The guys went to drop off our coats. "Greg is really nice," she said, smiling.

"See. I told you… just give it a chance." I said.

Emma was about to say something but stopped, her smile disappearing. She looked stunned. I followed her gaze. Henry. Emma looked like she was about to faint. Grabbing her arm, I tried to make a move before he saw us, but it was too late.

"Emma, Kate, fancy running into you both!" Henry said as

he approached us. He sounded nervous. Henry wasn't a bad-looking guy: tall, with mousy-brown hair that looked good without him doing anything to it.

"Henry," I said coolly. His eyes flickered a bit. Emma stared at him, still shocked, unable to say anything. He seemed to be waiting for her to greet him. Did he really think she would run into his arms like all was forgotten and he was forgiven.

"Henry, what a surprise to see you here," Emma managed, pulling herself together. I loved that she looked so beautiful tonight. If she had planned it like I had with Jack, it wouldn't have worked.

"Yes, well... I actually... I came here tonight hoping to run into you. I know this is your favorite opera, so I took a chance, seeing as this is a special performance. You were always trying to get me to come and I never made the time," he said, looking slightly embarrassed and sad at the same time.

Emma didn't say a word.

I frowned. Great, so *now* he was doing the things that she had wanted them to do together?-I was angry watching him dig himself into a deeper hole.

"How are things, Kate?" he asked, trying to make conversation as neither of us was responding.

"All is well, thank you ..." I answered coldly. *You bastard* is what I really wanted to say. *You cowardly, inconsiderate prick.* I had plenty to say to dear Henry, but this was neither the time nor the place.

"How are you?" He asked, turning back to her and ignoring me, his brown eyes seeming lost. I stood there, watching the two of them in their awkward moment.

"I'm good, thank you," Emma said finally.

"You look amazing," he said, making her blush. Ridiculous! Did he actually think that all it took was a couple of nice words? Men! They thought a compliment or two would make us melt. This was total nonsense, yet I could see Emma was falling for it.

I pulled on her arm. “We should really get going and meet the guys. The opera is about to start.” My words went unheard as she stared at Henry like a lost puppy.

“I’ve tried reaching you. I know you must be extremely busy. You haven’t changed your number, have you?” he gushed.

“No, I haven’t, I just haven’t had time to call you back,” Emma said.

I beamed at her. Well done! I wanted to applaud her.

“She’s busy in her new job after she resigned from the old one,” I threw in for good measure, reminding him of what his actions had caused. He looked down and passed a hand through his hair. At least he had the decency to look embarrassed.

“I know,” he said, taking a deep breath. “Emma, when you can speak *alone*, please, call me...” He stared at me. “I have things I want to say…”

“Ladies, are you ready?” Mark asked. I turned around, wanting to kiss him for this perfectly timed interruption. Greg smiled at Emma.

“Yes, we are, gentlemen. Emma, shall we?” I smiled at Henry. *Take that, you dumper.* I wanted to stick out my tongue at him—childish perhaps, but it would have been satisfying.

“Of course, how foolish of me, you’re on a date,” Henry said, eyeing Greg disapprovingly.

“Greg, give me a moment, please,” said Emma.

Greg stood by me.

“I’ll wait for her,” I said to them.

“Are you sure?” Greg asked. I nodded. He hesitated before obliging, but not without giving Henry a look. Bravo, Greg.

“Henry,” Emma began. Henry stopped her, shaking his head, “It’s all right… there’s nothing to explain. I deserve as much, if not more. Enjoy your evening, Emma.”

For a moment, Emma looked like she was about to bolt after him.

"Let him go, he's almost certainly here on a date as well. Don't allow him to ruin our evening," I said, making her turn to me. She had hidden it well but she was clearly still hurting.

"You're probably right," she said, brushing her tears away. I pulled her to the side, letting other people pass us.

"Hey, no need to cry. You were absolutely brilliant back there!" I opened my clutch and handed her a tissue.

"You think so?"

"Yes! When I saw Jack, I ran like a scared rabbit. Well done you!"

That made her laugh.

"That's better. Are you ready to go back in, or do you need another moment?"

She took a deep breath. "I'm all right."

After we sat down, I scanned the theatre and spotted Henry taking his seat. He had to be here with someone—I waited to see who he had bought to Emma's favorite opera. But as everyone took their seats, no one seemed to be talking to him. It was clear he came here alone. I watched Emma talking to Greg. Henry was a Collins, and this one nice effort wasn't going to change that or fix the damage he had caused. In my opinion, once a Collins, always a Collins, and my dear Emma deserved much better than that!

Sundays in London are quiet and the shops close early. I had errands to run and I had less than an hour to get everything done. The moment I stepped outside, it began to drizzle. What else was new? This was when I missed New York: there, everything stayed open late, which made it possible for people who worked to get things done. I looked at my watch. 5:45pm. I had fifteen minutes before the store closed. I shut my umbrella and pulled on the door. It was locked. The sales girl looked at me and tapped her watch, taking the key with her.

"I have fifteen minutes!" I knocked on the glass. She doesn't look up. "Bollocks!" I complained to no one. The ringing of my mobile distracted me from my grievances. I looked at the screen and began to talk immediately.

"Why is it that every store in this city feels the need to shut its door before closing time?"

"It's Sunday, people want to get home. You should know better," David scolded me.

"Since when did you become my mother?" I asked, walking up the block, trying to find another store.

"If I were your mum, you would be in therapy right now. Get a taxi and come meet me at The Source, Richard is playing tonight." That explained the music I heard in the background.

"Richard? You're still seeing him? I thought last week you were going to break things off for good?" I said. David had met him at the opening of some gallery where Richard had been working as a waiter. He was an aspiring musician—David was into that at the moment.

"Please, spare me the lecture, I know. I was, but I felt sorry for him."

"Oh, whatever, you're still shagging. That's it, isn't it?" I knew David very well and there was no other reason he wanted to stay with this Richard guy.

"*Catherine,* I'm offended." He sounded surprised.

"Uh huh… I've known you for how many years now?" I asked.

He sighed. "If you must know the shagging is incredible. Just last night…"

"I can really do without the details. I don't need a mental picture." I shuddered.

"I need you here," he insisted. "He said he wanted to talk. This morning, he tried to convey that he had feelings. Naturally, I avoided him, but I don't think I can do that tonight. He is going to say the L word you silly girls like throwing around like it means something. I'm going to be forced to tell him that I don't feel the same. He may cry and you know I hate scenes."

I rubbed my forehead. He was right. There would be tears and the only one crying would be Richard.

"David, break up with him, put him out of his misery. It's not fair to string him along."

"But..." David began.

"No buts! I don't care how amazing shagging him is. I can't believe you're calling me to be your chaperone so that you can avoid having him tell you he loves you. You're unbelievable sometimes."

"When you put it that way, you make it sound so dirty and cheap...you know me so well." I could *hear* him grinning. "Come on, I would do it for you," he pleaded.

I raised my hand, signaling a taxi. "Fine, I'll see you in a few." I had barely sat down when my mobile went off again. "Jesus, I'm on my way, the taxi doesn't have wings," I said.

"Remind me again why I got married," a small voice asked.

"Olivia?" I looked at my mobile, making sure. She sounded like she was crying.

"I've been informed—no, more like instructed—that I am on an allowance. An allowance! Have you ever heard of such a thing? It would be one thing if I was spending thousands of pounds in one shopping trip. I have never, ever, done that. Not even my parents placed me on an allowance. How am I supposed to survive? Am I supposed to walk barefoot because my husband says so?" she wailed.

I was trying to put together the pieces of the puzzle as she talked and cried at the same time. It was hard to follow her. "Olivia, stop. Take a deep breath and tell me exactly what happened from the beginning."

She gulped for air. "Brandon found my new pair of shoes this morning, the ones David got for me. I left them in the bag stashed in the cupboard in the hall."

I laughed. This was not catastrophic. I leaned my head back on the seat. Saying I told you so was not going to get us anywhere. But she had a point: for her, being given an allowance would be a form of torture.

"Don't laugh, Kate, this is serious. My life is over as I know it. He was angry, he couldn't believe that I didn't last the month without buying a pair of shoes. I tried to explain that David had bought them but he wouldn't listen. And when he saw the price, he lost it. He asked me why I would need another pair, that he barely owns six pairs himself, as if that qualifies him for some kind of knighthood. We argued and then he went upstairs to check exactly how many pairs of shoes I actually have…" She started crying again. "What am I going to do?"

"Olivia, it can't be that bad."

"He stopped counting at forty-five, he was appalled. I explained to him that half those shoes are old and I wouldn't be caught dead wearing them. I meant to donate them, I've just been so busy. That's when he found the two pairs of Louboutins I got at Harrods on Boxing Day. He said I needed help and stormed off to work without saying goodbye. Why should I be ashamed of how many shoes I own? He has a lot of junk around the house that I don't complain about."

"Babes, calm down. You're right, you don't need to justify yourself. It's your prerogative to own as many pairs of shoes as you like," I said, silently thankful that I had no one telling me what I could or could not buy.

"Kate, I have never seen him this angry. He said the last time he checked, a woman had two feet and could only wear one pair of shoes at a time. Then he demanded that I show him my receipts from now on. He's gone completely mental!"

This was not going to be resolved over the phone.

"Why don't you come join me, I'm meeting David at The Source. You sound like you need a nice glass of wine."

Olivia sniffled. "Okay, I'll see you there."

I hung up, closing my eyes. Between the two of them, I was going to need something

stronger than wine.

Chapter Nine

David waved me over the moment I walked through the door. Richard was on stage singing a ballad—and he was surprisingly good. He almost had a Coldplay vibe going. The handful of times I had been around Richard before, there had been something familiar about him that I couldn't put my finger on. And now that I saw David dressed in what I was sure was a designer version of grunge clothing, it hit me.

I sat down next to him. "You know, I've never realized until now how alike you and Richard are. It's really uncanny," I said looking back and forth between the two of them.

David looked at Richard, eyed him up and down and shrugged. "I don't see it."

"Look at him," I pressed. "The hair, the nose, the body… that is totally you." I said.

David pressed his lips together in thought. "Well, *maybe* there are similarities," he said, picking up his drink. "That would explain a lot actually."

"How so?"

"I am the hottest person I know, and he's as good in bed as I am..." he started.

I rolled my eyes. "Is that really all you think about? Can't you have a conversation for, say, five minutes without talking about sex?"

David smiled, crossing his arms. "Has it been that long for you, darling?"

"What are you talking about?" I asked, eyeing the menu. I hated when he was right.

"Don't play dumb with me, being bitter is a sign. You're just jealous of my Guatamaleness."

I refrained from laughing for fear of encouraging him even further. "Enough with the *Bird Cage* quotes. It was funny the first couple of times, now it's just annoying."

"Being a bitch, another sign," he taunted.

"Hey! Be nice. You dragged me here, remember? I could leave, there are a few good shows on tonight that I'd rather be watching."

"I take it back. But seriously," he said, placing his head on my shoulder, "go get laid."

"Jerk," I mumbled underneath my breath.

"I heard that," he said.

"You were meant to," I replied. Richard's band picked up the beat and I found myself tapping my foot along to the music. "When are you breaking up with him?"

David shrugged. "I was thinking about doing it tonight but now, looking at him, I don't think I'm ready for that."

"But you're not in love with him."

"No."

I stared at Richard, feeling sad for him. I may not have

known him well, but I knew what he was feeling. It was painful, being the one who wasn't loved back. Was that how Jack had responded if anyone had asked him if he loved me?

"Let him go. What are you holding on to him for, David? You're stringing him along and it's not fair. We've talked about this, remember?" This was way too familiar. I shifted in my seat uncomfortably.

"What has gotten into you? Who said I was just stringing him along?" he demanded.

"Isn't that what you're doing by not breaking up with him?" I asked.

"I've never promised him anything, Kate. He knew from the beginning what he was getting himself into."

I knew I was being unfair in comparing my situation to his. David was pretty up-front in his relationships. This was about me feeling that Jack had strung me along. But before I could apologize to him, Olivia made her way towards us, wearing a pair of dark glasses.

"There she is… the lovely bride!" David said.

"Oh, belt up. I want a drink, something strong, not some fruity thing," she said, throwing her handbag in the corner and sitting down next to me. David gave me a baffled look. Olivia was not one to drink hard liquor—but Olivia had never been placed on an allowance before either.

"Drinking on a Sunday, Olivia? To what do we owe this unladylike behavior?" asked David.

She stared at her feet, the infamous pair of shoes. They were hot, worth getting in trouble for. "My initiation to the Collinses, that's what," she said, pushing her shoulder-length blonde hair back. "My *husband* has turned out to be Mr Collins—he placed me on a shoe budget," she told David. She lifted up her feet. "Take a look: these are probably going to be the last new pair of gorgeous shoes I'll ever own again." The waiter brought over the drink David had ordered for her. “No straw?” she asked, cautiously taking it.

“You wanted a man’s drink, there are no straws,” he responded. She threw back some of the drink, making us stare in surprise. She took off her glasses, her eyes wide, and she shuddered, making a face. Her eyes were bloodshot from crying.

“David, tell me, can I get a divorce on the grounds of shoe cruelty?” Olivia asked.

David pondered the question.

“I’m sure Brandon was just upset, Olivia, he didn’t mean it,” I intervened quickly before David had her racing off to divorce court.

She took another sip. “No, he was pretty serious. We have a joint account. He can look even if I don’t show him the receipts.” She gulped back her drink. “I think I need another one of these, I’m not numb enough yet.”

“I’ll get you another.” David ordered her another drink. I gave him a disapproving look.

“What happened to my identity when I got married? I mean, when have you ever know me to wear Collinses? I didn’t think I was marrying Mr Darcy, but I did think I had married Mr Bingley. Today, it’s shoes; what will it be tomorrow… my hair? These natural highlights aren’t cheap.” She touched her perfect blow-dry. “You men want us to look good all the time, but it’s expensive,” she told David, accusing him.

“Not me, darling, I understand,” he assured her. ”The more you spend on your looks, the better, I say.”

“Do you know that they say the first year of marriage is supposed to be the happiest? That can’t be true, can it? I want my glass slipper, what’s wrong with that?!”

I squeezed her hand in support. David took the drink from the waiter and handed it to her.

“Olivia, darling, look at me and listen very carefully to what

I'm about to say." He leaned in. "Take another sip before you hear this, because it may come as a shock… the slipper you desperately desire is made out of glass. That is the first clue about what is wrong with the entire scenario. You want to walk on glass." He laughed. "Have you ever seen anyone walking on glass? You both… and I am including you in this, Kate, are intelligent, modern women. You have to know that it's impossible to do without cutting the shit out of yourself. If you want to try, I'll crack open a bottle and see how you do. Do you understand me?"

I opened my mouth to protest but stopped. He was right. Were we women too delusional to see that?

"What is wrong with wanting the fairy tale?" Olivia moaned.

"Nothing! There is nothing wrong with wanting the fairy tale. You can have it, but you have to tweak a few things so that the prince remains clueless. Do you want my advice?"

"Yes!"

"No," I quickly added.

David rolled his eyes at me and took Olivia's hand. "It's quite simple. Hide your money." He looked at us, straight-faced. "Open a separate bank account, nothing too obvious but put money in here and there. Does he know how much you spend on groceries? *No*. Does he care how much your monthly bills are? No! You spend hundreds of pounds on beauty products. I mean it's endless the way you spend money. So I propose: hide some. That way, you can buy your shoes. I don't want you only to wear Collinses, darling, not you. You're too good for that."

Olivia was nodding her head in agreement. I crossed my arms over my chest as David continued.

"And another thing… I'm going to take a guess: he found the bag and box, correct?" he asked.

"Yes," Olivia answered, looking surprised.

"From now on, when you buy shoes, throw out the bag and the box before bringing them home. Honestly, I'm sure you could have thrown them in your wardrobe and Brandon would not have even noticed. He's a straight man, what the hell does he know?"

"You're right," said Olivia.

David reached down and lifted Olivia's foot. "I look at your shoes and I see Christian Dior. When Brandon looks at them, he sees black heels. He can't tell the difference. If he *can* distinguish between them, *then*, my darling, you have a lot more to worry about than your shoe budget!"

Olivia smiled for the first time. "David that's brilliant, you're a genius!"

"Don't encourage him, this has disaster written all over it," I said. Her eyes had a hint of glitter in them and I knew I was losing her.

"Do you have a better solution?" David asked, staring me down.

"She needs to let Brandon calm down and talk to him rationally," I offered.

"Ha! A rational straight man—when have you ever seen the likes of that?" he asked.

I puckered my lips, thinking. He had a point. I had not. I was not in a situation to know what I would do.

"He's right on this one, Kate," Olivia said. "What started this mess was him finding the shoe box and the receipt. If I had got rid of them, he never would have known."

"Precisely. It will save your marriage," he said. The two of them clinked their glasses together and laughed, plotting away.

"It's deceitful," I pointed out.

"It's called survival, Miss Single Lady." David looked towards the stage. Richard had finished his set and was staring at David with daggers.

"Great, I didn't realize his set was done. Now I have to go and make him happy. Bollocks. Be right back."

David walked off towards the stage. I turned to Olivia. "Is this really all about a pair of shoes?"

Her blue eyes shifted down to her glass. "No, I suppose not. It's been a series of things. I'm going mental. The other night, he left the toilet seat up. I went to the toilet half asleep and I fell in." Caught off guard, I couldn't help but laugh."It's not funny, Kate. Wait until that happens to you. He moves my things around, I feel like it's not my home sometimes. I hate feeling like that."

"I'm sorry, honey."

"Then there's the hideous mounted deer head that's currently at the center of my living room, a wedding present from his grandfather, which of course I didn't see until we came back from our honeymoon. I asked him if we could move it to storage or something until we got a country home, and he said no, that they had hunted it together and it was a great honor. Honor? It's a dead deer, beheaded. It stares at me every day with sad eyes, Kate. I swear it looks right at me, blaming me."

"You have Bambi's mother on your wall," I said.

"Oh my God, you're right, he killed poor old Bambi's mother. I married Bambi's mum's killer."

I had never seen Olivia so disheartened. "Olivia, I was kidding."

"It might as well be, Kate. What I am going to do?" She looked up at me helplessly. I needed to find an answer quickly.

"Okay, look at your new shoes." She did. "Are they hurting you?" I asked.

"A little. The alcohol is numbing the pain," she giggled, taking another sip.

"Well, did you think about returning them?"

She shrugged.

"But you didn't. You know why? For the simple reason that they are hot, just like Brandon. Forgive me for the comparison, but you get what I'm saying. You are not a quitter, Olivia. You want something and you keep it. Eventually, they get better, no?"

She looked at them pensively. "They are gorgeous, aren't they?"

I hid my smile. I was talking about Brandon but whatever

worked. "Yes, they are, and, honey, Brandon loves you to bits. Are you going to let him go because it hurts?"

"He does love me, doesn't he?" She looked hopeful.

"Yes, of course he does. The two of you will adjust, give it time," I said, mentally crossing my fingers. After all, I had never been married, what did I know about this? She got up and gave me a hug.

"What have I said about public displays of affection? We are British, stop embarrassing me," David ragged, pulling us apart. "Honestly, I can't take the two of you anywhere. Come on, let's go somewhere else."

"Is Richard coming?" I asked.

"Nope." He took some money out and left it on the table. "Just broke up with him. I'm in the mood to shop if you know what I mean," he winked, guiding us towards the door. I looked behind me at Richard who was standing on the side of stage, his face all red. He looked angrily at us and stuck his middle finger up at David.

David just laughed. "I'm so over him already."

"Another one bites the dust," I said, following him.

Chapter Ten

"Don't look up. You won't believe who just walked in!" Gemma, my quirky but lovely co-worker whispered, barely containing herself as she lifted her sunglasses to the top of her head. We were up on the roof terrace of our office building, enjoying the rare appearance of the sun. I shook my head and smiled. I didn't have to look to know whoever it was male. Gemma was boy crazy, and given how excited she looked, I wanted to see who it was. I looked slowly, trying not to make it obvious.

"Don't make it obvious, Kate!" she said, excited. I still wasn't sure who she was referring to. "It's Philip Spencer and he's walking this way." She dug quickly in her bag, took out a small tube of perfume and sprayed it all over herself.

"What? He's actually coming to mingle with us commoners?" I hissed, reaching for my mobile and badge on the table. "I'm heading back down," I said, not wanting to stick around and wait for him—especially after our last disastrous meeting.

"Philip, over here," Gemma the traitor called. She waved him over, not giving me an opportunity to escape. Philip Spencer, pompous aristocrat, tailored blue suit and all, had spotted us and was walking our way. Everything about him was immaculate, even his blond hair was perfectly combed back.

"Good afternoon, ladies." He smiled, holding a lunch tray uncomfortably, something he probably hadn't done before. I had always pictured him with a bell in his hand, ringing for his meals to be brought to him.

"Come and join us," she invited, patting the empty seat next to her.

"Thank you, Gemma, very kind of you," he said, accepting the invitation.

"I'm surprised that you get your own lunch," I said to him. I couldn't help myself. His eyes met mine and I looked down. Perhaps that had been a bit harsh.

Gemma gave me a quizzical stare. "When did you get in?" she asked, batting her eyes at him shamelessly. She had no idea how much I loathed him.

"I got in yesterday," he said, smiling at her.

"I'm surprised you even know this place is here," I said again, not being able to control myself.

This time, Gemma looked at me in shock. Philip just looked cross and I actually smiled at him, pleased I was able to get under his thick skin. Match point to me. There was an awkward silence.

"Isn't this weather brilliant? Kate and I ran up here trying to enjoy some of the sun," Gemma said, leaning in towards him.

Philip kept his eyes on me a little too long before turning to Gemma. "It certainly is. I'm glad you ladies are enjoying it. I hope the weather holds for the polo match this weekend. That's why I'm back in London."

Gemma began to gush about the celebrities the firm had managed to attract this year and I zoned them out and began to eat my salad. If I kept my mouth occupied it would stop me from insulting him. I couldn't be held responsible for any truth I uttered that would sound offensive. Gemma gave me a curious stare as I shoved more salad in my mouth. The last thing I wanted to do was discuss polo with Philip.

"Are you coming to the tournament?" I heard Philip asking. I glanced at my hands. I desperately needed a manicure. I only had a couple of meetings this afternoon, I could go today after work. Gemma kicked me under the table.

"Oh, you're asking me?" I said, startled. He was biting back a smile. He thought it was funny. There was nothing cute about Philip at this moment. "I don't think so, Americans don't belong on the grounds. I've been told we somehow draw the wrong attention. Who knows what I might say that may be considered rude and inappropriate," I said, reminding him of what he had told me the first time we met.

Philip smiled, coolly. He knew exactly what I was talking about. Gemma, of course, did not.

"Don't be silly, you're the most proper person I know," she laughed.

"Apparently not proper enough for some," I smiled at Philip.

"I'm sure you can be taught the rules of the sport," he said.

"That's a marvelous idea Philip, we can teach her!" Gemma said, getting excited about the prospect of being attached to him at the event. But as much as I liked Gemma, there was no way I was going to get stuck with Philip for her.

"No, thank you, I already had a lesson a couple of years ago, and I'd rather not have it repeated."

Philip pressed his lips together and almost began to shake his head. His face was turning slightly red.

"Oh my, look at the time, I totally forgot I have a deadline to meet," I looked at my watch and got up quickly, bumping the table.

"Which account are you working on?" Philip asked, crossing his arms.

"The Thomson account." I threw out the first name that came into my head. He reached for his inside pocket and pulled out his mobile.

"That's one of my accounts. Funny, I haven't been notified with regards to a deadline."

Busted! I could feel my cheeks turning red. He was challenging me, waiting to see how I was going to get out of this one.

"Well, you work out of New York, this is a London matter," I snapped, and began to take my lunch tray, but Philip rose and took it from me.

"I've got this, I wouldn't want you to be late for your deadline."

I looked away from him, mumbled to Gemma that I would see her later and rushed out. *How could I have been so stupid?* I kept asking myself moments later when I made it to the safety of my office. Once I'd shut the door, I let out a deep breath. I'd just made myself look like an idiot and a liar in front of Philip. I might as well start packing my stuff and looking for a new job.

There was a knock on the door a few moments later, but I was too preoccupied with my thoughts to answer it. When the door opened, I didn't bother to look up.

"What the bloody hell was that all about?" Gemma asked, closing the door behind her. I opened my drawer, searching for my aspirin bottle.

"I don't like him, he's so stuffy and pompous," I mumbled, taking a pill out and swallowing it quickly. "Really, who cares about a stupid polo tournament? Some of us are actually busy and perhaps have something else to do on a weekend."

"Did something happen between you and Philip?" she asked, eyeing me curiously.

"No, of course not. Don't be silly. Jack will be there more than likely and I don't want to run into him," I said half truthfully.

"That makes sense, totally understandable, but Philip doesn't know that. I'm not saying you have to kiss his ass but pretend to like him a little when you're around him. He is the big boss' son. Don't ruin a career opportunity over Jack."

I sighed. "I suppose I have to go to the tournament, don't I?"

She beamed. "Yes, you do. But I'll be there. Just make an appearance. If Jack is there and approaches you, I'll come and rescue you. Deal?"

I nodded, knowing I was going to regret this. I would have to go to the tournament, but this time I knew better and wouldn't wear my good shoes.

I got lost in my work for the rest of the day. Philip was in my last meeting and I tried to bolt as soon as it ended.

"Kate," he said. I stopped in my tracks, mentally cursing as I turned around. "Could I have a moment?" he asked, walking towards me.

I put on a fake smile, remembering what Gemma had said. "Sure. What can I do for you, Philip?"

He watched a few people pass us before speaking. "I wanted to let you know that I would like you to be at the tournament."

Now that was surprising. Was Philip about to apologize? That would be a first.

"Your clients will be there and it would be good if they saw you. We want them to feel at ease and have their questions answered if any should arise."

"Of course, whatever the company needs," I said, sounding too sincere.

"Good. See you there." He gave a nod as if that settled everything. The two of us stood there awkwardly, unsure of what to do next.

"Is that all?" I asked. "I have loads of work to finish up."

"Yes, of course. I don't want to keep you from your work. Have a good evening, Kate." He walked away. I could never figure that man out.

Chapter Eleven

The day of the tournament came quickly. This time, I was appropriately dressed in a smart jacket, white blouse, blue jeans and brown riding boots. I took in the crowd around me, laughing and enjoying the festivities and the beautiful day. It was easy to spot the newbies, whose heels were sinking into the ground. I sympathized with their looks of horror, realizing how naïve I had been and how far I'd come.

Spotting Gemma, I waved. She was mingling with a few co-workers and made a sign that she was heading towards me. Taking the opportunity, I casually scanned the grounds for Jack, as some of the players were starting to take the field. I might as well get it over with. It would be easier to see him first than have him surprise me. But there was no sign of him. Philip, however, was walking in my direction. Our eyes locked and he gave me a polite nod. I mimicked him. I had to admit, he looked quite the English gentleman in his uniform. His looks weren't the problem—just what came out of his mouth when he opened it.

"Creep ex-boyfriend is behind you," Gemma said, standing next to me.

"Thank you," I replied, but since my back was now toward the field, I had to take her word for it.

"He's staring this way, flip your hair to the side and laugh like I'm telling you the funniest thing ever." She nodded, encouraging me to do as instructed. It was silly but I did it anyway, laughing a bit too loudly.

"Perfect! He's looking right at you. Don't turn around. I'll tell you when." I looked at Gemma, not believing I was playing high school games. "You can look now," she said.

I turned around casually and looked across the field. There he was, looking dashing as he mounted his horse.

As the match commenced, I stood on the sidelines with Gemma and pretended to pay attention, but all I was really doing was staring at Jack. Philip got control of the ball and hit it toward his teammate. Jack rode by him, trying to get the ball back. Jack was good, but Philip was the better player, and he took the ball from Jack and scored. I found myself clapping for Philip. He rode by us and smiled.

"That man is hot," Gemma whispered.

"Jack?" I asked, surprised she would say so, even though of course he was.

"No, Philip! You want to make Jack jealous? Go out with Philip," she grinned.

"Philip? Me? Please, he's not my type," I responded. I could feel eyes on me and looked up expecting to see him, only it was Jack watching me.

"I think I'm going to get something to drink, it's gotten quite warm out here. Would you like something?" I asked Gemma. I was still being a coward.

"No, thank you. Give it a thought, won't you? I'm telling you, that would be the best revenge," she said sweetly. I waved off the suggestion and walked away, putting distance between myself and Jack.

An hour later, after the match had ended. I found the perfect spot under a tree and took a seat. I pushed my sunglasses back over my head and pinched the bridge of my nose. This day was giving me a headache.

"Kate, join us at the tent," Gemma called. I nodded, taking the liberty of enjoying a few more moments. I couldn't help yawning as the breeze hit my face.

"I hope we didn't bore you too much."

I looked up, squinting against the sun, at Philip, who was red-faced. His hair, for once, was in disarray. "No, not at all. Well done, you," I said. His eyes flickered in surprise at the compliment. I started to get up and he offered his hand. I looked at it, unsure, but took it and he helped me up.

"Thank you. I'm pleased you came today," he said, giving me a warm smile—another first for him.

I dusted off my hands on my jeans. "Well, it's a company event and all, I couldn't exactly say no," I said with a laugh.

"I suppose not." He sounded disappointed. "You know, Kate, that first match you attended…"

I shook my head. There was no reason to bring back that embarrassing moment. "I've learned since then."

He looked down at my boots, grinning. "Yes. But it could have been handled differently." I raised my eyebrows in question. "*I* could have handled it differently," he corrected himself. "Did you fall off your horse?" I asked, surprised.

"No." He laughed like I had never heard him before.

"Too much sun?" I continued, teasing him.

"I suppose I deserve that." He scratched the top of his head, looking shy. Perhaps Gemma was right, I needed to be nicer to him. This was my opportunity to clear the air with him once and for all.

"About the other day," I began, but stopped mid-sentence as Jack approached us.

"Philip, excellent match, mate!" he exclaimed, shaking Philip's hand and slapping him on the back as if they were pals. Only I knew they weren't.

"Yes, it was, wasn't it?" They had a brief, senseless discussion before Philip excused himself, leaving me alone with Jack. Part of me wanted to run after him and leave but I needed to face Jack and get it over with.

"That guy is a piece of work," Jack said, turning to me.

"He's not that bad," I said, watching Philip walking towards the tents.

Jack stood in front of me and blocked my view. "Since when are you defending him?" he asked with a laugh.

I shrugged. "I'm not defending him, I'm just saying perhaps he isn't as bad as he seems. I'm beginning to think it's a bit of a facade with him. Given who his family is, I can't say I blame him, really."

Jack looked annoyed. "You haven't crossed him yet… Wait until you do, then come back and tell me you sympathize with poor Philip," he said.

I sighed. "Well you know him best…" I said. "I should get back to my friends."

Jack held his hand to his chest. "Truce? Let's not get into an argument over Spencer; I know you have a certain degree of loyalty."

"Loyalty? Don't make me laugh," I said, putting on my sunglasses. That was about as much as I was going to be able to handle today. I turned to leave.

"Why don't we have a drink?" he asked, stopping me.

I didn't respond. Every part of me was saying, *Keep walking, don't let him see that you care*. But I hesitated and he saw it.

"For old times' sake, Kate," he said, his dark eyes finding mine. "Please."

"Okay," I managed, and followed without a word as we headed towards the tents.

"Seeing you here today brings back so many memories," he said finally after getting us drinks.

I put my drink down. "Let's make it clear, Jack. I didn't come here for you. It's a work function. Why wouldn't I be here?"

"Yes, I know it is, but it's significant for us, no?" His eyes softened as he said that. Did he really need to ask? Of course I knew it was significant to us, this was where we had met.

"Why can't we talk about the lovely weather we're having or the match or whatever it is acquaintances talk about?" I said.

"I thought we were friends," he insisted.

I laughed. "Given the circumstances, I don't have a clue how you can actually believe that or say it with a straight face."

Jack closed his eyes, inhaled deeply and took my hand. I was startled. I hadn't been expecting him to touch me. He closed his fingers around mine.

"I've missed you, Kate. I've missed us." He opened his dark eyes and I tried not to stare into them but it was hard not to. "How things have changed since we met at this event, haven't they?" he said, almost to himself.

Inside, my stomach did a somersault. I had envisioned Jack saying that he missed me hundreds of times... But somehow it fell short ...there was still more I wanted to hear from him.

"Are you fighting with your girlfriend?" I asked with a cheeky grin.

He let go of my hand. "Why must you bring it back to that?" he said.

I stared at him in disbelief. And there he was, the true Jack. I had almost believed that he had changed his ways.

"Are you still with her?" I asked.

His silence gave me my answer.

"It doesn't change that I've missed you," he said finally, looking unsure.

"Incredible, you almost had me," I laughed, throwing up my hands in exasperation. "It doesn't change that you've *missed* me?" I leaned in. "You say Philip is a piece of work but at least he shows you that he's an ass. You, on the other hand, are a Wickham!" I began to get up but he grabbed me.

"There's no need to make a scene," he said through gritted teeth, glancing at the crowd.

Part of me wanted to make a scene—after all, he deserved it—but, let's face it, the one who would look crazy would be me. I pulled my hand free from his grip and grabbed my bag. I faced him.

"I've been breaking my head trying to figure out what I could have done differently, was there anything I could have done for us, but right now, hearing you, I realize there was nothing."

Jack got up, towering over me, looking angry for a change. "You broke up with me, Kate, you're the one who called it quits. I didn't. I wanted to stay."

I leaned in closer. "You chose her over me and you cheated. How many times do I have to remind you of that fact? That's your problem right there, you have a selective memory. It only remembers what is done to you and not the harm you cause others—in particular, me!"

"I never said what I did was right," he said.

There was no way I was backing down from this one. "Funny, you never said it was wrong."

He took a deep breath, realizing he wasn't going to get me to agree with him. "I wasn't the ideal boyfriend. Fine, I admit that. I can't explain what happened between us. I thought something was missing. Something didn't feel right."

I pushed my hair back absent-mindedly. "So that gave you the right to drop your trousers? Wow, thanks for explaining that to me. Now it all makes perfect sense," I said. "I'm done talking about this. The next time you see me, do us both a favor and don't approach me!"

"Kate!" he said, but I ran out, tears blinding me.

"Hey, are you all right?" Philip asked, as I bumped into him. He held on to my shoulders. "I'm fine," I muttered, shrugging off his hands and keeping my gaze down. I did not want Philip to see that I was crying. Silently grateful that he didn't try to stop me, I walked away quickly. I needed to hide before everyone saw me crying like a fool over a man I had stupidly allowed back in only to have my heart ripped out again. I ran behind the stables to compose myself.

Jack was making his way towards me. "Let me explain," he said.

"Please leave. What else is there to explain? You've pretty much summarized it with 'something was missing'." I wiped my tears away angrily.

"I didn't say that to hurt you," he said, taking his thumb and slowly wiping away my tears. Every part of me wanted to push him away but I stood there frozen. He tilted my head up and looked into my eyes.

"You never do but that's all you wind up doing," I said. "I just wish you would have said so from the beginning before I invested..."

"I love you," he said, pulling me closer to him. He began to kiss me there against the stables, not caring if anyone walked by. I stood up on my tiptoes, kissing him back eagerly, allowing myself to admit that I had missed him, that I still needed him.

"Kate?" We broke away from each other. Philip was standing there, frowning, and clearly noting that he had interrupted our make-out session.

"Give us some privacy, won't you, mate," Jack said with a soft laugh. I didn't say a word as I came back to reality. Philip stared at me angrily and with disappointment. I could tell it was taking everything he had not to say something. Shaking his head, he walked in the opposite direction.

"That guy is always at the wrong place at the wrong time, I

swear," Jack laughed, pulling me close again. Of all the people who could have found me making out like a teenager, Philip was the last one I wanted or needed it to be. I pulled away slowly. This was ludicrous, and I couldn't let Jack kiss me.

"You shouldn't have done that, Jack." He tilted my head up and grinned. Without another word, he kissed me again.

Chapter Twelve

As I made my way down Regent Street, maneuvering through the Saturday crowd, I watched them all running with bags. I realized that we shopped to show off to other people. As much fun as it was to buy things for yourself, if you had no one to show it to, what was the point? Sometimes, we made outrageous purchases. You know the ones: they make you feel guilty the moment you leave the store. You try justifying it, but the bag just feels heavier with each step. You hold off telling your friends because at least one of them would tell you to take it back. They would bring to the surface what your subconscious was already telling you… it was a mistake. That was how I'd felt for the past week since my make-out session with Jack. I had kept that a secret. I wasn't ready to confess to the group. It was like keeping a pair of Collins in my closet. I would be questioned, and I was not ready for the confrontations.

I turned the corner facing the Tudor building that was the home of Liberty, one of the oldest department stores in London, and texted David to let him know I was there. He, of course, was already inside. I was meeting him to shop for a birthday gift for his Great Aunt Margo. David always got her a gift from Liberty. He would buy her scarves with one of their famous floral prints—it was a tradition her father had started, and David, since he was a little boy, continued it. Quite darling of him, but he would never admit that. He adored her—and I had grown quite fond of her myself.

I entered the store. I always loved the smell of it, the dark wooden spiral staircase and floors that creaked like an old manor.

"This looks like her, doesn't it?" David asked as soon as he saw me. I stared at the beautiful dark pink floral scarf.

"Am I allowed to touch it?" I said.

"Are your hands clean?" he asked, inspecting them.

"I was actually joking," I said in protest. He handed me the scarf. It felt like heaven. As the saleswoman showed us a few of the newest prints and my mind wandered back to Jack and all that had transpired in the last few weeks since the polo tournament. I was starting to believe that I was out of my mind.

"Oh, look at this one," David cooed, eyeing a white and navy blue orchid-print fabric.

"Hm?" I barely acknowledged what he was saying. I was too preoccupied with my own world.

"Are you listening?"

I nodded, not really paying attention.

"I'm seriously feeling ignored, Catherine. You know I need your undivided attention while I'm spending money or else what is the point of you being here?" David asked, staring at me suspiciously. I needed to be on my game with him. David missed nothing.

"You're so dramatic. Honestly, you've missed your calling,

you should have been an actor," I said, picking up one of the scarves. "Should I get her something for her or for the house?" I asked, distracting him before he asked any awkward questions. I might as well shop for her here too as I needed to get her a gift.

"I can add something else in the same print from the two of us," he said.

"Does she still think we're a couple?" I asked.

He shrugged. "Possibly."

"*David*, you have to tell her. Remember the last time we were here with her? She was practically creating a wedding list, choosing upholstery fabrics and everything."

He leaned back on the counter. "Why ruin it for her? The only crime she has committed is enjoying *EastEnders* a bit too much; it's a ritual with her. Besides, it's her eightieth birthday. She has, what, five good years left?" he said without a blink of an eye.

"I can't believe you just said that."

"It's true. Perhaps I should get her a better gift this year, you just never know."

I shook my head in disbelief.

"What?" he protested. "Don't give me that look. Why disillusion her? If this was my mum's birthday, then I would be all for ruining her party. It reminds me of when I came out to her. I did it on New Year's Eve at the stroke of midnight." He grinned, remembering.

"You did not."

"I did. It was at a lavish party she was hosting, of course. Her really snooty friends were there and she was complaining and correcting me all night. At the stroke of midnight, I turned to her in front of all her friends and said, 'Mum, I'm gay! Happy New Year!"

"Stop lying."

The saleswoman tried to disguise the fact that she was laughing as David handed her his choice.

He crossed his heart. "I swear," he said. "I've never told you this? She blamed the devil, also known as my father, for being too liberal with me, and I blamed her for putting me in military school." He took the package the saleswoman was holding out to him and linked his arm through mine. "She said she knew it was a phase and it would rub off. I told her, 'Oh, it rubs off, believe me.'"

I laughed. "You're horrible," I said. I thought about his mother and the shock that must have crossed her face when he said that.

"Why are you so surprised? Did we just meet? Anyway, Aunt Margo was there for me through the back-and-forth legal battles my parents had, being passed from one to the other. She was the only consistent thing in my life, never missing a birthday, school play or graduation. She was there for me for all of that. If she wants to believe that we are an item then so be it. Besides, I am one hell of a catch, Kate. I'm successful, wealthy, a fabulous dresser, handsome...what more could you possibly want?"

"Hmmm, let's see, shall we... You're gay," I said, pointing out the obvious.

"Beggars can't be choosers, darling. I don't see you having a better offer. Actually, I'm the best offer you'll ever get. I would never cheat on you with another woman, I enjoy shopping for shoes with you... It would be an ideal situation: you could run off with other men and so could I," he smiled.

"As tempting as that sounds, I'll have to pass," I said.

He stopped, checking his pocket. "I forgot my glasses, be right back," he said. "You don't know what you're turning down... Here, make yourself useful, take the bags. It's the least you can do after ... breaking my heart."

I took the bags and shook my head.

"I know you're only with me for my money," he called, teasing me.

"You got that right. Who else can take me shopping like this but you?" I called back, bumping into someone.

"Sorry," I turned around and found myself looking up at Philip, who had obviously heard what I had just said to David.

"Hello, Kate. Shopping I see," he said, looking at David's bags. I hadn't seen much of him since he'd caught me making out with Jack. I could still see the disapproving glare he had given me.

"Yes, is that a crime in this country?" I asked, lifting up my chin, ready to confront him.

"You don't seem the Liberty type," he said. I bit my lip. Part of me wanted to lash out but I was still slightly embarrassed. I hadn't seen him since he caught me making out like a teenage girl behind the barn.

"Why is that? Is this store only meant for posh people like you? I wanted to bite my tongue the moment I said it. No matter how hard I tried, his presence turned me into a rude individual. I couldn't help myself around him.

He pressed his lips together. Finally, I had hit a nerve with the jerk. I turned to look at David, who had struck up a conversation with some man and was oblivious to my current situation.

"That's not what I meant, just that this type of department store… You know what? Never mind."

"Oh, come on, Philip, don't back off now, please enlighten me as to what you were going to say."

"It's best I don't," he said.

"It's funny, if you asked me, I would say you didn't seem like the department store type either. I always pictured you sending someone to shop for you or having a tailor fit you at home for suits and stuffy tweed jackets, that sort of thing," I said.

His look was making me feel uneasy. I had pushed it too far. I knew I needed to apologize.

"You have a strong opinion of me, don't you, Kate?" he asked, his jaw tense.

"Just like the one you have of me, Philip. If you'll excuse me, I want to continue shopping in peace." I turned on my heels and walked towards David, upset at myself for letting him unsettle me like that.

David was staring at us, having caught our little exchange, and was still looking at Philip when I reached him.

"Who is that and where have you been hiding him?" he shot at once.

I looked back at Philip, who was giving me a deathly stare. "It's not like that at all. He's a colleague. Philip Spencer."

"Spencer as in Spencer & Lockhart?" he asked, not missing a beat.

"That would be correct," I answered.

David glanced at him again. "His family practically owns the whole firm," he pointed out. As if I did not know that fact.

"I am fully aware of that. Don't let that fool you. He's the most pompous man I've ever met!"

"Well, honey, aren't we all? He looks quite good from where I'm standing."

I pulled his arm. "Stop looking at him. I don't want him thinking we're talking about him."

"But we are talking about him," David said, putting his arm around me. He continued checking him out. I allowed myself a quick glance in Philip's direction. He was over at one of the counters looking at something. Even in a department store he looked quite serious—almost stuffy. He looked like he'd rather be anywhere else but here.

"I've been observing him. He doesn't play for my team… definitely not."

"How could you possible know that just by looking at him?"

"I just can. What a pity for me but lucky for you." David put his glasses on with a grin.

"And this is relevant to me why?"

"A straight man—hot—and you need to ask? This is exactly why you are still single, Catherine," He turned to the salesman for back up. "Right?"

Ignoring him, I looked quickly again at Philip, who stared back at me stony-faced.

"Maybe I should go over there and introduce myself," David grinned.

I gasped. "Don't you dare!" I hissed. "Let's get out of here, I want to go to another floor."

"What did you do to him? He's practically throwing daggers at you," David said.

"We don't get along. I don't want to get into it. Let's just leave," I insisted. We had to walk past Philip in order to get out. I dashed by him as David took his time inspecting him. The moment he got near arm's length, I pulled him away.

"You have some serious issues," he finally said as we went into the perfume and make-up area. Everything on the floor was laid out as if one was home—bottles on the counters, everything accessible. I picked up a bottle and sprayed it on, trying to be casual even though inside I had unexplained emotions.

"I don't like him, he's full of himself, and could we please just drop it?" I said.

"Fine, take my fun away. Which reminds me, fancy going to Sketch tonight? You and I haven't gone out prowling together in ages."

I hesitated, quickly formulating an excuse. There was no way I could tell him I was seeing Jack later. He was waiting for an answer.

"I can't join you tonight, sorry. I have plans," I answered, fully aware I had revealed too much. I knew him well enough to know he wasn't going to leave it alone.

David stared at me curiously. "With whom? Elizabeth didn't come into London this weekend, Emma is out in the country and Olivia is at some family event, which leaves me as the only person you should be busy with… u*nless* I have some gorgeous twin brother that I don't know about." He flashed me his biggest smile. But he was right. The chances that I wasn't with at least one of them on a weekend were minute.

"I have other friends besides you," I said, clearing my throat. I mentally crossed my fingers that he would let it go and move on to something else. A normal person would do that. But there was normal and then there was David Cunningham.

"Please, don't make me laugh," he said as we made our way to the café. I loved afternoon tea—the thought of it was the only thing making this disastrous shopping day worthwhile. I followed him to our seats next to the neon pink geese.

I sighed. "What do you think I do when you're out with one of your many admirers?" I said.

He shrugged. "Stay home, dying of boredom?" He glanced over the menu. "What do you

think? A glass of Perrier Jouët?"

"None for me, thank you. And listen… look at me." I waited until he looked up from the menu. "I go out on dates, you know. I may not mention them all the time… but I do."

"Uh-huh, so you do have a date?"

The couple arriving caught my attention. "Philip," I said through gritted teeth.

"Philip? You're going on a date with Philip?" His eyes opened in surprise, unable to contain his excitement.

"No, dimwit, he's here!" David turned around. "Don't look at him!" I exclaimed.

David turned back to me. "Calm the fuck down, I'm not flagging him over here, am I? Have a glass of champagne, you need it."

He continued complaining but I ignored him and, doing exactly what I told him not to do as curiosity got the better of me, I eyed Philip. He wasn't alone. The cute brunette he was with laughed at something he'd said as he pulled out a chair for her. She had those bouncy curls that everyone wanted. I knew Philip, he wasn't funny. The fact that she was laughing like that already told me something was wrong with her.

"Now who's staring? Is that his girlfriend?"

"How the hell should I know? It seems like it," I said, looking away from them before I was caught looking. "Anyway, I'm not going on a date tonight, I'm just saying I go out on dates that you don't know about." David knew me well enough to know I was lying. Worse, he knew I was keeping something from him and now he was lurking around like a shark that had smelled a drop of blood.

"You're hiding something, I can tell."

"You're so annoying sometimes, you know that? I don't want to go out tonight," I lied, hating that I was doing so. "I don't grill you when you say you have plans, do I?"

"What is up with you? Is it that time of the month?" he inquired.

I punched him lightly on the shoulder. "Ouch," he said loudly, rubbing his arm. It caught Philip's attention and he looked over at us. Without any acknowledgement, he looked away, paying attention to his date or whoever Miss 1,000 Watts Smile was.

"I say, what did you say to him downstairs? He's giving you the look I reserve for my mother," David said.

"Never mind that," I said, annoyed.

"Whatever, go ahead and keep your secrets. You know I'll eventually find out. Remember that time you bought those silly shoes?"

"What does that have to do with anything? And for the record they weren't silly, they were cute," I answered, placing the napkin on my lap as we ordered.

"Cute?" David said once the waiter was gone. "No. I told you not to get them. They were plastic or some man-made material, and did you listen?"

"Don't be a shoe snob. Some designer shoes hurt you know," I said.

"Yes, but the pain is worth it. If I'm going to bleed, let it be for Salvatore Ferragamo or Tom Ford, not some plastic bottle someone placed a bow on and called a shoe." I rolled my eyes at him. "But that's beside the point," he continued. "You looked straight in my eyes and lied. *'Oh no, I won't get them.'*" He tried to imitate my voice.

"First of all, I don't sound like that," I said defensively.

"Oh yes you do, record yourself one of these days. You bought them regardless of what I told you and tried to keep it a secret until that day you wore them and they gave you blisters, remember that?"

I cringed. How I could forget, it was the worst shoe experience of my life. *This is what Jack breaking your heart is going to feel like—a big blister.*

"Is there a point to this?" I said quickly, trying to shut the thoughts out.

"The *point* is, I found out. I knew it the moment you came to brunch wearing flip-flops. Flip-flops, for God's sake. After we had gone over why you were not to wear flip-flops unless you were at the beach, coming out from a pedicure or at home. I knew immediately you had bought those hideous shoes."

"And this is relevant how?" I asked, distracted by Philip, who was laughing and looking quite relaxed as she touched his hand. Was that how Philip acted on a date? I pushed the thought away before I had formed an answer. It was none of my business.

David held the champagne glass in mock toast to me. "You are hiding another pair of shoes and it's only a matter of time before you come running to me in a pair of flip-flops."

Making my way home, I thought about those painful shoes David had reminded me about. When I had bought them, I didn't know they were going to hurt like hell. No one went out for shoes that deliberately pinched, gave you blisters or pain. I had simply fallen in love with the shoes, been blinded by the sparkling little jewels. Yes, there was always a risk that a shoe would be intolerable at first, but in that first moment, one did not think of that. You went by emotion. It was like love at first sight—you just fell head over heels. The bonus was when people admired them and even envied you for wearing them. That made one take the pain. I sighed. Jack had already caused me pain—was I know the fool blinded by the glitz? The difference was, this time, if I got hurt, I had no one else to blame. I had tried on that pair and knew there were consequences. Jack had left me scars that had temporarily healed. I was about to reopen them—only, this time, I knew there was a chance the pain would be worse.

Chapter Thirteen

A few hours later, I was dressed and ready to go. It was amazing what a shower, makeup, a hot dress and shoes could do. The dress was emerald-green silk, a Gucci number I had got at a consignment store, and it was one of my favorites. I kept it for special occasions. My one-strap Jimmy Choo gold sandals added the glam effect I was looking for. The best thing about the dress was its plunging neckline. Tonight, I wanted to be daring. The final touch was a thin, delicate gold belt. I smiled, anticipating the look Jack would have on his face when he saw me.

The doorbell rang, and I looked up at the clock. He was a bit early. I gave myself one last look over, fluffing up my hair a bit, before I opened the door and stared at David, who was holding a bottle of wine. I was totally busted.

He grinned. "Oh, liar, liar, pants on fire," he sang, coming in. "Someone has a very hot date tonight." He gave me another look. "Is this your idea of no plans? Or are you bored and playing dress up?"

"I can explain," I finally said.

"I can't wait to hear the explanation. While you think of something I'm going to have a drink. You look stunning, by the way. Now before you get your knickers all bunched up, I am not here to spy on you. I simply came because you said you had no plans, and my date cancelled on me. I don't think that I've ever been stood up, have I?" He paused, trying to remember. I closed my eyes, mentally cursing. I needed to get rid of him ASAP. Jack would be here in fifteen minutes.

"Ah, uni, Mike Atkinson: he stood me up! Maybe I should see if he's on Facebook,"

he mumbled going into the kitchen.

I walked after him. "I don't think you should start searching for your exes on Facebook, David. Don't go looking for trouble."

"Who said anything about looking for trouble? I want to see how the last few years have treated him. Maybe he's fat and bald. It would serve him right for standing me up." He opened my cabinet, taking out two wine glasses. "So, there I was at home, shocked that I had been stood up, for the second time in my life, and I thought of you sitting here alone again on a Saturday night. I can't even comprehend how you can handle this every weekend."

"Handle what?" I asked, wanting to take him by the arm and tell him to come back tomorrow.

"Stay home with no date, it's horrible. You're used to it now so it doesn't even deter you, but I can't be home on a Saturday night. I feel like someone is slowly choking me. So… being the good friend that I am, I took one of my best bottles of wine and thought, 'Let me make my very best friend happy with my presence.'"

I rolled my eyes. "Wow, what a lucky gal I am. How lovely. How could I turn down a proposal like that! I actually like being home alone sometimes, thank you very much."

"I don't. It's unnatural, which is why I am here to rescue both of us with a 2009 Marchesi Antinori Tignanello. We can order in. I'll even let you choose some romantic chick flick and we can have a lovely evening together." He opened the bottle. "Let it breath for a few minutes."

I didn't have a few minutes. I took the bottle and poured each of us a generous glass.

"Hey, you have to let it breath for a bit," he protested, taking the glass and the bottle from me. I clicked mine to his.

"Cheers!" I said, taking a big gulp.

"Honey, that is so unpleasant, especially when you're looking so classy. We sip, we don't gulp it back like it's a tequila shot."

I said nothing. David took a sip, eyeing me carefully. "How many times have you worn that dress? Three times… at most?" He was close. It had been only twice. "That dress does not come out unless it's a special occasion. And since you haven't mentioned you've met an incredible man, I'm going to go out on a limb here. Either you're suffering from short-term amnesia since you saw me earlier today… or you're going to see *him.* That is the only other possible explanation for why you lied to me today. Why you didn't tell me?"

"Why would you even go there?" I asked nervously.

"Because I know you, Catherine. You've been acting elusive, and now you have plans you forgot to mention—only a man would be worth your only Gucci dress—and, right now, you look like a child who's been caught with her hands in the cookie jar. So whose jar are your hands in, hmmm?"

"Let's just drop it," I said quickly.

"Oh, come on, I know it's Jack. I might as well stay and say hello to the bastard."

"That is it!" I placed my glass down. "I love you, but you have got to go." I took his glass, pouring it out in the sink.

He looked at me, appalled. "I was drinking that!"

I recorked the bottle and handed it to him, taking his arm and pulling him towards the front door. David took the bottle and placed it against his chest, looking at it then back at me.

"I can't believe you just threw out my drink—an expensive glass at that. You could have at least let me finish it."

"I'll buy you another," I said. "But it's best if you left."

He passed his fingers through his hair. "You're actually kicking me out over the sample sale Jimmy Choo? I thought we were better friends than that."

"Stop calling him that. And what is wrong with a sample sale Jimmy Choo anyway?!"

Laughing, he put his arm around me. "There is nothing wrong with the sample sale, honey. They are, after all, the real deal—only not the ones you want. What you don't seem to understand is that you are not going to find the Darcy you seek there. You're settling because you want it so much."

I didn't have time to analyze any of what he had said, I just knew I needed him to go. He sighed. "Fine, I'll go, but you had better have a really good explanation for how this little situation came about. AND I expect to be told over dinner at Nobu—your treat," he grinned.

"Nobu? And you wonder why I go shopping for sample sale shoes," I said.

"I'm actually being quite fair." He sounded as if he thought he had given me some sort of deal.

I laughed. "Okay, I'll make the booking tomorrow. Now, please, I mean this with no ill intention, but you have to get out of here." I quickly ushered him out of the door.

"Sample sale, Kate, sample sale—don't settle, remember that. You need to think about stepping up your game."

"Goodnight, David." I closed the door and leaned back against it. That had been a close call. Jack was not a sample sale. I didn't care what David said. Sample sales were real designer shoes. The soft pounding on the door made me groan.

"Christ, David! Nobu, I got it, I will make the darn reservations. Now bugger off!" I said as I opened the door.

"Should I come back?" Jack asked, smiling. "Everything all right?"

"No, please, come in. Sorry, I thought you were David, he just left. You know how he is," I explained, letting him in. I felt shy all of a sudden in my dress. Perhaps I had overdone it, I had no idea where we were going.

"Yes, we just ran into each other downstairs. He didn't say a word, just handed me this." He lifted up the bottle of wine.

I sighed. "Sorry about that, he can be a bit difficult. It could have been worse."

"It could have, but he's got excellent taste in wine. Mind if I pour myself a glass?" he asked as he inspected the bottle.

"Sure," I said.

"Maybe he likes you and is switching sides…"

I opened my mouth to berate him, but he lifted up his hands in defence. "I'm kidding. I actually like the way he's overprotective of you. After we broke up, I ran into him at an event and he ripped me a new one."

"*What?*" I looked at him, stunned. David was not the confrontational type at all, and if he had been, he would have at least told me about it.

"He warned me to stay away from you. Pushed me against the wall and everything. I think I was more shocked that he had it in him, which gave me time to calm down and not start a fight with him then and there." He saw my expression. "Relax, I didn't touch him. He was quite angry for my having hurt you."

"He never mentioned it," I said softly. I had the urge to call him right now and tell him what a stupid thing that was to do and at the same time hug him.

Jack placed his arms around my waist and pulled me close to him. "I don't really want to spend the evening discussing him. Do you?"

I smiled. "No."

He lifted my chin with his forefinger. "I must apologize,

sweetheart," he said, almost touching my neck with his lips. I held my breath, all thoughts ceasing.

"Why? For David?" I asked, my mouth dry.

"No, for not telling you how incredible you look tonight." He kissed my neck slowly. I closed my eyes. God help me. This man was going to be the death of me. I became jelly whenever he touched me. And now, feeling his lips at the base of my throat, I couldn't care less about what had happened in the past.

"We have dinner reservations…" I stopped short as he lowered the top of my dress.

"It's your fault for looking so delicious. I think I'm fine right here. How about you?"

Chapter Fourteen

Going out to dinner was overrated in my opinion. I glanced at the corner, where my dress was in a heap along with my shoes. Jack turned on his side and smiled, scooping me up in his arms. I had missed him holding me like this. These were the moments I had taken for granted when we were together, and I was grateful I had them back. We had been seeing each other regularly since the polo tournament.

"So much for dinner," I said, giving him a kiss.

He pushed my hair back. "Do you want me to try to get us a table?" He lifted his head, glancing at the clock. It was late.

I shook my head. "No, I like it here. We can order something delicious like pizza and have the wine."

He laughed. "Not quite the fancy dinner I had planned for us. I've never been around anyone else who can have pizza all the time the way you can," he said, running his fingers up and down my arm. "I don't get it."

"Are you kidding me? Pizza is the food of kings. I thought everybody knew that," I said, matter-of-fact.

"I'm afraid not. But thankfully, I have someone as clever and beautiful as you to show me the light." He turned me over on top of him, making me squeal as I grabbed the sheets.

"Yes, you are a very lucky man, Jackson Barnes. What would you do if I wasn't around?" I looked down at his deep brown eyes, reality starting to creep in. But I mustn't think of what we were doing, of what I had compromised in order to have this moment. I didn't want to face the reality of what I had been hiding for the past few weeks. It was moments like this, when I thought about what was going on, that the guilt would sink in.

"Hey, what's the matter?" he asked.

"Nothing. I just really want the pizza," I said, trying to sound convincing. The shriek of his mobile made us turn. Jack pushed us both up. I placed my hand on his chest, pushing him back down. "Don't get it," I pleaded.

"It's probably Domino's. Don't you know I can telepathically call them now?" he joked. The phone stopped.

"Ha ha. Tell them I want green peppers on mine," I said when the mobile began to ring again. He looked at me and I frowned.

"It could be work." He leaned over, grabbing his jacket and getting the phone.

"Hello?" he said, getting up. I leaned back on the pillows, watching his body tensing. I didn't need to ask who it was. He looked at me, mouthing *sorry,* and I shut my eyes as I heard him picking up his clothes.

"I'll be there as soon as I can."

Biting my lower lip, I watched him and listened as he told a story about how he was working but would be there shortly. It was *her*. The truth that I had been avoiding from the moment he walked through the door. Jack was still dating Amanda, and now *I* was the other woman. We had resumed our relationship, only now it was an affair. We had reversed roles, Amanda and I. It was something I had been struggling with the entire time but I didn't know what do about it. There was a part of me that kept saying I was just doing this in order to get revenge. That I would be able to stop at any point. Jack sat at the end of the bed and hung up.

"Please don't give me that look," he said.

"I'm just looking, Jack, no *look*," I said with a bit of attitude.

He sighed, pushing his hand through his hair. "I..."

"You promised we wouldn't be interrupted tonight," I reminded him. I reached for my robe on the side of the bed, quickly putting it on.

"Kate, this isn't intentional. Her car broke down and she's alone." He didn't wait for an answer, just went into the bathroom. I heard the shower going on.

She was alone? Didn't he see that *I* would be left alone as soon as he left? I thought back to the day of the polo tournament. We had taken things too far. It had been a moment of losing complete control. It was foolish, reckless and stupid. I knew he was still with her, but somehow I foolishly thought I would be able to handle this no-strings-attached situation. *How's that working for you?* I asked myself as I looked out the window. Hearing him showering in the bathroom made me think of the way I used to call him, wondering where he was. Is that what he had told her when he had to leave to get to me?

Taking a deep breath, I made my way towards the bathroom without saying a word.

"I'm sorry, I had every intention of staying. I don't want you hating me, Kate," he said over the shower. I leaned against the door, wrapping my arms around myself.

"I know," I finally said.

"I'll make it up to you, I promise." He turned off the water and pushed the curtain open. I handed him a towel. Just like that, he had erased all traces of me. Every part of me wanted to turn to him and say, *I'm done with this, I'm sick of your excuses. I wish I just hated you or even better had no feelings left for you at all. Hit the road, Jack!* But, of course, I said nothing. Instead, I walked back to the bedroom, and sat at the foot of the bed, watching him get ready.

Jack momentarily stopped what he was doing and placed a kiss on my forehead, the tip of my nose and finally my lips. I hugged him tightly, putting my fingers in his wet hair and nuzzling his neck. I was struggling with my feelings, and at the same time I was angry at myself for being pitiful. Elizabeth Bennett would be ashamed of me.

"I'll see you soon, darling."

I watched him go and, for the first time since I started this affair with him, I began to cry.

"And there you have it. I've been seeing him—if that's what you call it—for nearly a month now. At first, this was all about revenge. I figured shag him then dump him. It seemed like a perfectly good plan at the time," I said to David. I hadn't told him that Amanda was still in the picture. "Have him feel what I felt when he did it to me, you know?"

David had both his index fingers resting on his lips in thought, just staring at me.

"Say something," I insisted.

"I don't know what to say, really, this is very unlike you, Kate. I'm still trying to process it all."

"I'm screwed. I have no idea what I'm doing. I tried to end it, but I can't. Whenever I want to tell him, I freeze. He's addictive, it's the only way I can describe it. I've been avoiding him the last couple of days to see if that helps me. But I think it's hurting me more than it's hurting him. I think I'm losing my mind," I confessed.

He took a deep breath. "Losing? Honey, you lost it the moment you thought you could use him and leave him. It's not you, and it doesn't work when you are still in love with the guy. I can be that person, *believe me.* I've been that many, many times. The kind of revenge you want only works if you don't have any emotions, and you, my friend, are all about emotions. It will never just be about shagging with him."

I looked at him, unsure. "Is this why you called him a sample sale Jimmy Choo?" I recalled.

David nodded. "Partly. The sample sale doesn't give you the one you really want. Understand? You're settling. Even though it is a pair of authentic Jimmy Choos, it's a shoe that you have to plan an entire outfit around."

"But they are still a pair of Jimmy Choos… on sale," I stated.

"True. You think it's a bargain at first, but you wind up spending a lot more money to make them work."

"Exactly how much wine have you had?" I looked at the bottle.

He waved me off. "I'm not pissed. I know you want to believe that he'll change or that he has but, in my experience, men like him don't change. If I thought he had, I would be the first to admit I was wrong, but I'm hardly ever wrong… Men like Jack will always have another woman on the side."

I looked away. This was not what I wanted to hear. I didn't want to believe that. Worse, I couldn't tell him *I* was the other woman, how far I had actually gone. I wasn't telling him because, deep down, I knew if I did, he would tell me what I already knew and was not ready to hear.

"You'll forget him. It takes time, but you will. What you need to do is go shag someone else to get him out of your system. Here's a thought, how about that Spencer bloke?" he suggested.

I made a face. "Great, you're telling me to replace a Darcy with a Collins?"

"Ahh… but who said Jack is a Darcy? And we both know Spencer is certainly not a Collins, keep telling yourself that. You need to make Jack a distant memory. Go to anyone—hell, go wear a Collins, literally. Maybe then you'll see your own worth."

I laughed. "Seriously, dude. How many glasses of wine have you had?" I had suspected three. That was usually David's limit before he went off on his self-proclaimed love guru revelations.

"I sound like Jeremy Kyle, don't I?"

"Yes, you do. You're scaring me, cut it out."

"Not as much as you've scared me. Cut him loose, Kate, for your own good. I really mean it when I say you can do better." He gently patted my hand.

"Is that why you pushed him up against a wall and warned him to stay away from me?"

He attempted to look shocked.

"Don't try to deny it, David. Jack told me that, shortly after we broke up, you told him off."

Shrugging, he leaned back in his chair. "I merely threatened to cut a certain part of him off if he hurt you again, that's all."

I raised my eyebrows.

"I'm kidding, lighten up."

"I know. It's just so sweet of you. Thank you," I said, meaning it.

"You're not going to get up and hug me, are you?"

I laughed. "Do you want me to?"

"Not necessary. 'Thank you' was sufficient. Besides, what are friends for? And as your friend, I really want you to consider forgetting about him. Jack is not a Darcy. He's a Wickham. A bad, bad Wickham. A hot one, I'll give him that, but that's the worst type because *he* actually believes he's a Darcy. Do remember one thing, Kate: in the book, Wickham never changed."

Chapter Fifteen

Ignoring Jack for the rest of the week proved to be extremely difficult. He sent emails, called, had flowers delivered to the house and to the office with simple messages saying to call him, that he was sorry. The last note still had me shaking. He had quoted Mr Darcy. "My affections and wishes are unchanged…" No signature, just the quote.

I thought about how the rest of the line went: "…but one word from you will silence me in this subject forever." The message was clear. My stomach instantly tightened into a knot. He would let me go if I asked. I felt my throat closing. I had to make a decision. Did I want to stop seeing him? Wasn't that what I was showing him by ignoring him? Did I want it to continue?

My meeting ended early and Jack's note was all I could think about. I looked at my watch: it was lunchtime, but I wasn't hungry. What I wanted was a distraction. Part of me wanted to tell him, "Yes, silence yourself forever on the subject and leave me alone." The other part wanted to tell him how corny but perfect that line had been and kiss him, beg him not to go. Still debating the matter, I found myself walking past the Jimmy Choo store and stopped in my tracks as I saw the tiny white *sale* sign in the window. I stepped inside, remembering the first time I walked in here; I had felt like I needed to whisper. I smiled for the first time in days and Jack was pushed from my thoughts.

Stilettos, each more gorgeous then the next, were lined up, calling my name. But I was focused and headed straight to the back for the sale shoes. This was heaven: the chance to try all these shoes and possibly end up leaving with one! I glanced down the row until my eyes came to rest on a pair of black corset-front four-inch stilettos.

I asked the sales lady for my size and as she headed to the back to check, I said a silent prayer. My mood lifted when she came back with the pale lilac box and placed it at my feet. I put the shoe on the floor, removed my own, and felt instantly happy. There was nothing like stepping into a fabulous pair of heels for the first time.

"They're fantastic," the girl next to me said with envy in her eyes.

"They are, aren't they?" I replied, staring at my feet. These were hot. It was taking all of me not to look like a silly schoolgirl and leave the store with the shoes on. The first pair I ever purchased took me a month to wear for the first time, and look how that had turned out. *Don't think of him!* I told myself. Of all the people to think about, Philip was not one of them.

"What size are those?" the girl asked, looking at them attentively.

"37 but I'm taking them," I said with a smile.

I took the bag and left the store. I had purchased a pair of £350 shoes for £175—it had just made my entire week! Not even Jack could dampen my mood today. Suddenly, I froze. Coming up the street was Philip. I tried not to make eye contact but it was too late. He had seen me and was walking straight towards me.

"Kate, shopping again, I see?" he said, looking down at my bag then up at me. He was giving me a look as if to say *why aren't you at the office*? I hated how his eyes pierced right into me.

"I just finished a meeting with the Warner team. I do get a lunch hour, you know," I said, feeling the need to defend myself. The luck I had when it came to this man was unbelievable.

"I never said anything contrary to that. Actually, I didn't say anything negative at all. Why is it you always take a defensive approach with me?"

So he had noticed. "That's not true…" I said.

"It is. In the office, even that day at Liberty… I watch you interact with other people and I'm the only one you treat this way," he said boldly.

"I think you're imagining things," I said, trying to look away, but it was impossible once his eyes held you.

"And I think you're being evasive." He smiled at me, waiting for me to look back at him. He was holding his briefcase tightly. Other guys had a shoulder case; not him. Old school.

"So, tell me, what have I done to offend you so?" he asked.

Here, in the middle of the street, he expected me to tell him what my problem with him was! Where did I start? If I told him exactly what I thought of him, we would both be standing here until nightfall…

"Perhaps you always catch me on a bad day. I don't know what you want me to say."

"I'm giving you a free pass here: tell me what I've done to be the only person in the office who gets looks like the one you're giving me right now." He waited for an answer.

"Just forget it, please. If you'll excuse me, I have to head back to the office."

"I suppose shopping at Jimmy Choo and spending a few

hundred pounds would make anyone want to run to the office," he called after me. If I hadn't been so angry, it would perhaps have occurred to me that Philip was jesting, but all I saw was red.

"Comments like that are *exactly* why I don't like you," I snapped.

He towered over to me, making me tilt my head to look at him. "Finally, the truth. You have to learn to trust people."

"You're a man; I don't trust you on principal," I responded.

He shook his head. "Seriously, Catherine..."

"Don't call me that, don't say my name like that..." I stupidly said. It was my name, after all. But at that moment, he sounded like Jack. "Why must you be so rude? You need to filter your thoughts before you speak," I said, beginning to walk away. He followed.

"And you are defensive and prejudiced. I was merely pointing out that you bought a pair of Jimmy Choos. It was a logical statement. I was actually trying to be funny."

"Not in the tone in which you said it. I know you, Philip Carlton Spencer." He grinned in an annoying way, noticing that I knew his middle name. "What is wrong with spending money? I'm not spending *your* money, am I?" I asked loudly. People were staring. It was ridiculous that we were having this conversation in the middle of Knightsbridge where anyone we knew might see us.

"Technically, it is my money," he said.

"Wow," I said, swallowing hard. I knew he was snobbish but not to this degree. So that was how he saw the rest of us.

Philip looked more shocked than I did. "That was extremely inappropriate. Forgive me, Kate." He pushed his hands in the pockets of his trench coat. I was angry.

"And you wonder why people don't like you. You sure know how to make a girl feel unwelcome... again."

"That wasn't my intention. I happened to see you as I walked down the street and instead of ignoring you I came to say hello and you instantly jump down my throat."

"Well, do us both a favor, Philip: unless it has something to do with work, do not approach me socially." I said, as I signaled a taxi and jumped in. I rested my head back against the seat, holding the bridge of my nose. What the hell had gotten into me? I had totally lost it and had allowed him to get under my skin. He thought he could speak to anyone however he pleased. Yes, there was a certain business etiquette one ought to follow with the boss, but he wasn't the boss yet. Just the son of one of the bosses. Did that give him the right to talk to me like that? And the middle name! How could I have let that slip? It's not like I fancied him or anything, I had looked up his bio the first time I met him and noticed it. Now he probably thought I was stalking him. Perhaps it was time to call the headhunters… just in case.

I sat in my office, contemplating whether to approach Philip again, but it wouldn't solve anything. I should not have to justify how I spent my money. Jack would never question it. He would have encouraged it. But then again, Jack was the flashy type. I sighed, leaning back. The worst part was that I was careful. I wasn't an overspender, but Philip clearly thought I was.

"Oh, lilac bag. Let me see!" Gemma said as she knocked on my open door and came in. She took the bag. "May I?"

I smiled, taking off my glasses. "Sure," I said, watching her open the box.

"These are gorgeous. You have great taste, Kate, great taste indeed."

"I was thinking of returning them," I admitted.

She looked at me, mortified. "Why would you do that?"

I couldn't tell her it was because Philip had made me feel guilty about spending 'his' money. "I have another pair just like these."

She sat across from me. "Babes, you can never have enough of 'another pair just like these'. These are perfection."

"Thanks. I needed to hear that." She was right. Why should I let pompous Philip take away my shoe joy? I was giving him way too much importance.

"You have such tiny feet!" she said, still inspecting the shoes. "Anyway, are you ready to go?"

I looked at her, confused. "Go where?" I asked.

"Philip sent an email inviting us all for drinks. You didn't see the email?"

I frowned, looking at my inbox. There was no email from Philip. So, that's how he was going to play it…

Gemma didn't miss a thing. She tried to cover for him. "I'm sure he meant to include you, minor oversight." I had to admit, it stung a bit. He was making me even more of an outcast.

"No worries, I have a lot to do anyway," I said, pretending I wasn't bothered.

"Come anyway, it won't be a problem, we could all use a drink," she nodded, trying to reassure me.

"I have to meet David later, but thanks for letting me know." I put my glasses back on. I certainly wasn't going to go where I wasn't wanted or invited.

"Okay, well, let me go get ready. If you change your mind, we're at the pub down the street."

"Cheers, hun, have fun." I smiled the best smile I could manage, not wanting her to see that I felt like my stomach had been kicked in. That little shit. It was taking everything I had not to storm into his office and finish giving him a piece of my mind. He wanted war? War I would give him! If he thought he was the only one who could make someone feel like an outcast, he had no idea who was messing with!

I'd had it for the day. I looked at the box and took out the shoes, putting them on. I instantly felt better. Part of me wanted to walk into the pub and show Philip he couldn't intimidate me. But I didn't dare, partly because I didn't trust myself not to walk up to him and choke him with his own tie.

Grabbing my bag and coat, I headed out, watching the group leaving. My eyes locked with Philip's as I walked towards the elevator banks. He looked up, surprised, about to take a step towards me.

“Hot shoes, Kate,” Becca, one of my co-workers, called out.

“Thanks.”

“You’re not coming?” she asked.

“No…”

Philip stopped in front of me. “Why, not?”

I couldn’t believe he was pretending he hadn’t invited me. The smile he gave me annoyed me. “I wasn’t invited, and I have a rule about not going where I’m not wanted. I’m a good worker, Philip. So if you want to get rid of me, you’ll need a better excuse than my shopping habits,” I whispered, not wanting anyone else to hear.

Without a word, he reached inside his jacket, taking out his mobile.

“Have a good evening,” I said sweetly and got inside the elevator that had just arrived.

“Kate, wait a moment,” he called, but I didn’t listen, pressing the close button furiously. The elevator doors shut. That round somehow went to Philip. I stomped my foot. I needed to control my mouth and temper around that man.

Chapter Sixteen

I'd been struggling for the past fifteen minutes to pull on a pair of cheap plastic leather pants. This was not the way I'd envisioned getting ready for the party. The first time I was invited to a 'fancy dress party' in London, I thought it entailed a cocktail dress and fancy shoes. Thankfully, someone had mentioned buying a costume. London was famous for them and, I have to say, I quite enjoyed dressing up. Frustrated, I picked up the phone and dialed David's number.

"Who chose these outfits?" I huffed.

"You must have ESP. I was about to call you and say isn't this the best costume ever?"

"Ask me that question once I've manage to put on these stupid pants," I said, trying to pull them up one more time.

"You're using those? I have my own leather pants I'm using instead… I have to admit, when you and Elizabeth said let's go dressed as *The Incredibles,* I had another picture in my mind altogether."

"Why?" I asked, still wiggling them up. Almost there!

"You said it was a cartoon. I was expecting to be dressed in something with bows, hence the mentally wishing you ill. But *this* costume, I'm digging."

"Of course you are," I laughed out loud.

"I bet you're wishing you didn't have dessert this week," he teased.

"You have no idea," I answered.

"Well, darling, cheer up. Tonight, we're going to have a blast."

I struggled again and finally managed to pull the pants on. The T-shirt was a tad on the snug side, too. Leave it to Elizabeth to pick out the smallest shirt. It would do, as long as I didn't eat anything else for the rest of the night. The last touch was the high black patent leather boots that fit like a glove. I stared in the mirror, placed on the eye mask and laughed… it was silly and fun. No one gave me a second glance as I got out of the taxi and walked towards the club.

Elizabeth spotted me when I stepped inside. "Damn, girl, we look good!" she said.

"There's David," I pointed. As always, he looked great. It made me wish I'd opted out of the plastic leather and actually had cool leather pants. He looked like *The Incredibles* meets *Rock Star*.

The club was pumping with great music and everyone was in elaborate costumes. We headed towards the dance floor, spotting Emma waving at us. At least, I thought that was Emma. She was dressed like a naughty angel in a black corset get-up, her red hair was spilling down past her shoulders and her make-up looked amazing.

"Wow, who did that?" I asked David.

"Olivia and I did," he said. "We did well, if I do say so myself." I recalled that he had picked out her outfit. She had complained to me all week about it but hadn't revealed what it was.

"Go you, she looks hot," Elizabeth remarked.

"Look at you guys! You look brilliant! Wicked," Emma said, attempting to hug us as she balanced her drink in her hand.

"So do you, honey." I said, watching as she took a sip from

a fruity-looking drink that looked suspiciously like a cocktail. "You seem cheerful."

"What is this?" David asked, taking the drink. Pushing her straw to the side, he took a sip. His eyes opened wide. "Wow, this is strong even for me."

Emma took it back. "It's quite delicious. I told the bartender I wanted something to loosen me up and make me forget a *certain someone*." She winked at me. "But I have to say, I don't feel any different." She attempted to take another sip from her straw but missed it. David chuckled.

"How many of these have you had?" I asked.

"Two, I think. I finished the first one quite quickly. Have I told you how delicious it is? It doesn't even taste like alcohol. Here, try it!" She handed me the drink. I took a taste and the liquid burned as it traveled down my chest.

"I think you should try some water…" I began. My voice was drowned out by the holler of delight as Cheryl's *Fight For This Love* blasted around the club.

Emma started jumping up and down, nearly spilling her drink over herself as she took another sip and handed it to me. "This is my song!" she squealed. One of the guys pulled her into the crowd.

"Hey!" I called out to him, but David stopped me.

"If I had known spirits did this to her, I would have spiked her tea a long time ago," he said with a smile. The three of us looked in the direction Emma was being taken and my mouth dropped opened. She wouldn't…

"Oh yeah!" Elizabeth called out when Emma was lifted on top of one of the tables. The DJ was mixing the beginning of Cheryl's song with Britney Spears.

"It's Britney, bitch!" Emma yelled. The crowd cheered her and she began to dance.

"Oh my God," I said, covering my mouth. Never had Emma let loose like this before. "David," I said, patting him on the shoulder. "Go over there and get her down before she hurts herself." David wasn't paying attention. I placed the drink on the bar. Emma was going to be mortified about this tomorrow. Not that it was a bad thing; she was having a good time shaking her booty up on the table.

"It's okay, let her, she's having fun," David yelled over the music.

"Too much of anything can make you sick, even the good can be a curse…" she sang along.

Olivia approached us, looking as astonished as we were. "What is going on?" she asked. She was dressed like Batgirl.

"Let's just say Emma has discovered alcohol," Elizabeth filled her in.

"She's good," said Matt, one of David's friends. "She's quite good."

"She doesn't even realize this is wasted on the men here," Olivia added.

"That's not necessarily true. The crowd loves her," he said. "If they didn't, believe me, she would have been jeered off a long time ago. She is totally dancing like the video, she's quite good." I had to agree with him, Emma was brilliant.

I glanced over at Elizabeth, who had her mobile phone out and appeared to be recording it.

"What are you going to do with that?" I asked suspiciously.

"Relax, *Mom,* I'm not going to post it on YouTube. This is for when she's sober. I want to show her how much fun she is drunk!"

Olivia was still looking at Emma in disbelief. There she was, still dancing to Cheryl Cole, only now she was accompanied by two back-up dancers. The DJ lowered the music and Emma started singing a cappella.

"*We gotta fight, fight, fight, fight, fight for this love…we gotta, fight, fight, fight, fight, fight for this loveeee…*" the crowd joined her, then the music started again to cheers.

"I didn't even know she knew who Cheryl was, never mind listened to her music. I love the new Emma!" David said, singing along.

"Henry has been calling her. She's having a hard time ignoring him," I said to Olivia over the music.

"Are you serious?"

"Yep, some nerve, right? Bless her, she's trying. But I suppose we should let her have some fun tonight," I said. My mobile began to buzz and I took a look. Jack's name showed on the screen and I shut off my phone. I knew I couldn't avoid him forever. I needed more time to decide what I was going to do. That's what I told myself. But secretly I knew the answer: I wasn't going to be able to turn him away.

The four of us were on the dance floor, laughing and having a great time. Emma was completely wasted. We had been dancing for quite some time and I was finally forgetting my problems and enjoying myself.

Olivia looked at her watch. "Well, it's time for me to go," she said, saying goodbye to us. I took the opportunity to round up Elizabeth and Emma.

"I want to stay!" Emma protested. This was the girl you usually had to force out of the house for a drink, never mind to go to clubs.

"I'll watch her," David reassured me. But the fact that he was deep in flirtation didn't fill me with confidence. He could easily forget she was there with him.

"I think the fallen angel has had enough for the night. Come on, sunshine, grab your wings, time to go home," I instructed.

Emma groaned like a toddler who'd been told it was time to go to bed. She pulled her wings back on, half slanted. Elizabeth chuckled, holding Emma up as we exited the club. With the biggest grin on her face, Emma looked up at the bouncer. "I danced in Heaven!" she said, spreading her arms out.

The bouncer smiled at her. "Yes, you did, angel."

"I danced in Heaven," she repeated, holding on to me, stumbling a little.

"Oh boy, let's get a taxi…" Elizabeth hailed down a cab. "Careful, babes," she said, helping Emma inside.

I gave the driver directions while watching Emma, who immediately leaned her head back and closed her eyes.

"Emma, honey, are you okay? You're not going to be sick, are you?" I asked.

The taxi driver gave us a warning glare.

"No. I'm dizzy, though."

"Just keep your eyes closed until we get to your flat, we'll be there in no time," Elizabeth reassured her. "I'll stay with her tonight," she turned to tell me. "She's going to have one hell of a headache tomorrow morning."

"Don't let her drunk-dial Henry," I warned. That's the last thing she needed to do and would instantly regret it when she was sober.

"He's a jerk!" Emma said, opening her eyes at the mention of his name. "I gave up a great opportunity for him. For what? How could he do that?" she moaned.

"It's his loss," I reminded her.

She nodded vigorously. "It is, isn't it?" She closed her eyes. "I wish he could have seen me tonight. I was totally wicked, wasn't I?" she asked with a grin.

"Yes, you were, honey," Elizabeth answered, giving her hand a supportive squeeze. Poor Emma. I hoped it would get easier for her.

The taxi dropped them off first. I had the driver wait until they were both safely inside the building and turned on my mobile. I had over ten texts from Jack. Should I call him? I didn't have the drunk-dial excuse… As I looked at his name, ready to tap the screen and call, the taxi stopped, startling me. I was home.

As I got out of the taxi, I opened my clutch, looking for my keys. There was no point in calling him. It was late, I knew where he would be… with her.

"Haven't I told you to have your keys ready before you get to your front door?"

I stopped in my tracks. My heart felt like it was in my throat. I looked up at Jack, who was leaning against the wall. "Nice costume, by the way," he added. Ignoring him, I looked around at the deserted street.

"What the hell are you doing here? You scared me! How long have you been waiting here?" I rambled.

"Long enough. I was beginning to think you weren't coming home." He sounded annoyed as he pushed himself off the wall. "You've been ignoring me and this was the only alternative. I had to see you," he said, shoving his hand through his hair. I finally retrieved my keys, my hands shaking. My stomach felt like it had hundreds of little butterflies fluttering inside, betraying the bravado I was displaying.

"Jack, we've been through this before, I thought you would have learned by now. When someone ignores your calls and texts, that means they don't want to talk to you," I said, avoiding his eyes. His eyes always made me go against what I wanted to do.

"I've upset you and I'm sorry. It was completely my fault. I promised you that entire night and I went against my word," he said. I still refused to look at him.

"Some things never change. I'm used to you going against your word. Please go home. I'm tired. I had a very lovely evening and I don't want it to be ruined by you," I said, heading towards the door. It was only by a thread that I was holding back the impulse to throw myself in his arms and kiss him.

Jack blocked the entrance. "I know that and I've been trying to explain myself to you and apologize."

I laughed. "Since when did you start giving a shit?" Finally, I looked at him. "Please, move."

Jack shook his head. "No, I want you to listen to me." I opened my mouth to argue but he continued. "If you didn't mean anything to me, would I be here in the middle of the night waiting for you, taking the chance that you could have got out of that taxi with some guy?"

Part of me felt validated, happy that he hadn't assumed I would be here alone. He leaned in, closing the gap between us.

"I've been standing here for the past hour, going crazy, running that particular scenario over in my head and wondering how I was going to have the power to contain myself from punching him in the face. And you know what I realized?" he asked, not waiting for me to answer. "That the one who needed his face punched in was me for what I've done to you." He pushed my hair back softly from my face. I closed my eyes, feeling all my defences coming down as he kissed me.

Chapter Seventeen

I must admit, not even the best shoe can duplicate the feeling of waking up with Jack's arms wrapped around me. I moved and he snuggled his face into my neck, making me sigh with contentedness... I had missed this most of all, waking up in his arms, feeling the sense of security. Trying not to disturb him, I sat up and stared at him, admiring his perfect features and resisting the urge to pass my fingers lightly over them. He took my hand and kissed my fingers softly, startling me.

"Lie back down," he grumbled.

There was nothing I wanted to do more than stay in bed with Jack. But I had made plans with the girls to have brunch and, given last night's events, they would be eager to meet and discuss it. Part of me wanted to text them and say I was feeling unwell or too hungover. But I knew them well enough: they would wind up at my apartment at some point later on to check on me.

"I have to meet the girls soon," I said. He opened his eyes and gave me a smile.

"Cancel. Tell them you have better plans, like being in bed all day with me," he said with a devious look. I couldn't help but grin. "It's a better offer and you know it," he teased. I grabbed my robe and put it on as I got up.

"Let me give them a call and tell them I can't make it," I said, giving in. "Do you want some coffee? I asked, heading towards the door.

"What I want is for you to come back to bed," he said wickedly.

"I'll be back," I promised, and headed downstairs to phone Elizabeth. Her mobile went straight to voicemail and I sighed in relief. It would be easier to cancel to a voicemail than to Elizabeth, who would have had a million questions. I gave her the excuse of a headache and exhaustion, and a promise to make it next time. I stared at the phone, feeling guilty: I should be able to tell Elizabeth the reason and not have to lie. Yet again, the little voice in my head I'd been ignoring was making its way to the surface.

I looked out my kitchen window as I started up the coffee maker. The sky looked promising. Perhaps I could convince Jack to head out later and grab a bite on the river by the old bookstore we loved, just like old times. The woman heading towards the building seemed familiar… I looked closely and panicked. Emma! Emma was making her way up the street towards my building. *What was she doing here?* I ran to the living room, picking up Jack's clothes and mine—scattered all over the floor—as quickly as I could. Nearly tripping up the stairs, I pushed the bedroom door open. Jack had gone back to sleep and didn't stir.

"Jack! Get up quickly and get dressed. Emma's on her way up," I said in a panic.

He pulled a pillow over his head and groaned.

"Come on, get dressed! I'm not kidding." I threw his clothes on the bed. The buzzer echoed downstairs. Grabbing a pair of jeans, I looked around for a sweater. Jack lifted up his head, watching me hop on one foot as I tried to pull them on.

"She's not coming up here, is she? Wake me up when she's gone," he mumbled and rested his head back on the pillow.

"You have to get dressed!" I stressed again. But he ignored me and closed his eyes. He was not appreciating the urgency of the situation.

"Jack!" I tried to pull on his arm but he didn't move. I gave up trying to get him out of bed. "Fine, just don't come out until I tell you," I hissed and shut the door quickly behind me.

The buzzer rang again and I ran downstairs. Out of breath, I picked up the receiver and the camera came on.

"Emma, what a surprise," I managed.

"I'm early, I know, but I knew you would be up." She looked up at the camera. "Are you going to let me in?" she said with a laugh.

I buzzed her in and ran to the bathroom, throwing water on my face and pulling my hair into a ponytail. I grabbed my ballet flats and headed towards the door, quickly looking up the stairs and praying silently that Jack wouldn't come down.

When I opened the door, there was Emma, wearing dark glasses and looking a bit pale.

"Why in the world did you let me drink so much?" she groaned as she came in. "My head feels like it's going to split in two." I scanned the room and saw Jack's shoes in the corner. Thankfully, Emma went straight to the kitchen. I took the opportunity and grabbed the shoes, lifted up the top of the coffee table and threw them in.

"Do you have any headache tablets?" Emma called.

"In the bathroom," I replied. "I'll get you one." I spotted my bra on the floor. I grabbed that as well and shoved it into a drawer, then headed to the bathroom to get her some aspirin.

Emma came back with a glass of water. "Did I do anything embarrassing last night? Be honest with me, I can handle it. All

I remember is asking the bartender for a drink, and the next thing I know, I'm in my flat."

"Let's just say you were quite lively," I said, relaxing a little. Emma looked at me in a panic. "Nothing that would ruin your reputation," I teased, and filled her in.

She groaned and shook her head. "How embarrassing," she moaned, covering her face.

"It was not. Everyone loved you. But to be honest, I'm surprised you're up at all," I said. "Actually, I just left Elizabeth a voicemail saying I wasn't feeling up to going out today."

"*Oh no* you don't, no excuses. If *I* managed to get out of bed today this hungover, you can come out. Besides, it's sunny! We have to enjoy it while we can. Elizabeth is getting ready. You know how long she takes, and I got restless so I told her to meet us at the restaurant."

I mentally cursed the fact that I was an early riser. She wasn't wrong in assuming so, it was no secret that I got up at the crack of dawn even on the weekends. And she was already here—if I tried to back out, it would raise suspicions. I wasn't ready to confess and that left me no choice but to go.

"Okay, I just need a little time to get myself together. Do you want a cup of tea?" I asked, looking up the stairs, hoping Jack would remain there.

"That sounds lovely, I'll make it. Go and get ready."

"I'll be down in five minutes," I said and ran upstairs to the bedroom. This had potential disaster written all over it. Jack needed to get dressed and stay out of sight. Only, when I stepped into the room, the bed was empty. The bedspread was on the floor but there was no trace of Jack.

"Kate, your mobile is going off," Emma called. "It's Elizabeth."

"Go ahead, answer it, I'll be right there!" I shouted, panicking. "*Jack,*" I hissed. I could hear Emma coming up the stairs. I froze, unable to react. Deep in conversation with Elizabeth, Emma didn't notice my distress. She sat at the foot of the bed. I closed my eyes, waiting for her to scream, Jack had to be under there. My heart felt like it was about to jump out of my chest. Emma finished the call and got up, handing me the phone.

"She'll meet us there so hurry along. I'm going to drink my cup of coffee and see if it helps with this bloody headache." She headed back downstairs and I immediately closed the door, locking it.

"Jack…" I whispered louder, leaning down to check under the bed. Strong arms lifted me off the floor and I held back a scream. Jack turned me around, smiling.

"The last time I had to sneak around and hide I was a teenager," he said.

"Shh… lower your voice! Where were you?" Relieved, I hit him on the chest.

He pointed towards the window. The thick curtains dragged on the floor. "I barely had time to put on my jeans, and the closet was too risky."

It was hard not to stare at his bare chest. *Must not think about that now*, I warned myself. I handed him his shirt. "Put it on. She might come back up here."

"Next you'll make me climb out the window," he said, pulling the shirt over his head.

"The thought had crossed my mind," I said. He chuckled softly, pushing me on the bed. I fell on my back.

"Stop it. I need to get ready," I squirmed.

"Tell her to sod off and come back to bed." He kissed my lips softly, making it very difficult for me to think straight.

"Mmm… I need to get up," I argued. I didn't sound convincing. "You can leave after we're gone…" He sighed, helping me up. "I'm sorry," I said, and scurried to the closet, pulling out a blazer and scarf.

"You have very inconsiderate friends," he said, helping me put on my blazer. I got on my tiptoes and gave him a kiss.

"We'll talk later," I promised.

At brunch, I kept wishing I had stayed home with Jack. And the girls noticed I was distracted. When they suggested walking down Motcomb Street, I agreed—I didn't want to head back to an empty flat.

"Kate, what's with the long face?" Elizabeth asked.

"I'm just tired," I replied.

We stopped in front of the Christian Louboutin store, and I couldn't contain my grin as I looked at the display. The shoes in the window were exquisite. I wanted to place my hands on the glass like a kid and press my face against it.

"Is this your way of telling us you want a pair for your birthday?" Emma laughed.

"What?" I asked, surprised. "Oh, yes, my birthday, I'd forgotten that was coming up."

Elizabeth turned to face me. "Since when? You're usually reminding us weeks before. What's the matter with you? You haven't been yourself the last couple of months."

Emma nodded in agreement. "Is it work?" she said.

It was the perfect excuse. "Yes, I've been under a lot of stress, nothing I can't handle… but you know what, I'd rather not get into it now and ruin our lovely afternoon," I answered quickly, and focused back on the glittery arrangement of shoes. I adored them all. "Guys, I think I'm in love. Have you ever seen anything sexier than that?" I said, pointing to one pair in particular.

"A man, six pack, tall, dark, handsome?" Elizabeth offered. "Am I the only one, people?"

"Only you," I said, rolling my eyes. "Forget men for a second, look at them—they are so Wickhams." I pointed to the towering five-inch stilettos. They looked dangerous to walk in, but who cared about something minor like that? They said look at me, hear me roar!

"How could someone walk in those and not kill themselves?" Emma asked.

"You have no sense of adventure, Emma. It's worth the risk," said Elizabeth, taking my arm. "Why don't we go in?" she suggested, knowing full well that I had been avoiding this store. Had been avoiding it like the plague.

"I can't. It would be torture to go in there and not be able to buy anything!" I protested.

"You can look and try on a few pairs, Kate. There's nothing wrong with that," Elizabeth grinned. I looked at both of them, unsure. I had promised myself I would only go in there when I was ready to buy the pair I wanted. It was dangerous to go in now, unplanned, and do something impulsive.

"I can't." I already felt my palms sweating. Why didn't I have the nerve to go in and say, *Give me the black patent leather simple pumps!* Just thinking of all the outfits I could wear them with was giving me palpitations.

"Scaredy cat. Next time. All I'm saying is you committed to an expensive bag, remember? What does that say about you?" Elizabeth said.

"She's not ready. Look at her, she's lost her color," Emma teased.

"Keep your psychoanalysis to yourself, that was an investment piece," I said. "*And* I bought it in New York and I got the VAT back, not full price," I pointed out.

Elizabeth sighed. "Just don't take forever to do it. Remember every shoe you buy is a substitute for the ones you really want," she said.

She was right, but I wasn't ready to take that leap.

Once I got home, I was surprised to find Jack stretched across the sofa with the television on, watching a football match. There was a pizza box open on the table and he was yelling at the TV like he could somehow change the outcome of the match by giving the players instructions. He looked at me and smiled.

"You're still here," I grinned like an idiot.

"I want you to know that I'm being held hostage."

I leaned in and kissed him, then squealed when he grabbed me and pulled me against him. "Oh, and how exactly did I manage that?" I said.

He placed his hands on my hips. "You stole my shoes," he said. I stared at his feet. The only thing he had on them were charcoal grey socks. "They seem to have disappeared, I can't find them anywhere."

I got up. "I'm so sorry!" I said. I walked over to the coffee table, pulled up the top and retrieved the shoes.

He threw his head back, laughing. "How was I supposed to find them in there?"

"I wasn't hiding them from you."

"If you wanted me to stay, all you had to do was ask," he grinned.

I walked back to him, placing the shoes on the floor. "And if you wanted to leave, you could have called me."

"Perhaps I didn't want to leave. Luckily, I remembered the one place that does takeaway."

"Seriously, why didn't you text me?"

"I didn't want to bother you. Besides, the game was on." He nodded at the television. "So what did you ladies do today?"

I sat down, placing my legs over his. "We went for brunch and we window-shopped. I saw one of the most magnificent things on this planet."

"Besides me?" he joked.

I rolled my eyes. "Shoes are a totally different category."

"In which I can't compete, I get it." He took off my shoes. "Why didn't you buy them?"

"They're not currently in my price range at the moment. I suppose I could buy the one pair, but it's ludicrous, I couldn't justify it," I went on.

"What makes those shoes different from the other hundred pairs you have upstairs?"

"I don't have that many," I protested. Jack gave me an amused grin. "Classic red soles," I said.

Jack shook his head. "Women, I do not understand, nor do I think I want to. Red soles? Don't you have a pair like that already?"

"Yes, but not the simple black pumps."

"Then get them," he said, matter of fact. Of course he didn't understand the process I went through in order to buy shoes like that.

"I wish it was that simple."

"*It is* that simple. You make it difficult. I want something, I get it." He pulled me up against him. "See how that works?" he smiled.

"Not all of us have the cushy life you have. There's your world and there's mine, the working class," I said, giving him a look.

"*Oi*, I work," he said, pulling me in as close as he could.

"You do, but you have other means."

"I won't take offense at that. You want something, sweetheart, go after it. That's how we get what we want in life." He pushed his hand softly in my hair.

"I have this theory, you know, about how women date the type of shoes they wear."

"Is that so?"

"Yes," I said with confidence.

"Like walking all over a man is not enough? You need to do it in fancy shoes?" he laughed.

"Hey!" I laughed back indignantly.

"What type of shoe am I? At least say the expensive one." He grinned slyly.

"You're a type all of your own, I think."

"Get the shoes, Kate."

"I'm thinking about it."

"Well, while you are thinking about the shoes. I have something else for you to think about. Your birthday is coming up. Why don't we go away for that weekend?"

I looked at him, shocked and happy at the same time. "You're serious?"

"Yes, preferably somewhere your friends can't drop in and I get stuck in a cupboard!"

Chapter Eighteen

Kate, honey, you have to get up." I heard Jack's voice in the distance. He shook me gently. "Come on, sleepyhead, you snoozed four times already."

I pried my eyes slowly open. Jack was staring down at me, his hair slicked back, still wet from the shower. He was already dressed in a suit minus the tie.

"I don't want to get up," I groaned, pulling the covers over my head. Normally, on Monday mornings, I was up early. It was a way of just getting the day over with. Today, however, was different. Jack had gone home in the evening and surprised me yet again by coming back with a bag and spending the night. With those small gestures, he made it feel like old times. These were moments that I had truly believed I was never going to relive with him.

"I need to go," he said, leaning in to give me a kiss. "I should have been at the office an hour ago." I pulled him towards me and he started to laugh.

"We can call in sick," I suggested.

"Mmm, tempting, but I have a meeting that can't be rescheduled. Do you want to go to dinner tonight?" he asked, giving me another kiss. At that moment, I wanted to shout at the top of my lungs that I was in love again.

"I'm going to take that as a yes," he grinned.

I coyly pushed him away, "Get going, you idiot," I teased. I sat up on my knees and he leaned in, giving me a hug. "Have a good day at work," I said, giving him one last peck on the cheek.

"See you later." He paused. "Make sure you get up, don't go back to sleep," he warned.

"I won't, I'm getting up in a few," I answered, throwing a pillow at him. He grinned and gave me a wave. And then he was gone.

I stretched on the bed, the biggest grin on my face. Mondays were quickly beginning to be my favorite day. *I should get up*, I thought, and glanced over to the desk. No time like the present, I sighed, and grabbed the phone. Reading the messages, I felt the color drain from my face. I had less than an hour to get to the office. I had totally forgotten about the mandatory team meeting with Philip. Of all days to be late for work, today was not one of them.

Running like a madwoman, I quickly showered and began getting ready, throwing my makeup in my handbag, I would have to put that on later. I wiggled into my skirt and grabbed a shirt and a pair of black platform stilettos. Hopping on one foot, I put on one shoe then the other. It was warm enough to get away with not wearing stockings—in any case, I always had a spare pair in my bag.

Making sure I had everything I needed, I headed out the door in record time. I ran to the tube station. It would be the fastest way at this time. Only, when I got there, I was greeted by the message on the board: "Station is closed due to flooding." I cursed under my breath. Typical London and just my luck.

Now, I had to run back in the direction I had come from and take the bus. If I had known I would be running a marathon this morning, I would have rethought my choice of shoes. Luckily, I could run in these. I hesitated, wondering if I should try my luck and see if I could hail a cab, but I thought better of it. I would take my chances with the bus. It was just pulling up as I got to the stop and I quickly got on. A part of me knew I should call the office to let them know I was going to be late. Fifteen minutes later, the bus was only a few blocks down the road from my flat. I mentally began to pray that it would somehow grow a set of wings. I willed it to go faster, fly over the cars if necessary. I sighed, giving up. I was being silly.

I could no longer avoid it. I began to write an email. I was still typing as the bus approached my stop and, without looking, I stepped off. Only I didn't feel the ground. My mouth opened in a silent O as I felt myself falling forward, my mobile flying out of my hands. I landed on the ground, my hands and knees scraping the pavement. My eyes watered as I felt a burning sensation on my knees. I was startled, unsure of what had happened.

The other people who had got off the bus were just making their way around me, not bothering to help. I was roadkill in the middle of rush hour. I struggled to get up, then felt soft hands taking hold of me, helping me up. I looked up at the older woman, the Good Samaritan who had stopped.

"Oh dear, are your shoes all right?" she asked. I heard the words but didn't comprehend their meaning. I could feel warm liquid running down my legs but that wasn't important at the moment. Her words had finally sunk in. My shoes!

I looked at her in horror. Had I broken the heel? Panic mounted. These were my special slingback platform stilettos, they were my staple shoes! I straightened myself and carefully stepped on each heel. Okay, the heels still felt secure, nothing seemed to be broken and the ankles felt fine. I sighed in relief.

"Do you need to go to A&E?" she asked. I looked down at my knees and realized why she had suggested that.

"No, I'm all right… thank you," I finally managed.

"You'd better have that looked at," she said, blending back into the crowd.

I needed to get to the office pronto. I looked around for my mobile and spotted it lying a few feet away. The battery had flown off in the opposite direction. I winced as I bent down to pick it up. People were staring at me like I was crazy as I limped away towards my building.

Charlotte started talking the moment I entered the office. "Kate, Philip is…" she stopped as she took in my appearance, her expression changing to one of horror. "Oh my God, what happened to you?" She came out from behind her desk to help me with my bags, and opened my door.

"I fell getting off the bus. But never mind that… is the meeting still going on?

"Have you seen yourself? You…"

I waved her off, no time to stop. "Call Philip's office and tell them to pass on a message that I will be there in five minutes."

"Are you sure you don't need me to get you anything?"

I looked up at her as I headed to my desk. "No, thank you, just get that message to Philip." I opened the bottom drawer of my desk and pulled out a first aid kit. Peroxide, water, bandages, alcohol pads… I had it all. Finally, I took a look at my knees. Blood was dripping down both legs, and my hands were cut as well. Sitting down, I began to clean the blood off. The knock on the door behind me startled me, and before I could respond, it burst open.

"*Miss Seeley*, when an email is sent about a mandatory meeting, it means *your* presence is required. I don't need a note passed to me that you will honor us with your presence after the fact. I don't know what has given you the impression that you are not part of this team. Whatever differences we may have does not pardon you from..." Philip's voice dropped off as I turned my chair to face him.

"What happened?" he demanded, scurrying over to me.

"I fell, let's leave it at that. I'm sorry about the meeting. It was not my intention at all to miss it. I was rushing as quickly as I could," I gushed out.

He grabbed tissues from my desk and before I knew what he was about to do, he kneeled down and pressed them on my left knee. I held my breath—it was the pain that was causing me to do that, I told myself, and not the fact that he was touching my bare leg, lifting it to the adjacent chair.

"You need to elevate your legs," he said, taking my other leg.

I squirmed. "Philip, I can do this," I protested, feeling my face flush.

Ignoring me, he took the peroxide bottle and tilted it into a bunch of tissue he had gathered. I sucked in my breath, tears forming from the burning sensation as the peroxide made contact with my knee.

"Sorry, I know it must hurt," he said. I looked down at the top of his blond head. For the first time, I didn't know what to say to him. This was something I would never have imagined Philip doing for anyone, let alone me!

Charlotte walked in and stopped in her tracks, staring at me.

"Do you need me to get anything?" she asked, clearing her throat.

Philip lifted his head as if nothing was amiss. "Could you please call Dr Alderson and tell him I'll be stopping by with Kate. She really needs to get this looked at. I'll just put some plasters on and we'll be on our way."

"Right away." Charlotte gave me a sympathetic but curious glance.

"Philip, really, no need to go to all that trouble, I'm okay," I insisted.

"It's no trouble at all." He gently touched my knee. My thoughts escaped me. *Dear God. Pull yourself together, Kate*! I told myself. He placed his hand underneath the knee and my stomach bunched up in knots. His touch made me jump.

"I'm sorry, did I hurt you?"

"No," I said, practically ripping the second bandage from his hand before he placed it on. He looked at me, startled. "I got it, please, you've done enough," I added. I looked away as I placed the bandage carefully on. He turned over my hands. My palms were scraped too. I could see the gravel in them.

"You fell, you say? How in the world did you manage that?" He looked at me curiously.

"Yes, I fell… no, more like flew off the bus. I missed a step," I groaned. Philip looked at my feet and I knew what he was thinking. "It's not the shoes, I run in these. I wasn't paying attention. That's what I get for trying to type and walk at the same time."

He didn't look convinced. "Can you get up okay? I could have Dr Alderson bring up a wheelchair."

"No, totally unnecessary, see?" I got up quickly, biting through the pain. I could see

he was still unsure.

"It could have been worse," he said.

I nodded in agreement. "Yes, I could have broken a heel."

He grinned. "I was thinking more along the lines of your ankle but, yes, thankfully, your heels are intact."

My cheeks burning, I coughed. "Well, yes, that. I'm fine, my ankles are tougher than they seem." He stared at me, his blue eyes unreadable. I had just witnessed a side to Philip Spencer I didn't know he possessed… compassion. Suddenly, I felt foolish. "You must think I'm a klutz," I said, pushing my hair behind my ear.

"It can happen to anyone, I'm sure. Well, let's head out to Dr Alderson, shall we?"

"I can go by myself, Philip. Please don't let me keep you. You've done enough, really. I don't want to be a burden." I gave him a soft smile. He was looking at me as if he was going to insist.

"Please, I'll look less pathetic if I walk out of here unassisted. Much better for my pride," I added.

"It's not a burden, but if you think you're okay on your own..."

I actually felt a tinge of disappointment that he hadn't insisted again.

"I'm sure. Thanks again, and I'm sorry about being late."

He grinned. "The next time you want to get out of a meeting, just say you have a client. It'll hurt less and you won't have to put your shoes in any danger."

I frowned, then realized he was kidding. "Oh, you're making a joke," I said. I was unsure that he had any sense of humor at all.

"Which I have failed at miserably, it seems. I'm afraid humor's not my strong suit." He paused for a moment like he wanted to say something but changed his mind.

"Shall we?" I asked, reaching for my coat. Philip beat me to it and walked over to help me put it on. "Thank you," I mumbled. "I'll see you when I get back," I added, grabbing my bag.

"I'm afraid not, I'm heading out to Heathrow in about an hour," he answered.

"Oh." I couldn't seem to hide my disappointment. "New York?" I asked. He nodded. "Well it is where you live, after all," I said, following him out. He walked me to the elevator. "Are you ready to go back?" I asked, surprising him—and myself a little. I'd never made pleasant conversation with him before.

"You know, for the first time in ages, I've actually wanted to stay longer here in London. But I have a few things that require my personal attention, and I wasn't expecting to be out here this long," he said. We stopped in front of the elevator banks and he pressed the button, turning back to me. "Are you certain that you don't need any assistance?"

I shook my head. "I'm certain." I was in pain but I wasn't going to let him see that. "I'm tougher than I look," I added for good measure.

He smiled. "Of that I am certain," he said. The elevator

arrived and I stepped in and faced him. "Let me know what the doctor says," he said, his hand holding the elevator door.

"I will," I assured him, staring at his blue eyes.

"See you around, Kate."

I lifted my hand in a slight wave, not understanding the feeling of sadness that hit me when the door closed.

"Kate, you brilliant, wicked girl! Tell me everything! I heard Philip was blowing on your knees. Okay, that did not come out correctly," Gemma gushed, quickly shutting the door of my office.

I took my glasses off and leaned back against the chair. "What?" I started. "Who said that?" I asked, laughing.

"Patricia from accounting," she said, indicating with one finger. "Oh, and Rebecca from down the hall. They walked by and saw Philip on his knees caressing your legs or something."

"What a bunch of gossips!" I said, exasperated. "I fell and scraped my knees. He was helping me clean my wounds. *That's all.* He was not caressing or blowing on any part of my body. Please spread *that* around, will you?"

Gemma sighed. "Kill our fantasies, why don't you. Ouch!" she exclaimed when she saw my bandages.

"Nearly killed by stilettos," I said, elevating my legs. "The doctor said my knees had the equivalent of second-degree burns, that's how much skin came off."

She cringed. "Disgusting, I'm going to stop you right there."

She was right, no need to go into the gory details. "Can you believe a quick spill on the pavement would do that?" I asked.

"Babes, I would risk the pain and possible death if it meant a man like Philip would come to my rescue and blow on or clean my wounds. You are so lucky!"

"Trust me, not worth killing yourself over," I said. But I had to admit, despite what I thought of him, it was sweet that he had taken care of me. I couldn't deny that he behaved very much like a gentleman.

"Not worth it? I think you need a stronger prescription for those glasses. Honey, he is rich, good-looking, tall, and the way his suit fits, you *know* he has a nice body underneath. Did you manage to feel his biceps while he tended to your wounds?" she asked hopefully.

"No, sorry to disappoint you and the girls. And who cares how rich and good-looking he is? He did what anyone else would do in that situation."

Gemma crossed her arms. "Is that so? Did Charlotte come and offer to help you clean up? Was she on her knees as well?" she asked.

Perhaps she had a little bit of a point. Charlotte had disappeared when Philip had taken over. But that was because he had taken charge. There was no other reason but that. I really did not want to be listening to Gemma's gossip. And now she was giving me a look that said she knew I had understood exactly what she was trying to say.

"I was doing fine tending to my wounds on my own, thank you very much," I said.

"I rest my case," she said with a sly grin. "I rest my case."

I shook my head and laughed. "*You* should ask him out," I said. It was obvious she fancied him and made no secret about it.

Gemma stopped at the door. "I would, trust me, would have done so already. But I don't think it's me he wants." She winked and headed out.

As I finally made my way home later, I felt a bit disappointed that I hadn't heard from Jack. He had promised to stop by and take care of me. It seemed a bit uncaring compared to the lengths Philip had gone to. Jack, however, did not have a potential lawsuit to worry about, which was probably the only reason Philip had helped me. Rather than call him, I turned on my laptop and began working. I might as well keep myself busy until he came over.

My internal messenger from work popped open on the screen the moment I logged on.

PSPENCER: How are you feeling?

Smiling, I responded:

CSEELEY: Honestly…embarrassed!

PSPENCER: Why?

CSEELEY: Let's see, I showed my knickers to all who were there, I am covered in bandages like a schoolgirl. All because of my shoes and I must say it has not deterred me from wearing them again! I've never fallen like that before.

PSPENCER: Really? I'm astonished given the height of all of your shoes. Maybe you should consider something closer to the ground.

CSEELEY: Ha-ha, not funny.

PSPENCER: Women and shoes, not my area of expertise. I'm glad that you are okay.

I smiled again like an idiot, staring at the screen. What was the world coming to? Philip Spencer was actually making me smile.

CSEELEY: Thanks again for tending to my wounds.

PSPENCER: It was nothing.

CSEELEY: Are you at the airport?

PSPENCER: Yes.

I was sad to see him go. I looked up from the keyboard: had I really just thought that? It was possible the fall had affected my brain.

CSEELEY: Safe travels, Philip.

PSPENCER: Could I ask you a random question…

CSEELEY: If you must.

PSPENCER: I was going to wait until I returned from NY to ask you this...

I sat up. Was Philip Spencer about to ask me out? The fact that I was considering saying yes was shocking. The man made one kind gesture and I was letting my guard down? The bottom corner of the screen was flashing, he had written something. Okay, okay, I could handle this, right? I could play it casual. I took a look.

PSPENCER: Are you dating Jack Barnes again?

Not the question I had been expecting. "That is a personal question," I said out loud.

PSPENCER: I wouldn't normally ask, and I apologise for the intrusion into your private life. I was under the impression that he was seeing someone else but I saw the two of you together recently. Unfortunately, I can't divulge the reason but I need to ask.

How dare he?! Just because he's my boss doesn't mean he had a right to ask questions like this. If he thought he could bully his way in, he had another thing coming.

CSEELEY: You're right, it isn't a question you should be asking. My private life is not your business. What's this about? You know, Jack told me that you had issues with him and I never believed him but now I see he had a point.

PSPENCER: Jack is a man with many opinions, it seems.

CSEELEY: Rightfully so, what difference is it if I'm seeing him or not?

PSPENCER: Work.

CSEELEY: My performance has nothing do with him.

PSPENCER: It's not your performance that concerns me. It's what you choose to tell him.

I was angry at the implication. What would I tell Jack about his own company that he didn't know?

CSEELEY: I will not indulge this conversation any longer. You are out of order!

I immediately logged off. I was so angry my hands were shaking. How could I possibly have thought for one moment that Philip was actually a nice guy?

Chapter Nineteen

A couple of hours later, Jack arrived with roses, and I smiled, momentarily forgetting Philip's ridiculous accusation.

"Am I glad to see you," I said, hugging him. "I'm sorry, I couldn't get out sooner. Are you okay?" he asked, inspecting my wounds. "You need to be more careful," he added.

I gave him an annoyed look. "I didn't fall on purpose," I said.

He smiled. "Let me start over." I waited for him to apologize, but instead, he kissed me—a much better apology than words. "I'm sorry you fell and I'm glad you're okay," he said softly.

"That's more like it," I said with a smile. He handed me the roses. "These are beautiful," I said, lifting them to my nose and taking in the scent. "Let me put them in water." I went into the kitchen to get a vase.

"Is everything all right at the office?" I called out, Philip's words still echoing in my head.

"Yes, why do you ask?" He came into the kitchen. I looked up into his brown eyes. To hell with Philip, I wasn't going to ruin our perfectly nice evening.

"No reason, just asking."

"Do you mind if I stay over? I feel the need to take care of you tonight," he said with a wicked grin. I put down the vase and walked towards him, forgetting Philip Spencer.

By the time the weekend came along, the only thing reminding me of the accident were the scars. They looked quite ugly but at least they were healing. I was on my way to Olivia's flat, glad for the distraction. Every so often, Brandon invited us for dinner, where he tried out new dishes on us. We were all happy to oblige.

"Oh my God, when you said you took a spill, I thought you meant you tripped. You said it was nothing—that is *something*!" Olivia said when she opened the door and saw my bandaged knees.

I greeted her with a hug. "You can't see anything, how can you tell?" I said, handing her the bottle of wine.

"Because if it was nothing, you wouldn't have bandages on." She turned over my hands, inspecting them. "Your poor hands, bless. You're lucky you didn't break something."

"My shoe life flashed before my eyes," I teased.

The rest of the girls, minus David, were in the living room. "Where are the chef and David?" I asked.

"They're still at the football match. They should be here soon. But don't worry, he left us a little treat to hold us over until he arrives," she said, handing me a glass of wine.

"Kate, you're just in time for my questioning," said Elizabeth. "When you're in a relationship, are you the dominant one?"

I laughed, sitting down next to her. "Do you use that an opening line when you go on a date?" I asked. "Because if you do, that explains a lot."

"Honey, I ask a lot more than that. So, who's going to answer first?"

Olivia took a sip of her wine. "I am. How can you manage your relationship if you're not on top?" We all laughed and she looked at us and winked.

"So says the girl with the shoe allowance," Emma said with a small smirk.

"Oi!" Olivia said, hitting her playfully on the leg.

"Very well played, Emma—it's always the quiet ones!" I said, making myself comfortable.

"Well, Miss Emma, how about you?" Elizabeth asked, leaning forward to grab what looked like a cheese ball. "Given your behavior at the club last time, it makes me hope there is a naughty angel waiting to come out." Emma blushed and said nothing. "Oh, that says it all," Elizabeth joked as her eyes turned to me.

"Don't look at me, I have no answer for that one," I said, which, given my current state of affairs, was the truth. I had no idea what I was doing or where I stood.

"Well, I always dominate," Elizabeth offered. "It's the only way I'll get what I want. Could be the reason why I haven't been in a long-term relationship in ages."

"Aren't you seeing Patrick?" I asked, recalling a name she'd mentioned a couple of weeks earlier. Elizabeth was never "in a relationship".

"On and off, I'm too busy right now to get into anything serious," she answered. I gave her a curious glance, suddenly feeling bad that I was too wrapped up in my own mess to stop and ask her if she was okay.

"Be careful, Eli, don't be so focused on other people's relationships that you neglect your own," Emma said thoughtfully.

Elizabeth stopped, a cheese ball held close to her mouth. "What have you done with the real Emma?"

Olivia clapped. "Bravo, I like this new Emma!" she said.

"Give her a glass of wine and she's agony aunt all of a sudden," Elizabeth noted. "But if you must know, I'm not ruling him out completely. I'm just not ready to emotionally commit." Elizabeth was never emotionally ready. She was practically the female version of David. I looked at the three of them. This was the perfect opportunity to come clean about Jack. It was weighing heavily on me that I wasn't being open with them. But it never seemed like the right moment…

Before I got a chance to open my mouth, Brandon, David and a couple of other guys arrived. Brandon had invited male friends over? I glanced at Olivia and knew immediately that she was trying to play matchmaker with us. Brandon kissed Olivia and made the introductions.

"Did you guys have a good time?" Olivia asked.

"Yes, we did," Brandon, answered. "Right, guys?" They cheered in agreement, giving each other high fives, recalling the game.

Elizabeth leaned in towards me. "Should we be worried?" she asked, looking over at David, who was part of the huddle talking about the match.

"Does he even understand the game?" I asked.

Elizabeth shrugged. "You know him better than me, does he even play football?"

"The only thing David understands about football is that there are men in uniforms," I answered with a chuckle. I looked back at the guys. "Did you know about this little set-up?"

"Hadn't a clue, but they're hotties. I'm going to make friendly conversation," she said with a smile, and headed over to them. Leave it to Elizabeth.

"Why are you being antisocial over here in the corner?" David asked, coming over and putting his arm around me.

"I am not being antisocial, I was chatting with Elizabeth until she ditched me for them." I nodded towards the guys. In all fairness, they were quite good-looking, I noted, taking another sip of my wine.

"You should be there. Russell, Brian and John are great blokes… and single." He threw the last one in there fully aware that I was still seeing Jack.

"What were you two gossiping about anyway?" he asked, when I didn't take the bait.

"You, of course," I responded.

"Good answer," he grinned. "Come on, tell me which one you fancy. Olivia took great care choosing them."

"None. I hate it when Olivia forces this on us," I said. It never failed. When Olivia had her mind set on something, she would continue until either a) she got what she wanted, or b) she got tired of trying.

"Why? She's trying to be nice and get you a man. Perhaps if you told her you're sort of messing with one, she'd leave it alone."

"Keep it down!" I hissed.

He rolled his eyes. "If I were you, I'd set my eyes on the tall blond one," he said. For David, this was his peace offering.

"They are right there, shhh!" I said.

"*And?* Kate, sweetheart, there is nothing wrong with stating what you what, that's how it works. You want it? Go and get it. Look at Elizabeth, she's doing just fine talking to Russell."

"That's because the two of you are exactly alike and go after anything with a pulse…"

"Why, thank you, darling, I'll take that as a compliment," he grinned.

"You would, wouldn't you," I said. There was simply no use in arguing with him—or Olivia, for that matter.

Emma made her way over to us. "So David, are you going to trade in your Pradas for trainers?" she asked.

"For your information, Prada makes trainers. But I have to say, hanging out with straight guys isn't bad. I actually had fun with them."

Olivia brought David a drink, joining our little circle. "I'm glad you had fun," she said. "Not my idea of fun, though."

"I'm going to the next one with them too," he said, as if it was something he did every weekend.

Olivia and I gave him a quizzical look. "Let's see how long that lasts," she teased.

Brandon came over and put his arms around her, giving her a kiss.

"Sickening, isn't it?" David teased, nodding towards Brandon and Olivia.

"Totally," I lied. It was nice to see someone in love. It made you realize what was missing sometimes. I certainly wanted to be with Jack now. *But he isn't yours*, my inner voice reminded me.

"Catherine, take a look—something to strive for. No sneaking around, able to be with each other out in the open. Think about it," David said, motioning to them.

"I'm fine the way things are." His look said it all. He didn't believe me—quite honestly, I'm not sure I did either. "So tell me," I began, changing the subject, "Did you really enjoy the football match?"

David pretended to look hurt. "Yes, I did. Why is that so surprising? That is really offensive… almost," he smiled. "I'm a gay man not an alien. This may come as a total shock to you but some gay men love sports… and men in uniform, of course."

I laughed. "Of course, and the total straight man crush you have on Brandon has nothing to do with it."

"Is it that obvious?"

"I think he's quite flattered, actually." I placed my arm around him.

"Are you coming out with us tonight?" he asked.

"I can't, I have plans with…"

David placed his index finger over my lips. "Don't say his name, it's like 'he who must not be named', we don't want to summon him."

"He's not evil. He and I have an understanding," I informed him. "I like the way things are—there's no pressure. I see him, we spend some time together, and that's it,"

He stared at me. "If it were only that, my dear, I would believe you. I just think you're heading down a slippery path with him."

I shrugged. "I can handle it this time." I took a sip of my drink.

"I don't want to make you feel bad. I'm just looking out for you. What's going to come of this? Have you seriously considered starting a relationship again with him? To have us meet you guys for dinner and we're supposed to—what—pretend that he never broke your heart? Yet, you're totally jumping down Emma's throat the moment she mentions Henry. In our eyes, Jack did the same thing to you."

"Let's change the subject, shall we?" I said, not wanting to participate in the conversation any longer.

"Fine. If you don't want to discuss it, fine. On another note: what are we doing for your birthday? The girls have been asking and we have a few things we're considering."

"Actually, I'm going away for the weekend," I said. So much for dropping the subject.

David didn't miss a beat. "And just like that, he's moved up to birthday status. Nice… The girls will be disappointed. Emma's getting us tickets for that chic charity ball. I suppose we'll have to go without you. I'll be disappointed as well," he said, giving me his best puppy dog eyes.

"If he and I work out, I'll tell them. Agreed?"

"Whatever," he pouted but then smiled. "Just make sure to do it when I'm in trouble for something so it will take the pressure off me."

"What are you two gossiping about over there?" Elizabeth called over.

"Boys, what else?" David said, making the group laugh. He gave me a wink. Even if he didn't agree with me, he wasn't about to rat me out.

Jack was waiting for me the next morning at Waterstones on Piccadilly, looking devilishly handsome. He didn't see me right away and I paused for a moment, taking him in. Was it possible for us to start again? Or was I just afraid to let him go? I thought about a pair of suede black boots I had in my closet. They were beyond repair, but I couldn't part with them. They were super-comfortable and had survived all sorts of weather. I knew I had to get rid of them: the suede on the front of the shoe had worn away, water now seeped through no matter how many times I got them repaired, they didn't even look presentable… but we had an understanding. *I knew Jack.* Did I just get rid of him because he wasn't perfect? Hell, I was far from perfect myself. He raised his head and smiled, spotting me. Didn't I owe it to our past, to all that we had, to try again? But that was the problem. He hadn't asked me to start again. He was still very much in his relationship.

The voices of my friends crept in… *Once a cheater, always a cheater! He lied to you once, he'll do it again!*

"You look beautiful, as always," Jack greeted me, with a kiss, dismissing all the voices in my head. I couldn't help but smile.

"You're just saying that," I said, getting on my tiptoes to kiss him again.

I liked that in a man: not afraid of PDA. Though I wasn't a

fan of overdone public displays of affection, I didn't mind the occasional hug and kiss.

"What do you have there?" I asked, noticing the books in his hand. "I thought you'd given up and gotten one of those kindles."

"Not entirely. I still like to read an actual book I can feel in my hands. I'd forgotten how much I liked coming to this place with you," he said.

I smiled. "Nothing beats a bookstore," I joked.

"I missed that about you. You take something so simple and make it grand," he said and lowered his gaze. That was unlike him. Jack never looked unsure. I stared at him, puzzled. It almost seemed like he was nervous. Jackson Barnes was not a nervous kind of man.

"Are you all right?" I asked. His brown eyes locked with mine. I frowned. Whatever he was going to say, he was struggling. I swear, if he was taking me to one of my favorite places to end whatever we were, I was capable of assaulting him with a paperback.

"I was so stupid, Kate. We were good together, and I screwed that up so badly. The fact that you're here with me now … I don't deserve it."

"Why are you saying this now?" I asked, taken aback.

"I want us back together, like it was before," he said. "Not exactly like before—the 'us' before it went wrong." He leaned in, pushing me back against the books.

"What about *her*?" I asked, reminding him of where things stood.

"I broke up with Amanda," he said, revealing no emotion.

"You *what?*" I said. My voice rose—I didn't care that we were getting looks from other people.

"I broke up with her this morning."

I shook my head in disbelief. "And you wait to tell me now? Here?" I said, gesturing toward our surroundings. We had spoken earlier that day and he hadn't even bothered to mention or even hint at it. I looked at him angrily. Then I paused. Why was I angry? He had broken up with her and he was here with me…

telling me exactly what? Slowly, the reality of what he was saying sank in. I placed my hands on his chest, pushing him gently away.

"What does that mean?" I managed to ask.

"It means, silly girl, that I'd rather be here with you, in a bookshop, admitting my faults and asking for your forgiveness, than anywhere else."

"Are you asking me to be your girlfriend?" I asked in a small voice. I felt like I was back in high school all of a sudden.

He gave me a crooked grin. "Yes, it means that I'm asking you, begging you, here in the middle of the..." —he looked up to see where we were— "fiction section... to be my girlfriend."

I bit my lip. I wanted to shout at the top of my lungs here in the middle of the bookstore: *I, Catherine Victoria Seeley, have played my cards right, and have gotten my man.* My Mr Darcy was back!

Chapter Twenty

"Hello there," I said to Gemma, popping my head in her office with the biggest grin on my face. Gemma immediately knew something was up.

"Why are you smiling like that?" she asked, signaling for me to come in. I continued grinning like an idiot as I walked into her office. Gemma had candles behind her on the ledge. It always smelled like a perfume shop in here. I needed to tell someone how my life had changed since yesterday. I couldn't tell the girls or David. I'd contemplated calling them last night but I needed to make sure Jack and I were secure. What if it went wrong again and everyone said "I told you so"? I didn't want to jinx it.

"Is it a crime to smile at work? How was your weekend?" I asked, shifting my garment bag and placing it over my arm. I was heading out with David tonight and he had given "suggestions" of what I should wear to Aunt Margo's event.

"It's Monday. No one walks in that happy unless they got

some action—or in your case, the last time I saw a smile like that on you was when we took you to Fortnum & Mason for afternoon tea. My weekend sucked. So if you went to some teahouse again, spare me the details, but if you have something juicy to say, come on, spill it."

Laughing, I turned back towards the door. "Thank you, I had forgotten about that. We need to do that again." I winked at her and walked out.

"Oh no you don't!" Gemma exclaimed, following me down the hall. "You're up to something. Tell me!" I shrugged, knowing it would drive her crazy. "Also, have you heard that Philip is coming back this week? You haven't seen him since the little accident, have you? Promise me you'll shag him this time. Don't let that man go to waste."

I paused. "He was just here, why is he coming back?" I asked, ignoring the rest of her comment. The moment Charlotte saw me, she rushed over with a look of urgency.

"Kate, Mr Thomas wants to see you when you have a moment," she said. "And David called to ask you to wear the black lace Stella McCartney dress for tonight's event. He was very stern about that." She smiled, noticing my garment bag.

Mr Thomas wanted to see me? He was my bosses' boss. Normally, you didn't see him unless there was something wrong.

"Did he say why?" I asked. She shook her head no. "Tell his office I'll be there in a few minutes," I instructed. I turned to Gemma as we stepped into my office. "Do you know what's going on?" I asked, hanging the dress on the back of my door.

Gemma shrugged. "Maybe we're getting a new client and now that you and Philip are an item, they want you on it," she smiled.

"Not funny. Stop saying Philip and I are an item, someone might hear you and actually believe it," I replied, putting down my bags and picking up my pad from my desk.

"Why is the idea of dating Philip Spencer so absurd to you?"

"We barely get along, and you're trying to get me to date the guy? I told you, he's not my type."

"Honey, get your head out of the clouds," she said. "You could do worse than Philip Spencer. You need to be more concerned with your love life."

"Right now, I'm more concerned about what Mr Thomas wants than planning a date with Philip."

"I'm sure it's nothing. He probably wants to compliment you on a job well done," she tried to reassure me. "Maybe you're getting a promotion!"

"Doubtful. Well, let me go see him. I don't think I can wait around and be productive until I find out what it is."

Gemma wished me luck, and I took out my compact mirror, making sure I looked presentable before grabbing my glasses and heading to Mr Thomas' office. When I arrived, Andrew, the team leader, was there as well. This was starting to look more and more suspicious.

"Kate, come on in, take a seat," Mr Thomas offered, smiling. Okay, not a bad sign, he didn't appear to be cross, his appearance was welcoming. I sat next to Andrew, who was clearing his throat and fidgeting in his seat. He looked nervous all the time so his expression told me nothing.

"Gentlemen, to what do I owe the privilege of having an audience with the two of you?" I smiled, getting straight to the point. I didn't want any preamble if the news wasn't going to be pleasant.

Mr Thomas chuckled. "I like that about you, Kate, straight to the point, no time wasted."

Andrew cleared his throat again and scratched the top of his balding head. "That's our Kate," he tried to joke, but only succeeded in getting an annoyed look from Mr Thomas, who signaled to begin.

Andrew cleared his throat again. "Let me start by saying that we here at Spencer & Lockhart are extremely satisfied with your work. You've shown tremendous leadership and teamwork," he began.

A rehearsed speech could mean one of three things: a promotion, a raise (normally together in that order) or the pink slip. Andrew continued to speak, shifting in his seat. He went on and on about what a great asset I was to the company, how productive I was. The more he spoke and didn't arrive at the point, the more restless I became. I tapped my foot, hoping he would just get on with it.

"What Mr Harrick is saying," Mr Thomas finally interrupted —Andrew jumped, his papers dropping to the ground. I got up from my seat, helping him gather them.

"Thank you," he mumbled as I handed them back to him.

"Kate, we are making changes here at the firm and want some of our associates to get more exposure in other areas," Mr Thomas said. Leaning forward, he placed his hands together and pointed both index fingers forward. "We are taking you off the Lewis & Morton account and placing you on another one."

I leaned towards him. "I don't understand. Has someone complained? Is my work unsatisfactory?"

"No, not at all… On the contrary, your exceptional work is the reason that we are moving you. The Thomson account has substantially grown and we are expanding the team," Mr Thomas said.

"That's Philip's account," I said, looking at them both. "Does he know about this?"

They both looked at each other, taking a momentary pause.

"Yes, he was the one who suggested you," Andrew responded, shifting in his seat. "We need new blood to bring in ideas. I think it will be a great opportunity to work with him, as do the people over at Thomson."

"How many of us are being switched?" I asked.

"Just you," Andrew answered slowly.

Just me? That didn't make any sense at all. But it did. This had Philip's name written all over it. That little… My mind started rambling, silently calling him every name in the book.

"It will be a great, great experience to work with Philip," Mr Thomas added with a grin. I didn't return the smile. As far as Mr Thomas was concerned, the sun rose and set around his golden boy, Philip Spencer.

"You mean work under him. Mr Thomas, Andrew, I have worked very hard to have the Lewis team trust me. They know me. Why would it be okay for them to have me off their account? Who are you going to put in there?" I stared at the two men. They looked flushed, confirming my suspicions. Being a Spencer gave him the authority to do as he pleased, whether it was right or wrong. And to top it all off, I had to report to him. He would be watching my every move. This wasn't a promotion, it was a backhanded demotion.

"We have already spoken to the head of the Lewis account and offered them a perfectly good solution and replacement," Mr Thomas answered.

"I see. Well, I will work where I'm needed," I said flatly. They had thought of everything—or rather *he* had thought of everything.

They both seemed relieved. "I knew you would understand, Kate." Andrew said as he smiled, his tension evaporating. I set my eyes on him, letting him know this wasn't over. Philip disliked Jack and was making me pay for it. How dare he! This was my livelihood he was messing with, my reputation. It was none of his business whom I dated, it didn't affect my work. I was going to give him a piece of my mind. I excused myself and headed back to my office. My heels clicked angrily on the marble. There was nothing like a woman in stilettos ready for a fight.

I shut my office door and immediately grabbed the phone to dial Philip's number in New York. My anger was now boiling over. If he had been in the building, I probably would have stapled his tie to the desk.

Philip wasn't available. Now I would have to simmer in my

anger and wait for him to call. The coward was probably hiding from me. He must have known I was going to be informed today. Whatever the issues he had with Jack, they were not mine and now he had forced my hand. I thought about the past year and the work I had done. There had been no complaints, my revenues were up and my bonus had been very generous. What else could it be? This was personal. I was tired of letting him step all over me. I needed to act. And I knew exactly what it was I needed to do. I picked up the phone again.

"Charlotte," I said when she answered. "Could you stop by when you get a moment?"

Waiting for Charlotte, I opened my emails and dashed off a few replies. Philip Spencer had messed with the wrong American!

"Is everything all right?" Charlotte asked, appearing in the doorway.

I looked up from the screen. "You're not going to believe this," I said. She closed the door behind her and sat down with her pad. "I'm off the Lewis account."

"*What?* Why?" She looked just as surprised as I had been at the news.

"Your guess is as good as mine. But starting today, I'll be working on the Thomson account." I instructed her on what documents I needed transferred.

"I need one more thing," I added. "I need you to call Lewis & Morton and check if they can meet with me tomorrow morning."

"I'll get right on it."

I called Jack to meet me for lunch and quickly filled him in on what had happened.

"Didn't I tell you that Philip Spencer couldn't be trusted? He plays the family card to get his way," he admonished me.

I took a stab at my salad, imagining it to be Philip's black little heart. "I've worked my butt off, and he just takes it away because he has the right surname? I hate him."

Jack smiled. "You're sexy when you're angry."

I pushed my hair behind my ear. "I'm serious, Jack." I could still feel my blood boiling.

"So am I. Your nose twitches right there," he said, touching the tip of my nose.

"It does not." I pushed his finger away, my anger slowly evaporating. "I'll tell you what I want to do. I want to speak to the team and explain that I'm not working on the account any more."

Jack took the napkin and wiped his mouth. "That may not be a bad idea. Everyone likes you. Have you ever thought about leaving the firm?"

"You mean come work for Lewis?" I asked, surprised.

"Yes, among others… you can have your pick. You're good at your job. Maybe it's time to make some changes," he suggested. "I'm not saying you have to quit today, Kate," he said, noticing my hesitation. "Just keep your options open. They know what a valuable asset you are. Take advantage of that. Don't let Philip make you think otherwise."

"It is something to consider," I said, taking it in. He had a point. I was under no obligation to stay. I had worked there ever since I moved to London. I'd given 150% to the firm and look what they'd done to me. Perhaps it was time to spread my wings.

"I think Philip has in it for you," I said to him.

Grinning, he leaned back in his chair. "I'm sure he does. I've been dealing with Spencer for ages. Don't worry about me, I can handle him. This is what he does—he doesn't have the guts to do more."

"But everyone lets him get away with it," I pointed out, stabbing at the salad again.

"He's not going to get away with anything. That is what makes him bitter. I always beat him at his own game and, with my help, so will you." He squeezed my hand. "You don't seem convinced," he said. "He can threaten all he wants, but at the end of the day, business is business. He's still under his family's thumb and wouldn't risk embarrassing them. Speak with the team tomorrow. And have fun tonight with David—now *that* is a man I am afraid of," he said, trying to get me to laugh.

I looked at him puzzled. "Why?"

Jack laughed, signaling for the bill. "Unlike Philip, David has verbally threatened to physically harm me. More importantly, to harm a certain part of my body. I actually believe he would follow through."

"He's harmless," I said, defending David.

"Not when it comes to you," he said. "Don't give me that face. I admire his loyalty, I've said that before. But I still wouldn't turn my back to him in the street: I'd like to see the dagger coming."

"Oh, stop it," I laughed.

Have you told him about us yet?" His dark eyes stared, knowing the answer.

"No," I sighed. "He'll need some time to warm to the idea. I mean, we are still trying to see where this is headed, aren't we?"

Jack leaned back against the chair. "Kate, I know what I want this to be. When you're ready, tell him. I want us, and I want it to work. I love you, you know that, don't you?"

"I love you, too," I smiled. It was a requited love. That's the one thing even the best pair of shoes can never give you.

Chapter Twenty-one

"I'm in love," David announced the instant I walked into the gallery.

"Who's the lucky guy this time?" I asked, greeting him with a kiss as I scanned the room to see if I could spot the latest target. David's view of love was warped. It came and then it went as quickly as he had discovered it. I felt his eyes on me, inspecting my appearance from head to toe. Even in his hour of desperation, he managed to make sure I measured up to his standards.

"You look lovely. I don't think even Rachel Zoe could have done better. It's amazing how great you can look when you take my advice… and Rachel's," he said with a satisfied look.

"Don't start with me, you have no idea the horrible day I've had. I've been taken off my main account." I took a champagne glass from the waiter who whisked by us.

"Why?" he asked.

"I don't want to talk about it tonight. Tonight is about having a lovely time with Aunt Margo. Where is she, by the way?"

"She's over there. She'll make her way over. But back to *me*, Kate, I'm serious about this: I think I'm in love..."

"You're not. Right there, sweetheart, is the reason why you're not. You *think*? Tell me, are we talking about someone you just met a couple of minutes ago? Because you will fall out of it the moment you've had him and get bored. Which, knowing you, will be by the time this party is over."

He shook his head. "He's not here... I think I've screwed it up."

"*You*?" I laughed.

"Ah, there is my favorite great-nephew and his lovely girl!" Aunt Margo exclaimed as she approached us. She was dressed in a classic cream Chanel suit—even her low pumps were Chanel. Her silver hair was styled back in a perfect bun. She held on to a purse like the Queen. She looked impeccable.

"I'd better be, I'm your only great-nephew," David teased, kissing both her cheeks. "Kate is my mate, Aunt Margo. We've been over this," he reminded her.

She smiled, greeting me. "*Only mates*," she chuckled. "I know I'm old-fashioned, but I watch EastEnders, I know what that means. You look lovely, Kate darling."

"Thank you, how are you?"

"I'm well. At my age, it hurts here and there, but I just get on with it. You know me, I need to keep busy. I love organizing events like this. But there is *one* event I really want to plan." She patted my hand, giving me a glowing smile. I shot a look of desperation at David but, luckily for me, Aunt Margo got pulled away by another guest. David took another glass of champagne, looking unaffected.

"You really should tell her," I told him.

"Tell her what?" He looked at me innocently.

"Don't give me that look, you know exactly what I'm talking about."

"Why ruin it for her? She's happy. It's like when I ignore

that you are seeing Jack. I don't think it's a great idea. I *want* to tell you that you are being a complete fool to even consider letting him back into your life, but you know what I do?"

"Tell me anyway?"

"*No*, I smile through gritted teeth and hold back all the inappropriate words I want to use when referring to him. Aunt Margo always told me if I have nothing nice to say, not to say anything at all."

"I don't think your method of execution is what she meant," I said.

"How is the scoundrel doing?"

"He's fine. Actually, there's something I want to tell you…"

"God, don't tell me you're pregnant." He looked at me seriously, the color fading from his face.

"*No*, I'm not, David. Why must you go there? You're so dramatic sometimes."

"Which is why you love me," he said.

"I do love you. Why else would I put up with you?" I said, unable to help smiling back at him. Aunt Margo passed just at that moment and heard me. She was grinning from ear to ear.

"See, you made her happy," David pointed out.

I groaned, looking at Aunt Margo. She was practically glowing. He was right. Who was I to ruin that happiness for her?

"Fine," I said. "Don't tell her. But if she even remotely takes it to the next level of making some kind of announcement, you better stop her."

"We would get some great wedding presents… possibly even a flat in Notting Hill. That alone is worth getting married for, don't you think?"

"Are you listening to yourself? Do not, I repeat, *do not* let it get that far. Promise me."

"Whatever, sure, I promise... Now, what is going on at the office?" he asked.

I knew that, at some point, knowing David, I would have to deal with the matter of Jack, but for now I filled him in on what was happening at work.

"Maybe there's a good explanation for this. Have you spoken to Philip?" he asked.

"No, he's been avoiding me." I answered. "I called him a few times and he has yet to return any of my calls. This has something to do with Jack, I know it has. The last time we spoke, he asked if I was back with him. He doesn't like him and somehow I'm caught in the middle of their rivalry."

"Well, in that case, I'm team Philip."

"Oh, shut up, you and your teams. There is no team Philip or team Jack, this is not Twilight!"

"It's not just about Philip versus Jack. In my book, anyone who has the sense to see Jack for what he really is gets a guaranteed seal of approval from me."

"I'm dating Jack again," I blurted out. "Officially, that is."

David had an odd look on his face, like the time a salesman tried to sell him a pair of man clogs. He was speechless, which was a rare thing indeed. He opened his mouth to speak.

"Please, think about it carefully before you answer," I pleaded. Scanning the room, I knew we needed privacy, otherwise the whole gallery would know my secret. I pulled his arm, leading him out to the balcony. The cold wind made me shiver and I wrapped my arms around myself. The moment we were alone, he began.

"*Why*? Shagging him was one thing, but you're in a relationship with him again? Tell me I heard you wrong in there and that I've had too many glasses of champagne. You can't be serious."

"He's apologized for what he did and I believe him and I'm giving him another chance." I was going to stand my ground with David. But the look he was giving me was not one of anger but of disbelief, which I hadn't been expecting.

"Don't look at me like that."

He pressed his lips together, shaking his head. There was a pregnant pause. It was unnerving.

"Say something!" I demanded, throwing my hands up. Anything was better than the silent treatment—or worse, what I knew his silence meant.

"What would you like me to say?" he asked coldly. He wasn't happy with my decision, I knew no one would be, but it was mine to make after all.

"I don't know! Anything! Tell me that you hate it or that you think I'm crazy," I threw at him. He sighed. "I love him. You just told me that you're in love, or think you are. Well, this is what it's like. You don't have control over your emotions. It's confusing, and not always wrapped up in pretty gift box."

David's eyebrow lifted. "Stop it right there. Whatever experience you want to share, stop it now."

I looked at him and we both burst out laughing. It took us a few minutes to compose ourselves.

"I just hope you know what you're doing," David finally said.

"Honestly, I don't know what I'm doing any more. I don't know if it's right or wrong but I can't stop seeing him, I've tried. The heart wants what it wants."

"I get it. I don't agree with it, but I get it. When are you telling the girls?"

I shrugged.

"Catherine, you have to tell them. It's been months now. Just get it over with and move on, they'll be shocked but they'll accept it."

"I need more time for that. You can't say anything, not until I'm ready. Okay?"

"Okay… come here." He stretched out his arms and I went into them. He gave me the tightest hug.

"Thank you. He's afraid of you, you know." I said. I could feel David grinning, proud of himself.

"Is he? Glad to hear it." He tucked my hair behind my ear as we pulled away, always the perfectionist. "What am I going to do with you?" he asked, pushing me back to inspect me. "Just do me a favor and don't go committing yourself entirely. Take it slow, remember. Make him earn it."

He had a point. Jack needed to prove himself now that he wanted to be with me. But what exactly did that mean? He had chosen to come back, but I had a nagging feeling I couldn't quite place.

"What do I do about Philip?" I asked, changing the subject to a more pressing matter.

"Confront him. You need an explanation and he should give you one. You're a valuable asset to the firm. Remind him of that fact and, before you do, do yourself a favor and believe it. You really don't value yourself sometimes."

"Jack said the same thing."

"Don't try to put him in my good graces by having him defend you," he said, but his voice softened.

"I'm not! I'm just stating what he suggested, which was perhaps I needed to consider working elsewhere," I said. David had to know Jack wasn't all bad. He did care about me, despite what he'd done in the past.

"Wait until you get the answers before making any subtle moves. If that doesn't work, sue," he grinned.

"What is it with you and suing?" I asked.

"It's what you Americans do, darling. Come on, let's head back in before you freeze."

The next morning, I regretted having the extra glasses of champagne David had forced me to drink. I groaned. Okay, "forced" wasn't the right word, I willingly took them. I knew better than to drink like that on a work night and now I was paying the price with a splitting headache.

As I got to office, later than usual, Charlotte gave me a warning look and nodded towards my office. She had one of the other associates by her desk and I didn't want to interrupt her, but she mouthed something to me. I tried to make it out—find the motor? What was she talking about? My brain wasn't cooperating with her attempt at charades. I nodded, brushing it off. It was easier to get settled at my desk and come back out when I was ready.

The moment I opened the door, I wished I hadn't. I turned to look at Charlotte for help but she had left her desk. I took a deep breath, staring at the back of the person who was intruding in my space.

"Philip." I managed to control the venom in my voice. He quickly turned around.

"Good morning, Kate." His blue eyes widened, startled. He was the one in my office, if anyone had the right to be startled it was me. And I was. He was supposed to be in New York returning my calls not bloody standing in my office doing God only knows what. I took in his appearance: a charcoal grey suit, and today he was wearing a bow tie. A bow tie? Ridiculous! But on him, it actually wasn't, I noted. On anyone else his age, it would probably look out of place but on him it worked. I was getting side-tracked. Everything I had planned to say to him when he called was temporarily forgotten. My mind went blank. I placed my Starbucks cup on my desk.

"What can I do for you?" I finally managed to ask.

"I'm sorry I haven't returned your messages," he started. "I meant to but the last few days have been extremely busy. Anyway, I wanted to discuss the account."

"Which account, Philip? The one you had them remove me from? Or the one you're now babysitting me on?" I said, regretting it the moment I did. The one thing I didn't want to show him was that he'd gotten under my skin. I needed to be professional about this.

"No one is trying to babysit you. It's nothing of that sort," he said. "The Thomson account has more potential. There's more room for growth there. It's not a demotion, Kate, far from it," he quoted my words from the messages I'd left him.

I quickly closed my door. Philip was still standing by my desk, his fingertips resting on it. As per usual, his face revealed nothing.

"Is that how you see it? Because from where I'm standing it sure looks like it! You had no right to take me off without consulting me. My performance has been nothing but outstanding on that account. No one complained except you, and we all know why I was really taken off that account."

"That is not what is going on here, but since we are on the subject of complaining, I did not appreciate getting a frantic call from the manager at Lewis discussing your removal from the account. That was a decision made here internally that did not concern them," he said firmly.

Now that was a surprise—and my face must have shown it. "It wasn't you?" he said. But it was more a statement then a question. Jack had beaten me to the punch and spoken to the managers. "This is exactly the kind of thing we don't need, Kate. We don't need the firm's personal issues discussed in a public forum, especially to a client. If your boyfriend can't keep his mouth shut then you should refrain from telling him anything that happens at this firm," he snapped.

I took a step away, taken aback by his lack of composure. "You have some nerve coming in here and parading your authority!"

"I'm not doing anything of the sort. I'm doing what is best for the company. These are matters that are still confidential and only top management is privy to. And it is my *professional* opinion that you are better needed on the Thomson account."

"That is total bull. You're jealous of Jack. From what I've heard, everybody knows you've been jealous of him since university!"

"That is preposterous!" He towered over me.

I continued. "Then it's a personal vendetta against me. Ever since we met, you've made it no secret that you dislike me. I see your little side gazes, looking down on me. You don't want me here."

"Are you still holding a grudge over that polo match? You were actually quite improper. A few of the guests were offended, and I was quite polite," he pointed out.

I laughed. "Oh that's right, your version of being polite." I ignored the daggers Philip was throwing in my direction. "You had me fooled. I actually thought for a brief moment that when you helped me, tended to my cuts and bruises, you actually cared and were being a gentleman, but that was all a facade. You knew you were going to pull the rug from right under me," I accused him, not caring that he no longer seemed quite as composed. If I hadn't been so worked up, I would have stopped.

"How dare you?" he threw at me. I had crossed the line, I knew that, and now there was no turning back.

"The fact of the matter is you are a rude, pompous, conniving, intellectual snob and a spoiled brat…"

Philip grabbed my shoulders, making me gasp. He lowered his head and his face was inches from mine. We were so close, I noticed his eyes had specks of grey in them. He was angry, his jaw was tense as he leaned in, and I momentarily held my breath. This was a side of Philip I had never seen. My lips parted. The words were lost. If he kissed me right then, I would let him. His eyes rested on my lips as if he was reading my thoughts. Oh my God, I would let Philip kiss me!

The knock on the door made him immediately release his grip, and I staggered back. Philip looked surprised, as did I. His face turned a very visible red. I quickly looked at him, not saying a word, and opened the door. It was Charlotte.

"Sorry—Philip, Sam has a few calls on hold for you." Her eyes searched mine. She had heard us.

Philip cleared his throat. "Thank you, Charlotte. Tell Sam I'll be right there." Charlotte nodded and quickly shut the door.

Philip turned towards the door without looking at me. "Kate, please send all the Lewis information to Brian. He will be handling the account, and I'll see you at the meeting this afternoon. Good day."

Once he'd gone, I leaned against my desk, trying to figure out what had just happened…almost happened. No way had Philip been about to kiss me. What was wrong with me? Charlotte knocked once again on my open door. "Are you all right? I heard your raised voices," she said.

I felt my cheeks turn red, wondering if she knew more. But that was impossible, the door had been closed. "Yes, I'm okay, I'm just so angry with him! He has no right to do this. I can't believe he is going to get away with this."

"It will get better. Things work themselves out, no?" she said, trying to reassure me. I wished her words would calm me. I had never felt so helpless at work.

A few hours later, the phone rang. "Stop what you are doing and head over to the Caffe Nero on the corner," Elizabeth said when I answered the phone. At the mention of the cafe, my stomach grumbled. I had skipped lunch.

"You're there already?" I asked.

"Yes, and I've already called Emma and Olivia. David called and explained what's happening. So I figured you needed to talk."

I froze. I was going to kill him. He had promised not to tell them anything! I bit my lip. He knew better than this…

Giving him the benefit of the doubt, I wearily asked, "What did David explain?"

"Well, I asked him were things okay with you, you've seemed a bit off recently, and he told us that you've been having a tough time with work."

I sighed in relief—he had kept his word. "I wish we could meet for drinks," she continued. "But I have to head back again this afternoon. I have a paper due tomorrow. So hang up and meet us at Caffé Nero in about fifteen minutes."

For the first time that day, I smiled, thanking the heavens that I had such great friends. "I'll see you in a bit," I said.

Chapter Twenty-two

The brisk air that greeted me as I headed over to the cafe was refreshing. Elizabeth waved me over as soon as she spotted me. She was sitting at the corner table, smiling. But instead of feeling happiness, I felt guilt. David was right. I just needed to come out with it. Just announce it. But every time I thought I was ready, something held me back.

"You didn't have to come all the way out here," I said to Elizabeth, hugging her.

"Yes, I did. I've been worried about you. I feel like we haven't had a proper chat in ages. Besides, I needed to come into town anyway," she said with a wink.

"You're a good friend, Elizabeth." I said softly. It was now or never. "There's something I've been meaning to tell you…" I began.

"Speaking of good friends, look at those two," she grinned, getting up. I turned around as Emma and Olivia walked in. My mouth opened at the sight of Emma—she looked amazing.

"Look at you!" Elizabeth exclaimed. Emma's hair was no longer in her usual tight bun. Instead it was flowing loose over her shoulders. Her green eyes looked wider and softer.

"Do you like it?" she asked, passing her hand through her hair. "Olivia took me to her stylist today and he cut it."

"And you're wearing makeup!" Elizabeth noted.

"I am. You don't think it's too much, do you?"

"Not at all, babes. You're gorgeous!" I exclaimed, hugging her.

"I love it," Elizabeth said.

Olivia, however, looked exhausted as she sat down and flung her jacket over the chair. "Of course she looks gorgeous! It was a nightmare, let me tell you. I almost had to strap her down into the chair. He cut this much off!"—she indicated barely an inch with her index finger and thumb—"and I swear the screams were heard up and down Mayfair."

"I did not scream. Just… shrieked," Emma said as she continued to pass her hands over her hair. "He just started cutting without saying a word, I didn't know how much he was going to take off. For all I knew, he was going to shave my head!"

Olivia looked offended. "Roberto is an artist. He would never… and if he had, trust me, you would have looked amazing. Do you know hard it was to get an appointment with him at the last minute?"

Knowing Olivia's taste, I did not doubt that Roberto (whose real name was probably Steven) was the best.

"It looks incredible," Elizabeth agreed.

"Thank you—at least someone appreciates my hard work," Olivia said.

"Let me go get our drinks—the usual for everyone?" I asked. They nodded. I needed a few moments to myself before I came back and told them the truth about Jack.

"We had to sedate her in order for Roberto to finish," I heard Olivia say as I returned with the tray. I gave her a quizzical stare. "We made her drink a glass of champagne. Once she got to the bottom, he was able to cut her hair shoulder-length." She pushed her blonde hair behind her ears. "I'm exhausted, but it was worth it. She looks amazing, doesn't she?"

I agreed, giving Emma another inspection.

"So… why the makeover today of all days?" Elizabeth asked, eyeing the two of them with wonder.

Olivia's face beamed. "Brandon and I have set her up on a blind date!"

Emma blushed, shyly looking down and taking a sip from her tea. I looked at her, surprised. I had just spoken to her a few days ago and she hadn't mentioned a thing.

"When was this arranged?" I asked.

Her green eyes looked at me. "Last week. I didn't want to bother you with such nonsense. You already have so much going on at work, I didn't want to give you unnecessary stress by talking your head off about one little date."

I really felt bad. I'd been so caught up in my own issues, I hadn't even noticed. "Emma, you know you wouldn't be adding stress," I said. "That's big news! Please, I'd rather you interrupt me than have to deal with the bollocks at work." I gave her hand a supportive squeeze.

"It's really all right," Emma said. "But we're here for you not for me. What's going on at work? Is it still Philip Spencer?"

I nodded. "It's gotten so bad, I've been contemplating going to a headhunter. I should regardless, it's always good to see what my options are, right?" I waited for them to agree but they were staring at me like I had two heads.

"But you love your job," Emma said without hesitation.

I pondered for a moment. Did I really? Or was I there because it was one of those jobs that one inevitably got stuck in. "I do, but I'm valuing my sanity more these days. And let's face it, there's a major issue here. He is the great-great—I forget how many greats—grandson of the man who founded the company. Tell me, how am I going to compete with that? Seriously."

"Bastard. He's got it made. Don't him get the best of you. I'm sure we can find a perfectly good solution to this," Elizabeth said.

"I'm trying, I am. But it's so hard when all I want to do is strangle him," I said.

"Too messy," Elizabeth teased.

"You could just kick him in the balls," Olivia suggested. "Tell me that you wouldn't have got some sort of satisfaction kicking Henry after the stunt he pulled. I say wear the pointiest shoes you have and bam!" she slammed her hand on the table, making the three of us jump. "Make that twat feel the pain."

We all started cracking up and the other customers stared over at our table. Olivia grinned as she innocently took a sip of her cappuccino.

"You go, girl!" Elizabeth smiled, giving her a high five. "I like the sound of that!"

I chuckled. "As tempting as that sounds, I can't go kicking people left and right whenever they upset me."

"I can totally go and do it for you," Olivia offered. "Is he at least good-looking?" she asked, looking hopeful.

"I haven't noticed," I lied.

The girls looked at each other and I looked down at my nails, pretending to inspect them.

"You haven't noticed? *Please.* He has to be on the internet, right?" Elizabeth picked up her phone from the table and started quickly tapping away at the screen.

"What are you doing?" I asked.

"Looking him up on Google. There has to be a picture of him somewhere," she said without looking up. Would she actually find a photo of him? I prayed not.

"I don't think he's listed," I said. "He values his privacy." She wasn't listening. "Besides," I continued. "Let's not waste our time on him. His appearance is irrelevant." But by now, Olivia was searching on her phone as well.

"Found him!" Elizabeth exclaimed, making me jump out of my seat. She ogled the photo. "Kate, he's good-looking, you need to get your eyes checked, hun." She shook her head at me, passing the phone around to the girls.

"Looks are deceiving, ladies," I stated as the phone made its way to my hands. I didn't want to look but I found myself staring at Philip. His semi-permanent scowl was prominent, but it made him look almost mysterious. Amazingly, he was smiling in a way I had rarely seen.

"He's handsome," Emma said, looking over my shoulder. She was right, he was. I never denied that Philip was good-looking but it didn't matter, his behavior made him an ugly individual in my book.

"Yes, yes, we all agree, he's good-looking. Is he single?" asked Elizabeth, getting straight to the point.

"How should I know? I don't ask him personal questions," I said, acting as nonchalantly as I could. "I try not to converse with Philip unless it relates to work. Believe me, that's as much as I can tolerate…" And that was a true statement. Just thinking about the situation was getting me worked up again. *You also wanted to kiss him.* "Can we talk about something else?" I said, dismissing the thought.

"Relax, it's not like you're in the office making out with him," Elizabeth said. I started coughing. She patted my back. "What is up with you? This man has you going crazy." She looked at me the way she did when she had one of her ideas. Nothing escaped her… well, Jack had. There was a first time for everything.

"Let's move on to something more important," I said, composing myself. "Like who is this man Emma has a date with."

Now it was Emma's turn in the hot seat. "He's a buyer at

Sotheby's. Brandon has known him since secondary school." Her cheeks turned a deep red.

Olivia beamed like a proud parent. "He's a total Bingley, well-to-do, good looking, smart…" She showed us a picture of him on her phone.

"Cute. I like him already," Elizabeth said.

"Ladies, it's not all about looks. I just want him to be a nice man," Emma said quickly.

"I agree with Emma," I smiled at her. She was right, looks were not everything—we had enough proof of that.

"We need to set you up as well," said Olivia, turning to me.

"Yes, we do," Elizabeth added. "You need to go back on the market. This is exactly what you need to make you forget all the drama at work."

If I didn't change the direction this conversation was heading in, it was quickly going to get out of control. "No, please don't set me up." *I'm dating someone.* I wanted to confess and get it out of the way once and for all.

Olivia paid no attention. Her eyes sparkled with excitement. "Brandon has a new business partner at the restaurant. I can't believe I didn't think of this before!" she said. "I'm going to text Brandon."

"I really don't think it's a good idea," I heard myself say. But Olivia was on a mission.

"Let me see, I think there's a picture on the restaurant's page," she scrolled quickly through her phone. "Here he is. Take a look!" She held up the mobile so we could see. I didn't look.

"*Ladies*, please listen to me. I do not have the time nor the desire to be set up at the present moment. I have more important things to think about, like what do with my career," I protested once again.

"He's cute!" Emma said, looking at Olivia's phone.

"If Emma's going on a blind date, you have no excuse," Olivia warned.

They began planning a date I could not possibly go on. I could stop this right now if I just told them I had a boyfriend.

"I am not Emma!" I exclaimed, raising my voice a few levels higher. The three of them stopped mid-sentence and looked at me.

"Emma," I turned to her apologetically. "I'm sorry, I didn't mean to get worked up. I'm happy you're finally going out there. Don't get me wrong, it's just not for me at the moment," I explained, feeling like crap. This was my fault. All they wanted was to see me happy. They were good friends, unlike me. I was being a coward and a selfish one at that.

"It's all right," Emma said, giving my hand a supportive squeeze. "Olivia, she's not ready, let her be," she said, coming to my defence.

"Honestly, the two of you. What are we going to do with you? If you don't get any action soon, you might as well join the convent now," said Elizabeth, breaking the silence. We laughed.

"When did David join us?" I asked, making her smile.

"Come on, you know I'm right. I'm just concerned," she grinned.

"Is that a topic for one of your papers? It seems to me that we're your subjects again," Emma said.

"Maybe," Elizabeth answered. "Kate, you and Emma have to learn how to open up. Emma at least is in playing position. You, my darling, have not even set up your board."

"Oh, don't make it sound like this is a piece of cake. I think I'd rather buy shoes—less complicated!" Emma said.

I lifted up my coffee mug in salute. "Hear, hear, Emma! That is exactly how I feel."

We chatted for a bit more and Elizabeth looked up at her watch, taking a deep breath. "Ladies, it has been real, but I have to say adieu. I have a paper to finish." She got up, giving me a hug. "Call me if you need anything, honey. And remember, you are a stiletto-wearing intelligent woman, don't let that loafer get the best of you."

Chapter Twenty-three

Later that evening, I curled up on the sofa with Jack, who was watching the football match. He pulled me closer and I snuggled into the crook of his arm. But no matter how hard I tried to relax, I couldn't. I had so much on my mind and there seemed to be no solution for my problems in sight.

"Kate, are you listening?"

"Oh… no, sorry, what did you say?" I asked, coming back to reality.

Jack rubbed my back. "Wow, you are tense. Are you all right? You seem to be a million miles away."

"I was just thinking about the girls… I still haven't told them we're back together," I admitted. That was the cause of half my distress anyway. Jack seemed to relax.

"Does that include David?" he teased. I playfully punched him on the chest and he laughed. "Hey, I'm just trying to be politically correct!" he said, leaning back on the sofa.

"*Right*. Be nice." But I grinned and cuddled into him again.

"I was actually being nice, considering he's probably planning my demise as we speak," he said. His fingers softly tucked the hair that had fallen into my face behind my ear.

I giggled. "He is not. If he was, believe me, he would have done it by now..."

"Is that supposed to reassure me?" He raised his eyebrows, pulling me in closer. "You're not the one he threatened. Should I hire a bodyguard?" I laughed, throwing my head back. "I'm serious!" He smiled, knowing he had succeeded in making me momentarily forget my problems—and I adored him for it.

"David wouldn't hurt a fly," I said with certainty.

"That's what *you* think. He'd swat it immediately given the opportunity."

"He wouldn't." Actually, he would, but I wasn't going to admit that to him. I closed my eyes as his hands moved to my shoulders and began massaging them.

"Is this all about your friends and us?"

"I feel bad," I admitted softly.

Jack tilted my chin up. "Why? Where does it say that you have to tell your friends everything about your life? Tell them when you're ready, or don't tell them. It doesn't change my feelings for you. Does it change your feelings towards me?"

"No," I said without hesitation.

"Then there's no issue. We're both consenting adults, we don't need their permission. This is what men don't understand about the female species. We don't feel the need to discuss every little detail with each other. You know what'll happen when you tell them: they're going to give their opinions, all hating me, of course—but I don't care what they think of me… the only person I care about is you."

His brown eyes stared into mine, waiting for me to agree. Could it be that we girls made things difficult by discussing our problems? I didn't think that was the case. Not once did they tell me Jack was a bad man, until he cheated. I thought about the awful dates my friends had saved me from.

"I know that look, Catherine Seeley. I've said something to upset you."

"No, not upset me but…"

"No buts," he said, kissing my forehead, then the tip of my nose. "Tell them or not, we're happy and that's all that matters."

He began to kiss me and I forgot about everything. Nothing else mattered at this precise moment. "I just need to tell them," I murmured on his lips.

"Then tell them, get it over with," he said, slowly sliding his hand under my shirt. The doorbell made us both jump.

Jack groaned. "Are you expecting someone?"

"No." I quickly got up, fixing my clothes. I headed to the front door in my bare feet and took a look through the peephole. What was he doing here?! I felt like a deer in headlights, unsure if I should open the door or not.

"*It's David!*" I said, panicked. Jack just looked amused. I felt my face drain of color and began to tuck in my shirt and tidy my hair. I felt like a teenager busted for making out with her boyfriend.

"Catherine." David banged on the door and I jumped back. "Open the door. I can hear you breathing from all the way out here and, let's face it, you're not exactly light on your feet—I heard you stomping your way to the door. Open up." He banged on the door again.

"Go on, let him in." Jack said.

The moment I opened the door, David barged in.

"Woman, where have you been? I've been calling you. Don't you check your mobile any more? Thank God I wasn't lying in some alley dying and you were my last phone call. I even texted you 911 after you ignored 999, thinking perhaps you'd forgotten what emergency means in this country," he said in a rush.

He didn't see the look of bewilderment on my face. I wasn't so much surprised that he was here unannounced, he'd done that on more than one occasion—it was the fact that he was rambling. David never rambled. The man hated noise and disorder. What I was witnessing was a rarity. His hair was messy, his shirt was wrinkled and he hadn't shaved.

"I'm having a major crisis… Me. Of all people." He stopped and looked at me, noticing for the first time that I wasn't alone.

"Evening, David," Jack said, offering his hand. David looked at me, then at Jack's hand, as if it was a snake that was about to bite him. After a long pause, David shook it and I found myself breathing again. If there was one thing David possessed, it was manners. But what happened after the formalities were taken care of was another matter altogether.

"Jack, I should have known you were the reason behind Kate not picking up her mobile. I'd forced myself to forget you were back in the picture. Tell me, how long are you around for this time?"

I groaned inwardly. Jack, however, laughed, brushing it off. "Some things never change. Sorry to disappoint you, but I'm here for the long haul, better get used to it." He stood his ground. I was bursting. Jack wanted to be with me.

David smiled. "Really? Because you seem to come and go like the wind. The only person who's in Kate's life for the 'long haul' is *me*."

I shut my eyes. Jack placed his arms around me. "I understand why you're saying this, David. But I don't intend to lose her again. It was my own stupidity, and I've learned my lesson. I don't intend to make the same mistake twice."

"I will agree with you on one thing, your stupidity." David said.

My eyes snapped open. "Okay, that's enough…" I stood in between them. This conversation needed to end.

"No need for the drama," David said innocently. "We're just talking, right, Jackson?"

"Of course, just a chat between mates. Would you like some wine, David, or a beer?" He rubbed my arms.

"Do you have something stronger?" David asked to my surprise. I thought for sure he would turn around and leave.

Jack nodded with a smile. "I'll see what I can find. It's all right, Kate." He gave me a reassuring kiss. But I wasn't convinced.

"Prove me wrong and I'll apologize," David added with a smile. Jack grinned and left to the kitchen.

I spun around to face David. "What are you doing here?" I hissed, grabbing him by the arm and pulling him further into the room so Jack couldn't hear us. I gave him an evil stare.

"Oi! No need to be so aggressive." He rubbed his arm.

"You just came in here and insulted him. Can't you give him a little room?" I pleaded, taking a deep breath.

"You're right. I'm sorry. But I have an emergency. Isn't that what friends are for, to be there in times of need? I am in need, Catherine. My life is upside down at the moment." I frowned. But he mistook the reason behind it. "I don't understand why you're upset about what I told him," he said. "I actually think I'm being quite pleasant given the circumstances."

"He's trying. Don't you see that?"

"Perhaps he is. Let's hope so, for your sake. Forgive me if I don't buy his *I'm now the perfect boyfriend* act."

I was about to speak, but Jack strolled back in with a bottle of vodka and handed David a glass. He offered me one too but I shook my head no and he placed it on the side table. In silence, I stared as the unlikely pair headed to the sofa, drinking vodka like old pals.

Jack stretched his legs out in front of him, glass in hand. "So what's the emergency?" he asked. I braced myself for David to smart-mouth him but, to my surprise, he answered.

"Richard…"

"Whoa! Did you just say 'Richard'?" I said. I couldn't believe what I was hearing.

"Kate," Jack warned. "Who is Richard?" he asked David.

David turned to him with a serious face. "I think the love of my life." He threw back the rest of his drink and Jack poured him another generous one. They ignored the fact that I was staring at them with my mouth wide open.

"You've got to be kidding me? So you think Richard is your soulmate? Give me a break!" I exclaimed. "This is the guy you've been going on and on about? The one you've fallen in love with? *Richard*? As in the Richard you dumped a few months ago because he was getting all needy and used the L word? The same one you wanted nothing to do with? Oh man, this is priceless!" Of all the things David was capable of coming up with, I had not seen this one coming.

David actually looked hurt. "You can be such a bitch, Kate. Being a mean girl doesn't suit you. Perhaps Richard is my soulmate… and perhaps he isn't. The point is—whether you believe it or not—I have feelings for him."

I crossed my arms in front of me. "I'm finding it unbelievable because you dumped him—publicly."

"That's not fair, Catherine, I'm suffering here." David moaned.

Jack gave him a sympathetic look. "What happened between you and Richard?" he asked. I shook my head, not believing what I was seeing—these two were now acting like BFFs.

David leaned back on the sofa, his shoulders dropping, and began to tell his story. "We were dating for a brief time and I stupidly cast him off. I told him I didn't share the feelings he had for me. I thought him to be too needy, too emotional. What was I bloody thinking?"

"You panicked. It happens to the best of us," Jack began. I looked at David, who was giving me the same look—'compassionate' was not a word we would use to describe Jack. "The important thing is you realized your mistake," he continued. "You can't go back and change it. The only thing you can do is think about what you're going to do to rectify it."

David nodded along with everything Jack was saying. "You're right. I need a strategy to win him back." For the first time since he came in, he smiled. "What would you do?"

"Well, that depends," Jack started, and I got up, picked up the glass of vodka I had refused and took a gulp. This was freaking me out.

"Okay, that's enough. Honey," I turned to Jack, "I love you but please go take a walk or head to the pub for a bit. I can't talk to him while you're here giving him dating advice."

Jack grinned at me. Shit. I had used the L word. How could I have that let that slip? His eyes locked on mine and I knew he wasn't going to let this go. David, of course, was oblivious to what I had just done as he was still wallowing in his self-pity.

Jack got up and placed his hand on David's shoulder. "Hang in there, mate. I'm sure it'll work out. He'll come to his senses. Just give him some time."

"You think so?"

"I see how you care for Kate and what she says about you. I think he will." Jack leaned towards the table, picked up his wallet and, opening it, pulled out a card. "If you want to talk about it or just vent, give me a call."

"Much obliged," David said, taking it. This wasn't happening. I was in an episode of *The Twilight Zone*.

Jack tucked the wallet into his pocket and turned to me. "Call me when I can return." He leaned in and gave me a kiss. "I love you, too," he whispered in my ear, making me shiver. I waited until he left before turning to David.

"What did you kick him out for?" David groaned, placing his hand over his head and getting up.

"I just told him I loved him, what was I thinking?" Shaken, I grabbed the vodka bottle and poured myself another drink. There was no turning back now. It wasn't like I hadn't told him

I loved him before but this was different. I hadn't said it since we'd recommenced our relationship.

"This is not a problem—it's no secret that you love him. We all know you never stopped. The only person you're fooling is yourself. At least he loves you… Call him back! He was giving me good advice—he should know, he's been in this predicament before!"

"Pull yourself together. Are you listening to yourself? You are asking *Jack* for advice!"

"How am I supposed to do that?" He sat on the sofa, threw his head back and closed his eyes. "Do you think I like being this… this… fool? I tried to call him to apologise –"

"*You*? Apologize?" I asked in disbelief. This was serious. David apologizing to a guy he had dumped was unheard of. It was about as rare as a classic black Christian Louboutin going on sale. I had never seen it.

"I apologize! Not often, I'll admit, but I do."

"What did you say? Did you tell him how you felt?"

"No. I never got the opportunity. I called and began a very carefully rehearsed speech about why I ended things, and he didn't even let me get a word in. He told me to sod off. Just like that, he told me to do one and hung up on me! Nobody speaks to me that way!"

I laughed and immediately covered my mouth. It was a bit harsh to laugh when he was down but I doubted anyone had told David to 'do one' before. His blue eyes shot open. "You're enjoying this, aren't you?" He took the bottle of vodka and poured himself a healthy glass.

"I am not. I didn't mean to laugh… It's just, you look so disheveled, and this is so unlike you."

"What is happening to me? I can't think straight. I'm checking my mobile every three seconds, making sure it's still working when I don't see a call or text. I'm even on Facebook now. He's constantly on that bloody thing, liking ridiculous photos. I swear he's doing it to upset me. I'm practically stalking him on it." He threw back the rest of his drink in one quick gulp before continuing with his rant.

"For God's sake, I have grown a vagina! I'm going out of my mind. How do you stand it? Tell me how you deal with this every day? Am I going to transform into one of those Collins wearers now?"

I laughed and he gave me a look of death. "I'm sorry, I'm sorry," I said.

He threw his head back and began to laugh as well. "Look at me. I'm pathetic. Isn't there something I can do to make it all go away?

I placed my hand on his shoulder. "Well, you can finish the bottle of vodka, pass out and wake up feeling like crap tomorrow. Or you can go home, shower, shave and get yourself together. Tomorrow we'll go shopping for the hottest pair of shoes Prada has created."

He smiled. "You're so good to me, Catherine…"

I could see him picking out a pair of new shoes in his mind already.

"*Or* you can go and apologize to Richard in person and really mean it. Say you've been an idiot, that you made a mistake, and you'll do whatever it takes to make it right… even if that means wearing the Collins."

David turned his head and faced me. "Let's not get carried away. You had it right the first time. Shopping it is. I'm feeling so much better now. You have a point." He got up. "*I* am David Cunningham, I don't go begging, nor do I cry over any man. I'm the best thing that has ever happened to him. What am I doing drinking my sorrows away? I need to be out there meeting new people."

I sighed. "Okay, what just happened? How did you get from 'my life is over' to 'I need to go out there and prowl'? All I said is let's go out and buy some new shoes."

"It was a brilliant comparison, Kate. I can't ever settle for one pair, darling. What was I thinking? New pair and new man… screw him!" David grabbed his coat. "Thank you, you are brilliant."

"That wasn't what I meant by that, David," I said. But he was no longer listening.

"Tell Jack thank you. And good luck with the 'I love you' thing." He gave me a wink.

Chapter Twenty-four

The first pair of shoes I fell in love with sparkled. Ruby-red slippers that reminded me of Dorothy from *The Wizard Of Oz*. I was driven to them like a moth to a flame as they glittered on the table. I eagerly waited for the salesman to put them on my feet and I felt like a princess as he adjusted the straps. I remember how grand I felt as he took my hand and helped me up. I beamed… until I stood up. The shoes felt tight around my little toe. My mother instantly knew, as all mothers do, that they weren't compatible with my feet. She suggested a classic pair of black patent leather Mary Janes, and my smile faded as they paled in comparison to the glittery shoes. How could I settle for them after the sparkle? I pleaded with her and finally she gave in, warning me that the shoes would continue to hurt. But I insisted they wouldn't. I was in denial. And of course she was right. Even as a child, I had a knack for picking the Wickham out of a pile.

I found myself back in that place of denial. It didn't matter that I was now a grown-up. I was in denial thinking that my situation with Jack would suddenly take care of itself with my friends, and also in thinking that I was able to handle Philip without wanting to clonk him over the head with my shoe. Even David was in denial, going on a date every night, trying to forget the fact that Richard wanted nothing to do with him.

I looked at my feet: red patent leather stilettos. I knew when I bought them that even if I had them stretched, they would never be comfortable… some things never changed. But I felt powerful in these shoes, and today, I was prepared for battle. It was my first client presentation with Philip, and I had given myself plenty of time to get there, thinking I would arrive before him. But to my surprise, he was already there when I walked into the conference room. Did the man ever sleep? He looked almost normal, reading some documents as he passed his pen through his fingers with an air of confidence.

Sensing someone was staring at him, he looked up momentarily and almost smiled until his eyes rested on my shoes. Okay, I admit, they were a bit bright for work. They had seemed appropriate this morning given my mood, but the way his eyes lingered on them made me wish I had gone for a pair of old-fashioned black pumps instead.

"Good morning, Kate."

"Philip," I nodded. It was too early for pleasantries and I was thankful when he handed me a spreadsheet of the latest figures I had put together. Without skipping a beat, I placed my bags and coat on the seat next to me and plunged right into it.

"I went over the report last night, and I have to say, Kate… good work."

"Cheers." I placed my glasses on as I looked over his comments. Some of his suggestions made perfect sense and were actually better than mine in some instances. Even though I didn't want to be in the same room as him at the moment, I couldn't deny that he was good at his job. We ploughed through the figures together before meeting with the client.

The rest of the morning continued in much the same way. When I wasn't trying to kill him, we actually worked well together. It was nice not to be at each other's throats.

"Kate, do you want to go and grab a cup of coffee before we head to the next meeting?" Philip asked as we wrapped up.

I looked at him, surprised. "Coffee? You're a coffee man, Philip?"

He began putting his paperwork in his briefcase. "The Americans have converted me. What can I say?" he grinned.

"I never pegged you for a rebel. You must be causing all sorts of chaos in the universe with that one. I actually prefer tea." I tilted my head with a smile.

He laughed. There was something about his laugh that was quite pleasant. "Why am I not surprised? You are an enigma, Kate. So I gather that you're an afternoon tea drinker as well?"

"But of course, four o'clock on the dot," I said.

"In that case, afternoon tea it is," he said.

"Do you have a place in mind?" I asked, looking at my watch. He was right, we did have some free time before the next meeting. I could have headed back to the office and got some work done but, for my own amusement, I wanted to see what he would come up with.

"We're in Trafalgar Square, I'm sure we'll be able to find somewhere suitable around here."

I crossed my arms, laughing. Typical. Just like a man, not knowing where he was. I could immediately think of five places to go around here. We were in one of the biggest tourist spots in London.

"What's so amusing?" he asked.

"You don't have a clue what's around here, do you?" I dared him to say otherwise.

"Are you implying I don't know where we are?" His smile kept getting better and better.

"I believe you know where we are—I just don't think you know what's around here," I challenged.

"Oh, how dare you, you have no faith in me. I could name any number of places!" he said, amused.

"Go ahead then, what's around here?" I waited, crossing my arms in front of me.

"The National Gallery, the National Portrait Gallery..."

"Besides the obvious landmarks—every tourist knows them. Come on, Philip, you're a London boy born and bred, right?"

"Don't question my London soul, woman," he smiled, and began listing more tourist attractions.

"Pathetic," I teased. "I think I'm more of a Londoner than you are."

"Is that so? Then how about you pick a place in the area—one that I wouldn't automatically think serves tea, of course."

Immediately, I thought of one of my favorite places in the city. But did I want to bring Philip into my safe haven?

"Not so easy, is it?" he said, amused at my hesitation.

"I have a place in mind," I answered. It wasn't a secret place after all, it was open to the public. "I accept the challenge. Tea will be on you," I added.

"You're on." He extended his hand and I took it, my fingers tingling as we shook on it. I quickly let go and watched as he rubbed his hands quickly together before clasping them. For a brief moment, neither of us spoke or looked at each other.

"We can—" I began, as Philip began speaking at the same time. We both stopped.

Philip smiled softly. "After you."

"I was saying that I know just the place where we can sit and talk. It's one of my favorite places, actually," I said nervously. "But I'm warning you, if you tell anyone, I will have to hurt you." He bit his lip slightly and my heart began to beat faster. "If you make fun of me, you can forget about it," I said.

"No, no, I'm not making fun. I'm actually intrigued."

"That better be true or I *will* hurt you," I joked.

"I feel like I'm back in New York."

"Good, then you know I mean business."

"Oh, I believe you and your stilettos," he said, looking down at my feet.

The moment we stepped outside, I tied my coat, shoving my hands in my pockets. "It's chilly," I said, as we made our way across Trafalgar Square.

"Compared to New York, this is nothing."

"You're right—perhaps you're more of a New Yorker than I am," I said with a smile. I looked up at him, beginning to wonder what I was doing going for tea with Philip.

"Watch it," a woman said, annoyed, as we did an awkward dance to avoiding bumping into each other. I sucked my teeth, moving away to give her room, and she still couldn't figure out how to get around me.

"My apologies, she's American," Philip said. My head immediately snapped to look at him. He hadn't dared… the woman snickered. I punched Philip on the shoulder.

"I can't believe you said that. You are exactly like my friend David."

Philip laughed. "I like him already. I thought it was quite funny."

"Don't even get me started." I looked down at Trafalgar Square briefly, taking a moment. It always hit me, when I came by here and saw Big Ben in the distance, that I was in London. I never got tired of this view.

"Lead the way, mademoiselle," Philip said, bringing me back from my nostalgic moment.

"This way," I said, walking past the entrance of the National Gallery.

He looked a bit weary as we crossed the streets towards St

Martin-in-the-Fields. “Admit it, you have no clue either,” he said. “I knew it.”

“I know perfectly well where I am. This is where we’re going. You’ve never heard of the Crypt?” I said. We stopped next to the church in front of the glass cylinder that looked like it was emerging from under the ground, slightly out of place in the middle of the older buildings surrounding it.

“I know the church but had no idea about this,” Philip said, looking around as if he was seeing it for the first time.

His comment made me excited. I always enjoyed showing people new places. “Well, Mr Spencer, you are in for a treat. They have tea *and* coffee. I come here for concerts as well. You should try it.” My heels clicked down the spiral staircase and he surprised me by taking hold of my arm and guiding me down. “Always the gentleman,” I said, watching him turn a bit red.

“First and foremost,” he beamed. As we got to the landing, I felt nervous. It was simple, but beautiful in my opinion. I wanted him to approve of my choice.

“Follow me,” I said, stepping into the cafe. Its cobbled floor, lunchroom seats and high bar chairs dominated the space. We walked towards the back and I took a tray and handed it to him as we got on the ordering line. I looked up at the gothic ceiling and Philip followed my gaze.

“Did you know that Charles II was once buried here?’ I said, suddenly nervous. “We’re standing on gravestones. A bit morbid, I know, but there’s something quite poetic about it. Some of the stones have been here since the 1500s. Extraordinary, isn’t it?” I always rambled when I was super nervous.

“Wow, I didn’t expect a guided tour with my coffee. I’m impressed, Kate.” He sounded genuinely interested.

I blushed, hoping he didn’t think I was being silly gushing over the place. I asked for an afternoon tea and the man handed me a small silver teapot and a plate full of goodies. Philip ordered a coffee. I looked for a quick escape while I composed myself. What had I been thinking bringing someone like Philip here? I'd got carried away! I looked down, searching for some money in my bag.

"Please, put that away, you won the bet. A deal is a deal," he said. "Allow me." He took the teapot and plate from my hands and placed them on the tray. The small gesture was making me go soft. I really didn't want to like him. It was nothing but a pot of tea and a scone. Even the way he handled the tray was graceful… I needed to pull myself together.

I craned my neck and spotted an empty table. Philip followed me to it, looking around admiringly as we sat down. The soft lighting made it feel like we were in a room lit by candlelight.

"I like it," he announced. "I can see why you love it here. It's quite charming."

I smiled with pride. His words made me feel like I had won a prize. I poured myself a cup of tea.

"No milk?" he asked.

"No. I like my tea black," I grinned.

"And you claimed I'm the one with the rebellious impulses? The Chinese introduced us to tea, we Brits added the milk."

"And us Americans threw it into the harbor," I added. We both laughed and sat drinking in silence.

"Kate, I just wanted to say that you're doing an incredible job," he said as he set his cup down. "I know the transition hasn't been easy for you, but you've handled it quite well."

"But you still won't give me an explanation as to why I was taken off the Lewis account," I threw in, holding my cup between my palms.

He took a deep breath, his vivid blue eyes staring at me. "No, not yet, I'm afraid. However, you more than anyone should understand that changes are inevitable and at times beneficial in any company."

"Yes, you would say that, because it affects others... not you, of course," I said without thinking. I could see blotches of red instantly form on his neck.

"What is that supposed to mean?" he asked curtly.

"It means," I began, not backing down, "that if the company is making changes to better the accounts then that should include yours. The Thomson account is primarily a London-based operation. Yet you're running it from New York, which in my opinion makes no sense. The lead should be here but no one dares replace you and we all know why."

Philip just stared at me, expressionless. I winced when I moved my foot—these shoes were not meant for the amount of walking I had done.

"You really need to rethink your footwear sometimes, Kate," he finally said. My mouth dropped open and I looked at him in horror. No man had ever told me to rethink my shoes, not one. *The nerve!* And here I was about to apologize for what I had just said.

"Excuse me?" I said, my voice rising slightly.

"It's obvious that you're uncomfortable. It was apparent that you were in pain during the meeting, and you made the same expression just now. Why bother wearing them if they're going to cause you such misery? Tell me, is it worth it?"

Was he out of his mind? Men asked such stupid questions. That was like asking a woman how old she was or how much she weighed, you just didn't! It was common sense not to ask. He clearly hadn't been taught the rules!

"I'm fine," I managed through gritted teeth.

"Don't be ridiculous. You're not. If you want, you can head to the office and change into more sensible shoes before the next meeting," he offered.

Even if I had to go through the rest of the day bleeding and in agony, I was not going to give him the satisfaction of taking them off! It was as if his words had numbed the pain I had felt seconds ago.

"There's no need. If you'll excuse me, I have to use the ladies' room." I didn't give him time to respond and sprang from my chair in the direction of the bathroom. My feet were actually killing me and as I closed the door, I took one shoe off, feeling instant relief. I leaned against the wall, rubbing my poor foot. I placed it back in the shoe and repeated the process with the other. Taking a breath, I opened the door and headed to the sinks. I washed my hands, staring at myself in the mirror. I needed to pull myself together. How could I have been so blinded by a cup of tea to think that he and I could actually be civil? I could do this. The man would not defeat me. Taking a few more moments to wiggle my toes in the tight shoes, I headed back.

Philip was drinking his coffee, looking pensive, when I stopped in front of the table and picked up my things.

"I think we should head out if we want to make the meeting on time," I said, biting my tongue.

He looked startled. "You haven't finished your tea," he said.

"I think I've had enough tea for now," I responded coolly.

"I didn't mean to offend you," he defended himself. He stood up, holding the back of the chair, unsure of what to do.

I took a deep breath. "I actually believe that you don't mean to offend, but you just don't think the rules apply to you. If you took a moment, just one moment, to actually consider how the other person might feel when you say the things that you say, perhaps you wouldn't sound like such a snob."

His head snapped back as if I had slapped him. "That was not my intention, Kate."

"It never is! I supposed being a Spencer makes you think you have the right to speak to anyone as you please." I turned and headed towards the stairs.

Philip was right on my heels and took my arm at the top of the landing. "Must you always do that? If you have something to say, then say it, Catherine. I make no apologies for being a Spencer. I didn't choose what family I was born into."

"I'm not asking you to apologize for that, Philip. I am asking for you to *recognize* that you have it easy at the firm. No one questions you, no one moves you around. I've worked my butt off to get to where I am. I've worked hours upon hours proving myself at Spencer & Lockhart, yet here I am, being treated like a first-year. I've brought this company a lot of money as well, and no one is taking that into consideration," I said, finally letting out my frustrations.

"Of course we are! I value you… we value you. You're one of the best workers we have. But you're not being fair, I work hard, too, Kate. Do you honestly think that I have it easy because I'm a Spencer? I have to work twice as hard to prove myself. I don't like being treated differently, and I have earned my way as well. If you would take time to look beyond your situation, you would see that."

"Then why am I off the account?" I demanded.

"I'm not at liberty to say," he said.

Instead of responding, I marched out and across the street, back in the direction of the gallery. I could see he was following me. He made me so angry. I stopped short, making him jump back.

"Is this about Jack?" I asked, suddenly realizing this could very well have nothing to do with me.

"Jack? What does he have to do with this?" Philip demanded.

"You've made it no secret that you dislike him. And you were asking all sorts of questions about my relationship with him last time," I pointed out.

He looked annoyed. "The only concern I would have would be him obtaining inside information."

My heart stopped. "*What?*"

"I'm just stating the possibilities."

"You think I'm giving him information?"

"Damn it. You're twisting my words! That is not what I said." He was getting angry.

"It's what you're implying!"

"I am not implying that you are, but Jack is a sneaky character, I wouldn't put it past him. You, more than anyone else, should know that. He cheated on you, didn't he?"

I bit my lip. Philip cursed. "I'm sorry," he said. "That was out of order." I turned to leave, but Philip held me back. I began to pull away and my foot twisted… the heel snapped, stopping both of us in our tracks.

"Oh my… god," I gasped.

Philip looked down at my shoes. His face paled. I took a step and automatically limped—the heel was broken. Without hesitation, I placed my hand on his shoulder to balance myself and bravely inspected the damage. The heel had come off the hinges. Mumbling and cursing under my breath, I made my way towards an unoccupied bench.

"You could superglue it back together, I'm sure," he suggested with a nervous laugh, looking down at me.

I looked at him in sheer horror. "Superglue?" I repeated. Had he really suggested that I glue my heel back on? He had lost his mind. My perfect Dorothy shoes were broken, and he was standing there disguising his laugh with a fake cough. God, I hated this man!

"Superglue…" was all I could manage again.

"It's a perfectly fine solution. I could go and check if the shop across the street has any." He gave me a smile as if he had given me the best solution known to mankind. Part of me wanted to cry for my shoe, the other part wanted to take the good one off and hit him over the head with it.

"What is wrong with you?! I can't *superglue* these… Do you

have any idea how much I love these shoes? They don't sell them any more!"

He shook his head. "It's just a shoe. I'm sure you have another pair just like them back at home."

I gave him an evil look. Had he actually listened to a word I had just said? *They did not make these shoes any more.* He was about to speak, but I raised my hand to silence him.

"Please, Philip, shut up… just shut up. I really don't trust myself if you say another stupid thing." With my head held high, I got up and began walking, not caring that people were staring at me limping away.

I barely looked at Philip as we made our way back to the office. In the span of an hour, I had managed to go from bright worker to psycho. What was it about this man that made me lose my temper, my composure… worse, my professionalism? If anyone noticed my shoe, they didn't mention it. Throughout our presentation, Philip made eye contact with me only once, void of expression.

"Thank you for having us. I'm sure you will agree our proposal is quite fair…" Philip said, wrapping up the meeting. We were still smiling at everyone until we were finally left on our own. Then my daggers went back up and he knew it.

"I think that went rather well, don't you?" he said to me as we headed out.

"Yes, I agree," I answered coldly. We made our way to the elevator banks in silence. I could see that he was trying to say something. I'd been hoping he would drop it.

"About what happened earlier…" his blue eyes looked pleading as they stared into mine. I shook my head.

"Honestly, Philip, I don't want to discuss that. Let's pretend it never happened. I'm quite embarrassed, and I apologize for my behavior out there. But I will tell you this: I have never given Jack any information about my work."

"I know. I never thought you did," he said, taking me by surprise. "I apologize as well. I shouldn't have lost my temper like that. It was unlike me."

"You call that losing your temper?"

"I'm British, remember?" he grinned in a way that that made him look cute. I hated that. I also disliked the fact that I wanted to smile back—I should still be angry with him. "And I am really sorry about your shoes."

I mumbled something incoherent.

Chapter Twenty-five

The moment we got out of the cab in front of the office, we parted ways. I headed back to my office and took off my shoes, wanting to cry with relief. A few moments later, Gemma came barging in and shut the door. "Did everything go okay at the meeting?"

Not looking up, I sat with one leg crossed over the other, massaging my poor foot. "Yes, it went rather well. Why do you ask?" I asked.

"Philip came back and slammed his door. In all the years I've known him, I have never seen that happen."

That bit of information surprised me but I didn't let it show. "I have no idea what's bothered Philip. Maybe he realized his socks didn't match his tie," I shrugged, hoping I hadn't revealed too much.

Gemma looked at me suspiciously. "You know something," she said.

"I do not. The meetings went quite well. I think we may have landed the Smith account. He should be jumping up and down. Perhaps this is his way of showing emotion?"

"They *broke*?" she asked, forgetting Philip. She looked like she was about to cry as she watched me place the broken shoe in a bag.

"Yes, I'm still in shock," I replied, and pulled out the box under my desk in search of another pair of shoes. The Wickhams had done enough damage for the day, I thought, as I chose a pair of practical black pumps.

"How did you manage that? Do you think the cobbler could fix them?"

"It's a long story I'd rather not relive, but I hope they can be fixed," I said, wiggling my toes. The Collinses had won. My feet began to tingle—the circulation was finally returning.

"It's a shame. You're having no luck with shoes these days, are you?" she pointed out. I had to agree with her. I was a shoe disaster zone—much like my current situation with the men in my life.

"We're friends, right?" she asked suddenly.

"Yes," I answered, giving her a puzzled look. She continued to look at me like she was trying to figure out what I was keeping from her. Part of me wanted to burst out with what had happened, but I thought better of it.

"Good, then as a friend, I feel that I should warn you: if you don't jump at the opportunity to go out with Philip, someone else here will," she said.

I laughed. She was actually quite serious. "Gemma, I'm not interested in him in that way. Please feel free to tell whoever that they can have him, all of him, gift-wrapped."

Crossing her arms, she sat down in front of me. "Do you have a better offer?" She raised an eyebrow in question.

I smiled widely, unable to contain myself. "As a matter of fact, I do."

"Catherine Seeley! You have been holding out on me! Who is he?" she leaned forward in anticipation.

"I'm back with Jack."

"What!"

"Shhh! Keep it down. Long story, but I'm not telling anyone at the moment."

"I can't believe it. You've kept this from me of all people. You know I have to live vicariously through you!"

"Then that must stink for you because I really don't have an exciting life," I joked.

By the time the weekend came along, I was ready for some relaxation with the gang. I was on my way to Olivia's. She had managed to put together yet another dinner at her house and I was really looking forward to it.

Arriving at her front door, I heard some clutter and hushing noises. What was she up to in there? I pressed the doorbell again a little more forcefully. The door opened and a chorus of singing began. "Happy birthday to you… Happy birthday to you… Happy birthday, dear Kate… Happy birthday to you!" I clutched the bottle of wine against my chest.

"What is this? My birthday isn't for another week," I said, still startled. I looked up at the purple and silver helium balloons Olivia had filled the flat with. It was quite festive.

"We know, but you won't be here, so we decided to celebrate with you tonight instead," Olivia said, hugging me tightly. I hugged everyone as I made my way through. I didn't know what to say. *You could tell them the truth*, my conscience suggested.

"You're going to miss one of the best events. The charity ball will be the event of the season. Are you sure you won't reconsider?" Olivia asked. She did have a point. But I had a better offer—alone time with Jack.

"Ladies, ladies, let her settle in. Let's get her something to drink!" David saved me and gave me a sympathetic smile as he took the bottle of wine from me.

"Kate, would you like a drink?" Brandon asked, holding a plate of hors d'oeuvres.

"Yes, please! A big glass of wine," I said, knowing I would need it. He laughed.

"I'll get it," David called out.

Brandon placed the plate down on the table. "I am the chef for the evening, my lady," he grinned, giving me a hug.

"There goes my diet," I said, taking one of the crepes and savoring it. "Thank you, Brandon... Everyone, thank you. I wasn't expecting this. You guys shouldn't have," I said. Even the table was decked out in lovely shades of purple and pale pink, with white candles, and tiny crystals were scattered all over.

Dinner, of course, was grand. "Ladies and gentlemen, leave room for dessert," Brandon announced, coming in with a big fluffy chocolate cake. They began to sing Happy Birthday once more and I looked down shyly.

"Thank you, guys," I started. "This was unexpected but much appreciated. Brandon, once again, you have raised the bar. Dinner was delicious, and that cake... I have no words. To Brandon!" I lifted my glass and the others joined me.

"Let's take some pictures!" Olivia exclaimed. If there was one thing Olivia loved, it was taking pictures. We all got wrapped up in the moment, posing, Elizabeth taking on the role of lead photographer.

"Don't put any pictures up on Instagram or Facebook until I approve!" David called out. "Yes, please, no unflattering photos!" Olivia voiced as well.

"What's the point of putting up photos if you have to approve everything before I do it?" Elizabeth asked. They got into a discussion about selfies.

Elizabeth leaned over. "So where are you really going on your birthday that's good enough to make you ditch us?" Curiosity was written all over her face.

"I just planned a weekend trip. Long story, I'll explain later," I said, trying to change the subject as fast as I could. But with Elizabeth, that was asking for trouble. She was going to get an answer one way or another.

"Come on, you can say," she pushed, holding her glass of wine to her lips. "What are you keeping from us?"

"I'd rather not." I shifted in my seat uncomfortably.

"This has man written all over it. Why are you keeping it a secret if you're going away with someone? That's fantastic!"

"Just drop it, okay?" I said with annoyance in my voice.

The conversation at the table came to a halt. All eyes were on me. I was on the spot. And had lashed out at Elizabeth, who was staring at me, stunned. I folded my hands in my lap, taking a deep breath.

"I'm sorry, Elizabeth, I didn't mean to yell." I lowered my eyes. I was losing it quickly –it wasn't her fault that I was keeping my relationship with Jack a secret.

"You're overly stressed at work, I get it. But, honey, if work is making you that unhappy…" she began, being the friend she was and making an excuse for me, which only made me feel worse.

"It's not just about work," I said with a sigh. "I've been keeping something from you, from all of you." This wasn't how I had planned to reveal my secret.

"I've been seeing Jack again for the past four months or so." I gulped back my wine.

"What?!" Elizabeth was shocked.

"You're kidding!" Olivia said.

Emma stared at me with an unusual expression on her face: she was angry. "I saw you in the city with him a few weeks ago, and I thought perhaps it had to do with work, but you've been back with him?" She looked like she was about to cry.

"Emma…"

"Don't make excuses, you're a hypocrite. You've told me relentlessly to stay away from Henry because what he did to me was unforgivable," she said.

"It's not the same," I interrupted. "Henry broke you, or don't you remember?"

"But he didn't cheat on me! Why does Jack get a second chance and Henry doesn't?" Emma demanded.

"Girls, this isn't the time," Elizabeth said, but neither of us cared.

I looked at Emma across the table. "The difference between us, Emma, is that I was able to handle Jack. I didn't lose my job because I chose him. You barely pulled yourself together after that, and the best thing was for you to stay away from him. We all know that." I looked round the table, expecting everyone to come to my defence on this one.

Emma stood up. "But it's *my* decision to make whether I see Henry or not!"

I got up angrily. "Well, then finally make one!" I threw at her. "You've never made a decision. We make them for you. Olivia dresses you, Elizabeth counsels you… and I'm left to pick up the pieces Henry has left."

Emma seemed to go all shades of red—she looked at me as if I had slapped her. I had been cruel.

"All right, that's enough. *Downton Abbey* isn't until tomorrow night. Why don't we all have a glass of wine and chill?" David suggested, getting up.

Brandon got up as well. "Yes, that's a good idea. Let me get more wine."

Elizabeth for one was speechless. She was probably trying to figure out how she had missed this going on right under her nose. David was trying to give me looks, which I was managing to avoid.

Emma pressed down her skirt. "I'm sorry, Olivia, for ruining your perfect dinner party. Thank you for inviting me." She reached for her purse.

Olivia grabbed her arm. "Don't leave, this is just a little disagreement, we all just need a breather. Let's just take a few moments."

"She doesn't need a breather, she needs to be honest," Emma said, pointing at me. "You're so judgmental about everyone else but you don't look at yourself," she addressed me.

"I just wanted you to be happy. And I didn't want to see you hurt again by Henry," I said, softening my tone. Everyone's eyes shifted between the two of us.

"I didn't realize I was the laughing stock of the group. I may have made a mistake by not going to New York, but it's what I wanted; I wanted him and the life that I had with him. Look at all of us. Besides Olivia and Brandon, what are the rest of us doing on these pointless dates?"

"I'm having fun," David interrupted, but no one laughed.

"So where is Henry now?" I asked.

She threw her hands up in the air. "I don't know! Because I've been listening to you and not calling him back. I hate going on these stupid dates when all I want is Henry! He may be a Collins, but at least I know what I'm getting. I don't even like Jane Austen, nor do I care that much about shoes. That's your bloody obsession, Kate, not mine. Henry just got cold feet, and I haven't given him another chance because of you."

I felt horrible and placed my hand over my mouth. Olivia looked like she was about to cry. "I had no idea," I said, sitting down.

"No, you really don't know, do you? Because you've been so busy giving orders to everyone. I know you mean well, I do, but sometimes your advice is horrible. You need to let me make my own decisions. As shitty as they may be, all I need is for you to support them… all of you," she said, looking at the whole group. "If I make the wrong decision, all I need is for you to be there, just let me figure it out without judging me." She was shaking. "I know my shoes are boring and not exciting, but it's who I am."

"Honey, we don't mean to say you're boring," Elizabeth said, looking as bad as I felt.

Emma shook her head. "It's my own fault for not sticking up for myself, but that's enough, I've had it.

Elizabeth and I started reassuring her at once that we didn't think less of her, but all we managed to do was cause another argument.

"I'm pregnant!" exclaimed Olivia, instantly bringing everyone in the room to a halt.

"Oh my God!" I said.

"… You're not joking," said David.

Brandon smiled, standing behind Olivia. She shook her head, placing her hand on her flat stomach. "I'm not. I wasn't going to say anything yet, I'm only a few weeks along. But there it is, we're pregnant!" she grinned, looking up at Brandon. We all started congratulating them at once.

"That's wonderful!" Emma squealed, hugging her, forgetting that she was in the middle of taking off my head.

"Well, this deserves a toast!" Elizabeth said, lifting her glass. Emma and I avoided looking at each other as we toasted.

David and I headed back together at the end of the party. "That was intense back there. Why did you choose that particular moment to make your announcement?" he said the moment we were out the door.

"I don't know, because I panicked! I wasn't ready to have Elizabeth throw all those questions at me. And probably because I'm a crap friend," I said as I linked my arm through his.

"No, you're not. You're perhaps a bit of a cornball, and sometimes you can be annoying, but you're not a bad friend."

"Gee, don't hold back the compliments," I said with a small laugh. I took a deep breath. "Emma hates me."

"No, she doesn't, she's Emma. I knew with that red hair there had to be some fire in her. I'm glad she finally spoke up. Not at your expense, of course, but she was certainly holding in some frustrations. By tomorrow, she'll have called you to apologize and sent you some elaborate cupcake assortment. I hope it's from Lola's." He tried to make a joke but I didn't laugh.

He stopped walking, placed his hands on my shoulders and turned me to face him. "Lighten up, Kate. It'll be fine. Just let Emma be Emma. She has to do her own thing, even if it means going back to Henry. He's not a bad bloke, he just got lost. You women make it so complicated—which is why I stick to men."

"This isn't funny, David. Is it wrong that I don't want to see her get hurt again? Come on, you were there. You saw how devastated she was," I reminded him.

"Yes, I remember, and I also remember how broken you were when Jack hurt you, yet here you are back with him."

"I'm not getting hurt like she was," I said defensively.

David pulled me back as I took a step to cross the road. "Are you serious?" he smirked. "I didn't think you were delusional, Catherine."

I pushed my hair back against the wind. "I am not delusional. I know why I'm with Jack. I'm not an idiot like before, I have no expectations. Emma does! She wants the fairy tale."

"You have no expectations? Hun, wake up, look into a mirror and recognize who you are. You are the girl who's named the shoes you wear after the men in *Pride And Prejudice*, which has to be the most romantic book, movie, you name it, of all time. And you really believe you have no expectations?"

"Whatever," I said, and started walking.

"Lovely. Walk away, you can throw out all these rules for Emma but none can be directed at you?"

I stopped. "That's not fair. I just seem to be the only one concerned that she'll get hurt again."

David sighed. "And I don't want *you* getting hurt again either, but you'll do what you want and so will she. Only she's not wasting her time, you are." His words felt like a slap. David had never spoken to me like that before and it hurt.

"At least I can stay in a relationship." I threw at him. "You just shag everything in sight! How does that make you an expert all of a sudden?"

David looked angry, angrier than I'd ever seen him. "Don't make this about me. I sleep with whoever I want, yes, but I know that is all it is. I may not fit neatly into one of your boxes, but I'm honest with myself."

"That's a laugh. You're in denial about Richard. He hasn't called and instead of going and trying to win him back, you're out being a slag. And I'm wasting my time? At least I have real relationships. And you wonder why Richard won't give you the time of day! He shouldn't after how you treated him!"

"I could say a lot to you right now, but I'll keep it simple since you're being so blunt, let me give you a reality check. Jack will break you again. Leave him. It's only a matter of time, and he's never going to come to you with a ring. You're sleeping with a man who you took from the girl he cheated on you with. How pathetic is that? You want to know what the difference between you and me is, darling? When I get screwed, it's pleasurable. When you get screwed, you get completely fucked."

I gasped, watching him go. I wanted to go after him, but I was afraid that if I did, the argument would continue, or worse, I would actually start to see that perhaps he was telling the truth.

Chapter Twenty-six

"This is ridiculous! The three of you need to settle this. I don't recall any of us ever having fought like this," Olivia said as we worked out together at the gym. I held the bars of the treadmill and began speed walking.

"It's all my fault. I screwed up. I should have been honest about Jack from the beginning. What hurts me the most is the fact that I had no idea Emma was so angry with me," I said, increasing the speed on the machine. I really felt more ashamed than hurt—I hadn't realized I had ignored her wishes and probably hindered her chances with Henry.

"You're not the only one. I feel awful for having told her she needed an entire makeover. I forced her!"

I gave her a reassuring smile. "I don't think you have much to worry about. She's fine with you. I'm the one she's not talking to. I left a few messages but she hasn't returned any of my calls. And I can honestly say I wouldn't blame her if she never did."

Olivia gave me a sympathetic look. "Give her time. What happened with David? I thought you two were fine when you left the house."

I sighed. "We were, but we started talking about Jack and… you know what. Let's not talk about him. I really don't want to get into a fight with you over that and lose another friend. Let's change the subject. Like, I can't believe you just threw in your news in the middle of that chaos! Should you even be on that machine?" I asked, concerned as she picked up the pace. She was going much faster than I was.

She laughed. "The doctor said I should go on with my life as normal." She took deep breaths. "I wasn't planning on revealing it yet, but things were getting intense."

"Well, it certainly changed the focus of the argument," I said. "How are you feeling about it? I'm still in shock!"

"*You're* in shock? I'm stunned! I feel great, though. Brandon and I wanted to have children but we were planning on waiting until the restaurant was off the ground. Life had other plans. We're excited." She smiled. "*And* Brandon has lifted the shoe ban! He's so over the moon, he wants to make me feel like a princess and even suggested that I could buy more shoes."

I laughed. "Well, you will need more sensible shoes, I suppose."

She wrinkled her nose. "Not that I'll be wearing flats until I absolutely have to," she said.

"You need to be careful," I insisted.

"I am! You're the only one who falls in heels," she smiled. "Speaking of which, I have your birthday pressie at the house. With all the madness, I forgot to give it to you."

"You didn't have to do all that, the dinner was a gift in itself," I said.

"Well, it's from all of us. And besides, I didn't cook… Brandon did. The best thing I did was marry a chef."

"I agree!" I exclaimed. "He's the reason I'm on this darn thing," I pointed out.

She groaned. "Don't remind me. He's making me anything I fancy, and even things that I don't, but I want them the moment I see them … If it were up to him, he'd be cooking for me all day."

"He means well," I said.

"He does. I love him," she said almost to herself, looking all starry-eyed. I was quiet, letting her sit in her moment.

"I still can't believe you're back together with Jack," she finally said, looking over to me. "Are things are okay with you two?"

"They are," I said. "We're going away this weekend for my birthday. Ask me again once the weekend is over. Let's see how it goes."

"As long as you're happy, that's what matters," Olivia said. I pondered on that. Was I really happy? I should have been glowing but I wasn't. Things weren't going the way I thought they would. Olivia was right about one thing: I needed to fix the situation with Emma and David at some point.

The morning of my birthday was hectic as I packed my bags. Since I had no idea where we were going, I had to improvise. This was the first real couple thing we had done since getting back together, and I had to admit, I was nervous. It wasn't like we hadn't gone away before, it just felt like this trip had a lot riding on it. The chime of the doorbell interrupted my thoughts and I hurried downstairs to open the door. Jack stood there holding a red bag with balloons, and I giggled like a schoolgirl as I let him in.

"You didn't have to get me anything!" I exclaimed, secretly happy that he had. It meant he had taken the time to get me something all on his own without me having to ask.

"Happy birthday, darling, of course I did. This is for you, obviously." He gave me a kiss and handed me the bag. I desperately wanted to look inside but also knew that he liked to be on time, and my indecisiveness that morning had already put me behind schedule.

"Why didn't you leave it in the car? I could have opened it there. Or is this a clue?" I said excitedly. "I'm almost done packing. You have no idea how happy I am that we're getting away this weekend—and the sun is out!" I continued to ramble on, not paying attention to the fact that he was eerily quiet.

"Kate…" he said softly, and I stopped in my tracks and closed my eyes. I knew that tone of voice. It was the one he used whenever he was about to say something I wasn't going to like.

"Kate, sweetheart, I can't go. I'm so sorry, one of the partners pulled out from an event the firm is co-hosting this evening and asked me to step in," he started to explain.

I opened my eyes and laughed, placing the bag on the floor. This had to be a joke. "Good one, you almost got me there. I'll tell you what, if you give me a few more minutes, I can finish packing and we can head out. I'm starving. Can we stop to have a proper breakfast?" I said.

Jack lowered his head. "I wish this was a prank. I tried getting out of it, but I can't. I'm expected to be there this evening." His voice sought for me to understand his predicament.

I dropped my hands to my sides, feeling a coldness rush through my body. "Are you serious? Jack, this trip was your idea!" I reminded him. My heart felt like it had dropped to my stomach.

"We can go next weekend," he said, wrapping his arms around me for a hug that I didn't return. "If you still want to go today, you can. Why don't you invite your friends and enjoy the house on me?" he offered, as if that would solve everything. But it just made it worse. I shook my head and pushed him away.

"What friends?" I said. "Half of them aren't speaking to me because of you. Do you have any idea what they'll say to me if I tell them you cancelled on my birthday?" My voice trembled.

He took my hands and pulled me towards him. "I don't care what they say, I only care about you… I'll make it up to you, I promise. Come on, let's open your present," he insisted as he picked up the bag and balloons in one hand and took my hand with the other. He led me into the living room and tried handing me the bag again but I wouldn't take it.

"Please, I feel horrible as it is. I didn't want us to spend your birthday like this. Please take it," he insisted as he nudged the bag towards me. After what seemed like an hour, I slowly took it and sat down. Jack's eyes never left me as he watched me pull out the box—it was brown with white script… Christian Louboutin. I looked up at him, shocked. He grinned as my fingers shook and lifted the lid. I gasped, looking at the Decollete 554 Strass shoes. They were breathtaking—and also over 3,000 dollars. He hadn't!

"Do you like them? I took a risk, but the girl in the shop said these were the 'it' shoes to have. They reminded me of something Cinderella would wear to the ball," he said. He was right. This certainly was a shoe Cinderella would wear. But I couldn't accept it. It was too much. I couldn't even fathom the idea of wearing them.

Jack seemed to misinterpret my reluctance to take them out of the box. "Of course, if you don't like them, you can exchange them for something else," he added when I didn't utter a word. "The gift receipt is in the box."

"They're beautiful... but too much," I finally said. I should have been overjoyed, but this wasn't what I wanted. Jack hadn't heard me when I mentioned what I truly wanted. He didn't know me at all. It wasn't that I was ungrateful for such an extravagant gift. I'm sure any other girl would have been screaming in delight and hugging him.

"We can go to dinner on Monday and you can wear them. Try them on," he insisted. But instead, I closed the box and placed them on the sofa next to me. Didn't he realize the shoes didn't matter? I would rather have him spending the day with me than a pair of expensive shoes.

"Let's at least go for breakfast," he said quickly.

"I've lost my appetite," I said, getting up. "I think I'll go to the office and catch up on some work, if you don't mind."

"But it's your birthday!"

I shrugged. "I have nothing better to do now, I might as well not waste the day and get some work done." I knew I was trying to make him feel guilty but at this point I really didn't care. I was hurt.

Jack stood up angrily. "Jesus, Kate, I don't need the guilt trip. I can't get out of it!" he snapped. "What more do you want me to do? I'm trying here!"

"All I'm saying, Jack, is that I'd prefer to head to the office and work today instead."

"No, what you're telling me is you want me to feel like shit. And you're succeeding. I didn't plan on this happening today."

For a split moment, I did feel horrible. Wasn't he trying to find a solution?

"Why don't I come with you tonight?" I offered, extending a small olive branch.

He looked at me oddly. "Why?"

I shook my head. "Just forget it!" I grabbed my blazer, bag and keys. I needed to get out of here.

"Where are you going?" he demanded.

"I already told you… work. You can let yourself out." I was angry and didn't wait for him to answer.

"Oh no you don't," Jack took my arm, preventing me from

taking the elevator, and spun me around to face him. "Why are you being so difficult all of a sudden? You know I have work functions that come up at the last minute. You have no idea what I'm dealing with at work. Cut me some slack!" His brown eyes pleaded with mine but all it did was take me back to the times he used to lie to me.

"You know, when you used to say you had 'work functions', it usually meant you were with other women—one in particular! And I granted you so much slack that you went and left me for her!" I said angrily.

Jack was still holding my arm. "That was the past, are you ever going to let that go? I made mistakes but I have changed. You know that!"

"Have you? You know what they say: a leopard never changes its spots," I said coolly.

"Christ, Kate! Either you let it go now, because I can't do anything else to prove myself to you, or else..." he looked into my eyes and stopped speaking as he took in my anger.

"Or else what? Are you saying if I don't agree with you, we end this?" I prodded.

Jack slapped his hand on the wall, making me jump. "Damn it! Why are you making things so difficult? If I wanted out I would not have done this. Do you want out?"

I wasn't going to answer him. "Just leave me alone for today, Jack. Go to work and do whatever it is you're doing."

"It's complicated," he answered.

"What is so complicated?"

"I can't get into that now."

"Philip was right, you are up to something!"

He froze. "He said that?"

"Yes, he did. So what are you doing?" I demanded.

Jack took a moment too long to respond. I knew him well enough to know the man had a quick answer to everything. I didn't want to think that Philip was right. But his silence spoke volumes.

"And what did you tell Philip?" he finally asked. His voice sounded cooler and bothered.

"What would I tell him? I have no idea what you do or what you're up to," I said, staring at him in anger and confusion.

His eyes softened momentarily. "I'm going to start a hedge fund with some of the guys and a few of the clients are coming with us," he said quickly.

"*What?* You can't do that, aren't you prohibited by your contract?"

"There are always loopholes, Kate, you know that. I'm not doing anything illegal. This is why I'm going tonight. There's been suspicion, and we don't want them locking in the clients."

"So you're telling me you had a choice, and you chose to ditch me instead?" I said.

"It wasn't like that at all!" he groaned. "This is important."

"And I'm not?"

"Bloody hell… Let's not fight. I don't want to argue with you. I need to attend tonight. We'll go out tomorrow, just enjoy the shoes. Isn't that what you need a man like me for, to pay for shoes like that?"

I sucked in my breath, resisting the urge to strike him with all the strength I possessed. I had *never* made Jack buy me anything at all, especially not shoes.

"I didn't mean that, I'm sorry," Jack said, attempting to grab my arm when I moved to go, but I dodged him and didn't look back.

Chapter Twenty-seven

The office was like a ghost town at the weekend. Most of the lights were off and there was an eerie silence as I made my way to my office, not bothering to see if anyone else was around. Part of me wanted to go back home, tell Jack off and throw the tainted gift back at him. His words had hurt. Jack was a man who didn't like to argue, but when he did, his words inflicted pain.

As I rubbed my temples, I tried to stop thinking about him and threw myself into my work. I continued at a rapid pace, not realizing how long I'd been there until my stomach starting growling, reminding me I hadn't eaten all day. I spun my chair around to face the window and looked at my mobile—still no calls from David or Emma.

"This birthday sucks, men suck!" I stated loudly to no one. I threw myself back in the chair and covered my eyes.

"I agree, most of the time we do," an amused voice said with a soft chuckle. I nearly jumped out of my chair. When I turned around, I found myself staring at Philip, who looked quite relaxed in dark jeans and a fitted cream turtleneck sweater—and as I took in his appearance from head to toe, I had to admit, he looked quite good. When my gaze reached his eyes, they looked back at me, amused, knowing exactly what I was doing.

"I didn't realize anyone else was here," I mumbled, embarrassed.

He stepped into my office. "Did I just hear you say it's your birthday?"

I felt myself blushing. "Ah… yes it is, but ignore that bit. I have a habit of talking to myself. Not in a crazy way, but I do. You know what? I'm just going to stop now." I looked down, moving my stapler to a right angle, then to the left.

Philip chuckled. "I do the same thing. You're not crazy at all. But what I really want to know is why you're here? Surely anything you had could have waited until Monday?" he prodded, crossing his arms in front of him.

I shrugged. "I have tons of reports to finish and haven't had a chance to catch up."

He frowned and his blond hair skimmed over his eyes—it was lighter than I had thought, as it was absent of gel. I had never seen Philip looking so… cool and relaxed. I thought he slept in suits given how stuffy he was most of the time. I looked at his feet: great black boots, they were unpolished and worn, very unlike him.

"Even so, on a day like today you should be out celebrating with your friends."

"Everyone is busy," I looked at him quickly. "What are you doing in the office?" I asked, changing the subject.

"I had a few reports to finish as well," he gave me a crooked smile.

"Well, we can't say we aren't workaholics," I said. My mobile rang, interrupting my next thought. I hesitated to pick up but Philip nodded towards it.

"Take it. I have to get back anyway. See you later," he said.

I gave him a nod as I looked down at the screen. It was Aunt Elena wishing me a happy birthday. Olivia and Elizabeth immediately followed, but I let it go to voicemail. I didn't want to lie to them or break down crying that I had been a fool in thinking Jack had changed. I shut off my phone and continued working.

A knock on the door made me look up. Philip was standing there in a black leather jacket. "I'm heading out. Are you almost done?" he asked.

I shook my head. "I barely made a dent. I think I'm going to see what's open, grab a bite and come back here."

"That is completely unacceptable. You can't do that, not today. How about you take a proper break and let me take you out? It's a beautiful day outside, the sun is even shining."

I looked at him, surprised. He was the last person I had expected to be nice to me. I hesitated and looked back at my pile of work. "I don't know…" I started

"Come on, you need to get out and enjoy yourself. I won't take no for an answer."

I opened my mouth to answer and got distracted by what he was holding in his right hand—a black motorcycle helmet. I gave him a bewildered glance. What in the world was Philip Spencer doing with a motorcycle helmet?

"Is that yours?" I asked.

"Maybe, why do you look so surprised?" he looked at me with a cheeky smile. "Did you think I went to bed in suits since I seem so stuffy all the time?"

I momentarily froze. *Oh my God, had I said that out loud?* But given his demeanor, I knew I hadn't. I glanced at him again. He looked sexy. *For God's sake, Kate, get a grip*! I must be losing it.

"Kate?"

I wasn't listening, still trying to understand the thoughts crossing my mind—had I actually just thought he looked sexy? I must really be delusional, due to hunger…yeah, that must be it.

"Earth to Kate..." he said in amusement.

"What?"

He threw his head back and laughed. "Are you all right there? Where did you go? I've never seen you at such a loss for words before."

He had a point. I was struggling to think of a reply—I was still trying to figure out what had happened to the real Philip Spencer.

"Shall we go?" he asked.

"Go where?" I responded. I couldn't believe how thrown off I was.

"Anywhere that's not this office. Come for a ride with me. Let's get away from the stack of work on your desk, away from the texts and calls that you are obviously failing miserably to avoid. It's your birthday, let's celebrate! I keep a spare helmet in the office."

I smiled. "What do you ride? A Lambretta, Mr Pete Townsend?" I chuckled to myself. Leave it to Philip to act tough on a scooter.

He looked at me and grinned almost wickedly. "You'll have to accept my offer in order to find out. What do you say?"

I leaned forward, placing my palms on the desk and pushed myself up. "Sure, why not," I said.

Philip waited as I grabbed my blazer. I shoved my mobile in my purse and followed him out. He walked ahead of me and I couldn't help but stare at his back, not knowing what had come over me. It had to be the "mystery" and not "sex appeal"—I was clearly confusing the two at the moment. We made a quick stop at his office where he grabbed another helmet. It was different from his: where his had a full black reflective face, the one he handed me had a half clear face.

"Fancy," I teased.

We made our way to the elevator in silence and got in standing side by side. I couldn't help but look at his boots again. I had rules for every shoe type, but for some reason his didn't fit in any category. He had a rebellious look to him. Was it possible this was the real Philip? The ride down seemed to take forever and I could hear him breathing next to me, the smell of his cologne filling the small space. Who was this man? He was not the Philip I thought I knew.

Chapter Twenty-eight

When we reached the lobby, Philip stopped in front of me. "Could you do me a favor? When we step outside, close your eyes," he said, not giving me a chance to decide.

"Why?" I asked suspiciously.

"You're going to have to trust me," he said. Trust him? Was he for real? I was about to protest.

"Have some faith," he interrupted. "Just this once… a little bit of faith in me." His voice was very soft. I took a deep breath. He wasn't asking me to jump off a cliff or walk on fire. I was more curious than anything else.

"Okay." I obliged, closing my eyes the moment we made it through the revolving doors. I inhaled sharply when I felt his hand take hold of my wrist.

"Allow me to lead," he instructed, and I bit my lip, excited and nervous at the same time. *God, he smelled so good.* The unwanted thoughts resurfaced as I felt the breeze hitting my face.

"Stop," he said, and I stood still. We hadn't gone very far. He took the helmet from me, our fingertips touching for a moment. I was desperate to open my eyes, but keeping them closed was more exciting. There was a moment of silence and I could hear my heart beat against my chest. Once again, he took hold of my hand but this time he softly pulled it forward and laid it on what felt like a button.

He leaned in behind me, his lips very close to my ear. "As much as I love Quadrophenia, this isn't a Vespa… push the button," he said in the British accent I had always been a sucker for. I felt a shiver from my neck down to my toes as I did as he commanded and pushed the button. I wasn't prepared for the almighty roar, my eyes flew open and I gasped. In front of me was no scooter but an enormous, powerful and intimidating motorcycle with *Ducati Streetfighter* stenciled down the side. I looked Philip dead in the eyes and he looked back at me, smiling.

"She's a beauty, isn't she?" he said, and placed the helmet on my head, buckling the strap. "There, all set. Shall we?"

"*On that*?

"Unless you have a better means of transportation?" he said, getting on the bike. He indicated with his head for me to get on. I licked my lips, beginning to panic. I had never been on one of these before. And what the heck did Philip Spencer know about riding motorcycles?! As he pulled on his gloves, our eyes locked and he smiled. "I promise I'm a good driver," he said. The smile did me in. It was sincere. And I felt the rush of being a bad girl… even if it was just temporary.

Here went nothing. I took quick breaths as I climbed on the bike and wrapped my arms around his waist. He turned his head slightly to look at me before closing his visor, and at the same time, he kicked it down into first gear and revved it up a couple of times. The roaring sound echoed through the car park. *Show off*, I thought, saying a few Hail Marys as we drove off.

We had been driving down the road a few seconds before I dared open my eyes. I had taken a leap of faith, trusting posh boy here with my life. I had to be suffering from a case of stupidity mixed with a touch of rebellion to create this hot mess I currently found myself in. I wrapped my arms tighter around his leather jacket, not caring that I was probably cutting off his circulation. His waist was the only thing keeping my behind on the bike. Slowly, I began to allow myself to enjoy it, feeling a bit safer but still shaking. London flew by me in a heartbeat. The sun was out in full force as we drove alongside Green Park, down Constitution Hill. The name made me think of the States… but this was my home now. I took in the trees that were lined up on either side of us, blossoming in a mixture of greens.

The vibration of the bike gently shuddered through my body, which made me lean even closer to Philip. I tried to ignore how close we were by concentrating on the sights. I watched as the road turned into a tunnel, then what seemed to be a secret garden that opened out next to Buckingham Palace. To our right was the magnificent water fountain that honored Queen Victoria. With the clear blue sky and surprisingly light traffic, everything fitted together perfectly. Although the bike was moving very fast, my mind slowed down and I felt like I was experiencing these streets for the first time.

As we proceeded towards Birdcage Walk off St James Park, the sights continued to evoke those visions of London I had imagined back in New York before I moved here: black cabbies, green trees and white buildings. We powered down a long stretch of road, approaching the Houses of Parliament, and I kept looking to the side: this was it, this was why I had fallen in love with London. It was the sense of history, freedom and fear all wrapped into one that had driven me here… and of all people, Philip was the one reminding me.

He made a left up towards Trafalgar Square past Downing Street and, as always, it looked like a scene from a movie, the statues, the people, the museum steps… Birds fluttered up around us, making me look up, and my view got lost in the sunlight. For this brief moment, I forgot everything—Jack, the girls, David, my arguments with Philip. From the second I got on the bike, I had been free.

Philip pulled over on a side street near Charing Cross station, and I was a bit saddened to get off the bike.

"Wow, that was amazing!" I exclaimed as I took off the helmet.

"I'm pleased you enjoyed it," he said with a grin.

"What's not to enjoy? That was such a rush!" I couldn't stop gushing like a child but it didn't seem to bother him.

"I didn't scare you too much when I picked up the speed, did I?" he asked, locking the helmets to the bike.

"Not at all! I still can't believe you ride a motorbike. And you ride very well. I'm impressed, Philip," I said, blushing a bit at paying him the compliment. I scanned the area, wondering why he had chosen this place. "So what are we doing here?" I asked.

Philip grinned. "Well, I have it on good authority that you're keen on a place around here…" He paused and looked at my boots. "And since you have no chance of breaking another heel today, I'm going to take a chance."

I grinned like an idiot at the fact that he had been so thoughtful as to take me somewhere he knew was special to me. We walked to the Crypt, chatting about his bike. Once inside, he chose a table in the corner. The place was buzzing with tourists but neither of us minded.

"What can I get you—fancy a glass of wine?" he asked.

I nodded. "That would be nice, thank you." I leaned back in the chair, still taking it all in. Moments later, Philip returned with a small bottle of dandelion and burdock, a glass of red wine and some food that smelled incredible. He handed me the glass.

"Happy birthday, Kate," he said.

"You're not drinking?" I asked, taking note of his drink.

"I'm driving. Plus, it's very rare to find one of these.' He picked up the bottle and took a gulp, relishing it. It made me smile for reasons I couldn't place.

"So when are you heading back to New York?" I asked, sticking my fork in the delicious curry.

"In a few days. I should have left already but I had some loose ends to tie up. But I think New York may become a more permanent base."

"Oh," I said with disappointment in my voice. Normally I was ecstatic to see him go.

"What about you?" he said.

"What about me?" I asked.

"Ever think of heading back to the Big Apple? You must miss it."

"Sometimes. But I love London, there's just something about it… I can't really explain it."

He gave me a small nod. "I get it. I feel the same way about New York." He took a bite and I watched him. Of all the people who got my love for a city I wasn't from without any explanation… "When I moved to New York, I felt free. I could be myself and not be judged." I looked down as he said that—after all, I was one of those people. "My family and friends told me the novelty would wear off. But I found that every time I came back to London, I missed New York and wanted to go back immediately." I nodded, knowing exactly how he felt.

"So is that where you learned to ride a motorbike?" I asked. I was enjoying this session of finding out something new about Philip.

"No. I've been riding for ages. I've always had a rebellious nature, going back to secondary school… Let's just say whatever my parents thought was inappropriate for me to do, I did. That was my freedom."

I laughed. "You? No way! I don't believe it. I don't see you with a rebellious bone in your body."

Philip nodded. "Believe me, I was, my parents can attest to it. Never judge a book by its cover, Kate." He was right. Boy, did I have that cover all wrong. I didn't know what to make of all this. I looked at him, trying to picture a rebellious Philip, defying his parents and his upbringing. The Crypt began emptying around us. We had long since finished our dinner and drinks.

"You fancy a walk?" he asked, breaking the silence. I nodded, relieved he didn't want to part ways. We walked out on to the cobbled streets, making our way towards Embankment tube station. Evening had taken over and the temperature had dropped. I hadn't prepared to be out late when I left the house and found myself shivering in my thin sweater.

Philip stopped for a moment and I watched him taking off his jacket, not anticipating his next move. Without a word, he placed it around my shoulders.

"You'll freeze!" I protested.

"I'm not cold," he said before I could utter another objection. I gripped the jacket close to me, his scent was all I could sense.

"This looks like a dress on me," I joked.

"It's perfect," he said.

Before I got a chance to answer, I stumbled a bit and Philip grabbed me, stopping me from falling forward.

"Seriously, woman, you are going to break your neck one of these days," he laughed. "You're not even in heels! Are you going to be able to cross the bridge safely?" he said as we climbed the steps heading to the Golden Jubilee Bridge.

"For the record, that time I fell, the high heels weren't the reason—I missed a step because I was emailing the office, so it is technically your fault," I said teasingly.

"Of course, it's always the man's fault, just like the broken heel. I'm to blame for that as well."

"Exactly, I knew you were smart, Philip."

"Speaking of which, did you get ever get it fixed?"

"It has proven more difficult than I thought to find the right cobbler," I admitted.

"I may not be the son of a cobbler, but how difficult can it be? It's a shoe."

I laughed. "With that attitude, all the cobblers of the world are rejoicing that you are not their son."

"I have to say, I don't think I'll ever understand the obsession women have with shoes."

"Best you don't try," I said. In the middle of the bridge, we stopped for a moment. London was lit up, the lights reflecting off the river. We could hear a man playing a guitar and singing a beautiful song about losing a love.

"This is my favorite bridge in London," Philip said, looking over towards Parliament.

"Why?" I asked, already knowing the reason.

"It's underrated, but check out the view… it's beautiful," he said, turning to face me and looking into my eyes. I found myself holding my breath and waiting, trying to anticipate his next move. His eyes shifted up to the London Eye, and I hugged the jacket closer to me. I needed to pull myself together. How much wine had I drunk?

"You know, I've never been on the London Eye," said Philip, unable to take his eyes off the giant Ferris wheel. It was quite spectacular with its royal blue lights reflecting off the big white beams that matched the bridge.

"You never have?" I asked, surprised.

"I haven't had the time."

"It's one of the top attractions," I said disbelievingly.

"I'm not a tourist," he teased.

"Oh, poor excuse."

"And I gather you've been up?" he asked.

"Yes, a couple of times, when friends or family come to visit from the States. The view is incredible. It's worth trying at least once," I insisted.

He took my hand, startling me. "All right, you've convinced me. Come on, let's go. In honor of your birthday, I say let's do it."

"The queue's going to be ridiculous on a night like this, Philip," I said, feeling my hand tingling as he held on to it tighter.

"We have time. Unless you have somewhere else to be?" he asked, raising an eyebrow.

"I don't…" I hesitated. "But I don't want you to feel obligated to spend your evening with me, I'm sure you have plans."

"I don't feel obligated in the slightest and I have no plans this evening, so shall we?" he gave me a big grin and I returned it, feeling happy that even if he had somewhere to go, he had cancelled it to be with me.

Chapter Twenty-nine

As we approached the wheel, the crowd got overwhelming large. Philip was still holding my hand, leading the way as if it came naturally to him, and I followed him into the building that sold the tickets.

"I'll be right back," he said, letting go of my hand. I felt like it had been ripped away from me. I watched him go and my mind went into overdrive. This was wrong! I couldn't possibly be strolling along with Philip as if we were on some kind of date. But I was enjoying myself—why was I purposely trying to sabotage it?

"Are you all right?" Philip asked. I turned around to find him holding two tickets, a big grin on his face. "I got us express tickets." He sounded very proud of himself.

"Brilliant!" I answered, managing to get myself together. We chatted as we made our way towards the entrance of the wheel.

"I have a confession to make," Philip said. He looked at me with a bit of uncertainty, but before I got a chance to ask what he meant by that, a girl instructed us to move into the moving capsule. "I'm afraid of heights," he said, looking very unsure as the door was locked. The man next to us snickered.

"You're joking? Did you just figure that out now?" I placed my hand on his shoulder. He was tense.

"Oh no, I've known for years. I thought I could be tough and conquer my fear to impress you. So much for that idea." His face seemed to pale.

I looked at him in surprise. "This is from the man who drives a motorbike at 80 miles per hour." I shook my head.

"106 at times," he corrected me.

I stared at him, shocked. "And you're afraid of heights? The motorbike is more dangerous than this," I said, pointing out the obvious. But I saw my words went unheard.

"The bike stays on solid ground, when this starts moving upwards . . ."

"We've been going upward since we got on this thing," I interrupted, and watched him grow a little paler. I felt for him. He had done this for me... to impress me.

"Come on, give me your hand," I said reaching out mine, and he grabbed it tightly. "We can sit on the bench if you like?" I offered

His eyes focused on the bench. There were two little girls with their faces practically pressed against the glass and we both began to laugh.

"I can do this. I think I can walk around a bit," he said. I gave his hand a reassuring squeeze.

"I won't let anything happen to you, I promise," I teased slightly.

"How long is this ride? We're not even at the top yet."

"Thirty minutes. I assure you, we're perfectly safe."

I turned for a moment to look out towards the night lights that had taken over the city. The dome of St Paul's Cathedral was lit up, standing strong and timeless as it had done for hundreds of years. Philip stood next to me, forgetting his fear.

"Amazing," he said.

I agreed. London was lit in all its glory, a combination of silhouettes, moonlight, and streetlights below that looked like thousands of twinkling stars. Philip looked calmer as we walked along the capsule admiring the view.

"You know what I've been wondering?" he said.

"Why you decided to be all macho and get on this thing?" I laughed softly.

"Funny… but no. Why are you alone on your birthday?" he asked, taking me by surprise.

"Is this your idea of small talk?" I pushed my hair behind my ear. His question forced me to face what I had been avoiding.

"Well, it'll keep me distracted," he admitted.

I stopping and leaned against the pole for support. "How can I refuse to distract you. Let's see… for starters, I'm not on speaking terms with two of my best friends."

"That's a shame but I'm sure it's fixable."

I didn't say anything as I tilted my head up to look at him. "I hope so, they were quite angry at me."

"I'm sure they won't stay angry at you forever. You're stubborn but not unfair," he said with a smile. "And I'm speaking from experience."

I looked into his eyes. "Is that so?" I asked, raising my eyebrow.

"Look at you… It's no secret that you don't like me, and yet, here we are." He gestured around the capsule.

His words made me feel ashamed of my past behavior. "I don't dislike you," I said, blushing, and quickly started walking around. He followed.

"Come on, admit it, I'm not your favorite person in the office."

"I'll admit, sometimes I'm slightly prejudiced when it comes to you, but you're the one who has surprised me the most," I said pushing the sleeves of his jacket back towards my elbows.

"Why, Kate, that's the closest thing you've given me to a compliment… ever," he grinned. "I'll take it."

"I'm a horrible person," I said and turned back towards the lights of the city, looking over towards the Houses of Parliament.

"I beg to differ, you're not a horrible person but you're stubborn. And yet that's what I like about you, there's no pretense."

"Wow, you make me sound like a ball of sunshine."

"I always smile when you walk into a room, so yes, I agree that you are like sunshine that brightens up the room," he said, and quickly turned to look out at the city, away from my gaze.

"You always surprise me, Philip."

"Why? Because of my cheesy line? I assure you I'm not usually that sappy, it's the height thing."

I grinned. "I don't think there's anything wrong with being cheesy sometimes. I was referring to you taking your Saturday to cheer me up and saving me from seeming like a sad, lonely person on my birthday. Thank you for making it better," I said, genuinely meaning it.

"Any time," he said sheepishly. I followed his gaze to the floor, staring at the outlines of two feet, realizing where we were.

"We need to do this." I pulled him closer to the glass. He looked confused. "We have to take a picture of this to mark your courage." I pointed to the camera. To my surprise, he stood behind me, leaning in close and placing his hands on the railing as the flash went off. Even after the picture was taken, we stood exactly as we were, not moving. I could feel his breath slowly against my neck as he leaned in towards my ear.

"I'm warning you, I look bloody awful in pictures," he said, breaking the silence. I felt myself shivering and couldn't find the ability to speak. Philip took a deep breath and slowly let go of the rail. I turned to face him.

"Don't worry, I do, too," I said, clearing my throat. What was I doing? I shouldn't have forced him to take a picture with me. It was a foolish thing to do. Where exactly was I planning on displaying the photo? At the office? Half of the staff was already gossiping, if anyone got a glimpse of the picture, it would certainly give them something to talk about.

Back down on the ground, we stepped into the gift shop, and I lost Philip momentarily in the crowd. I was about to believe he had ditched me when I spotted him by the photos.

"You don't need to get them," I said quickly to no avail as he reached into his pocket and pulled out his wallet.

"I know. I want a reminder of my bravery." He began to chat with the guy who was cutting the wallet-sized pictures and I leaned over, staring at the photo of the two of us. It was quite lovely, and to the unknowing eye we actually looked like a proper couple. Instead of looking to the camera, it had managed to capture us staring at each other, smiling without a care in the world.

"We actually look good," he noted, handing me my set. I didn't say anything and shoved the picture into my purse.

"I guess I should be heading back home," I said quickly, breaking the moment.

"The night is still young," he said.

"I have an early start tomorrow," I lied.

He stopped for a moment as if to say something, but only nodded. "That's fine, let's head back." He sounded disappointed.

"Philip…" I tried to explain.

"No need to explain. You're quite right, it is late." He turned and began to guide us through the crowd. Pushing our way through, we made it out and headed towards Embankment.

"I can take the tube back to my flat," I said. Philip stopped.

"Have I done something wrong?" he asked, unsure. I couldn't blame him. I'd gone from hot to cold in a matter of seconds.

"Are you dating anyone?" I suddenly asked. Today seemed to be a day I couldn't control my mouth. "You don't have to answer that," I quickly added, not knowing what had come over me. It was none of my business.

"I'm not in a relationship if that's what you're asking," he answered, not seeming to mind the intrusive question. "I date here and there, no one serious."

"Why is that?" I asked, poking my nose where I knew I shouldn't once more.

He walked towards the side of the bridge, moving away from the oncoming pedestrians. "I work too many hours, and I travel too much. Not the best combination when you want to be in a relationship… on either side of the pond," he answered.

"I'm sorry. I shouldn't have asked that. It's none of my business," I said, resting my hands on the beams of the bridge.

"Why isn't Jack with you today?" he asked, saying out loud the name I had been avoiding since this morning. My heart started beating quickly.

"He cancelled on me because of work," I softly said, bracing myself for the lecture.

He shook his head. The "I told you so" never came. "Shame on him, your birthday should have come first."

I lowered my gaze. There it was, the truth, and it stung. I knew Philip didn't mean to sound cruel, but it hurt to hear what I knew deep inside. Jack should have been here. If it had been me, I would have cancelled anything to be there for him because it was his day.

"I didn't mean it to sound harsh, I'm sure he has reasons that are satisfactory," he added quickly, trying to make me feel better.

"You know what? Let's not talk about any of that," I said, not wanting think about Jack. I had already let him ruin a part of the day.

"His loss is my gain," Philip said, surprising me. I looked up into his blue eyes.

"Have I thanked you… for everything today… tonight?" I

said softly. He took a step and closed the space between us as the wind blew my hair over my face.

He gently pushed my hair back. “Yes, you have.”

“Philip…” I began, but I couldn’t find the words as I stared at him. No words needed to be spoken as he lowered his head down and kissed me. I froze, unable to react, and Philip put his hand around my waist to pull me in. I kissed him back as his lips molded into mine. My knees went weak. As cliché as it was, they did, and I found myself placing my arms around his neck.

“I’ve wanted to do this from the moment I met you,” he said against my lips, kissing me over and over again.

From the moment he met me? My thoughts immediately went to the polo match… Jack. Jack! I pushed him away, startling him with my force. I quickly touched my lips as I looked at him in disbelief. Since the day we met? That was impossible. He had hated me on sight!

“We shouldn’t have done that…” I managed to say, my lips still warm, I could still feel his lips on mine.

“I’m sorry,” he said, then shook his head. “You know what, I’m not sorry.”

“But you hate me!” I exclaimed.

He looked slightly defeated. “I don’t hate you, I’ve never hated you. What gave you that impression?”

“Your attitude towards me. Ever since I started at the firm. You never talk to me unless it’s about work. You avoid me. You’ve taken me off my accounts and won’t explain,” I pointed out a few of the most obvious things.

“That’s maybe how you view it, but that’s not how I’ve treated you. I’m guarded around you, that I’ll admit, and perhaps I don’t know how to express my feelings. But you can’t deny that you’ve always judged me—and I get it, yes, I’m a *Spencer,* but that’s all you’ve ever seen me as. I can never get you to see past the name.”

"That's not true," I interrupted.

"It is, Kate. I've lived with that my whole life, and I thought perhaps you would see me differently. I've liked you from the moment I saw you, wearing stilettos on the grounds and cursing in a very unladylike manner." He gave me a slow grin. I couldn't believe what I was hearing, had I fallen into a parallel universe? None of this made sense.

"We work together…" was all I managed to say.

He shrugged. "That doesn't stop people—there are many colleagues who date each other at the firm, you know that."

"Yes, but not everyone is you." I pointed out, still not believing that I was hearing this. It had to be some kind of joke. Philip didn't like me. It wasn't possible.

"You can't keep using my surname as an excuse."

"It is not an excuse, it's a fact," I said. "And I'm dating someone, Philip, have you forgotten that?" I threw at him—or was that more to remind myself?

"No, I haven't, but you should. He's a fool who doesn't deserve you."

I touched my lips again, still feeling the kiss. "You didn't kiss me to get back at him, did you?" I asked, afraid of his response.

"Of course not! Have you not heard a single word I've said to you?" His voice rose.

"I want to believe you…"

"Why is it difficult for you to believe? Are you so jaded that you can't believe someone can actually like you? Take a good look at me. I'm standing here on a bridge, blurting out my feelings for you against my better judgment, and all you can say is that I may be doing out of spite? I am not that man, Kate."

"And you think it's fine to tell me that, that it's against your better judgment? Why is that, because you are the almighty Philip Spencer and my little life doesn't measure up to yours?" I said angrily.

Philip shoved his hand into his hair in frustration. "No, don't be ridiculous. I have never thought you were beneath me."

"Yet you choose now to tell me? How about all the months that I was single, why not then? It's selfish of you to do it now when I have a boyfriend," I said.

Philip pressed his lips together. "It wasn't my intention to blurt it out like this, not here, not today."

"But you did, because you always feel entitled and didn't take into consideration what I would feel," I said.

"Is this what you think of me?" He seemed taken aback.

"It's all you've ever shown me until today, Philip. How was I supposed to know? I'm not a mind reader. And now what am I supposed to do with this?" I said. We both stood in silence, angry at each other, the air between us so thick you could cut it.

"Forgive me for unburdening myself to you, let's forget this happened," he finally said, taking a few steps back away from me, and in that moment I felt horrible. I had thrown accusations at him when all he had done was reveal his feelings for me.

"Philip…" I began to protest, but he shook his head.

"It's best to say goodnight, Catherine, before either of us says anything else."

Not waiting for me to respond, he turned and continued walking along the bridge towards the station. I didn't try to stop him or call after him. I watched him fade into the crowd. His words were still ringing in my ears. I looked out at the river and then at London Eye and I felt like crying. I stood there for a while, taking it all in. What had I done? I felt a breeze and shivered, realizing I still had his jacket. I needed to apologise and return his jacket, and as if my legs had a mind of their own, I began to run in the direction he had gone. By the time I got to where he had stationed his bike behind Charing Cross, all traces of Philip were gone. I held the jacket tightly around me as the tears I had been fighting began to slip down my face.

Chapter Thirty

I made it home, still astounded by what had happened on the bridge. I tried recalling all the run-ins I'd had with Philip over the last couple of years, looking for a clue I might have missed. From the moment we met, he had clearly showed his disapproval. I couldn't have been wrong all this time. I threw myself on the sofa closed my eyes, reliving the kiss. The fact that I had enjoyed it more than I should have was troubling me. Normally, at a time like this, I would have called one of the girls or David, but I didn't have the nerve to call and eat crow.

I opened my eyes for a moment and found myself staring at the bag containing Jack's gift. Sitting up, I reached for it, took out the box and placed it on my lap, opening it again. But all I could think about was Jack's comment about how I needed someone like him to buy me the shoes and I placed them back down. I could feel myself getting angry and hurt all over again, along with even more emotions I hadn't placed yet.

I went into my bedroom and kept replaying the scene with Jack as I made my way to my closet. I opened the doors—the sight of my shoes lined up on the racks would cheer me up. I had boxes on shelves and even more stacked up on the floor. Without thinking, I picked up a pair of super-pointy beige shoes that suddenly seemed completely impractical. I tried to slip them on, struggling to get my foot in. Had I actually forced my feet into these before? After one more push, I got them on, but immediately felt like they were cutting off the circulation. It was time to let these go.

On and on I went, removing shoes from the closet that I hadn't worn in ages, repeating the routine of trying them on and finding that they didn't fit any more—perhaps they never really had but I'd worn them anyway. What was the point in holding on to shoes I knew I wouldn't wear? After I'd finished with the closet, I took a deep breath and turned to the chest at the foot of my bed. I lifted the lid and found more boxes filled with shoes I'd long forgotten about. I picked up a pair of furry-looking heels. When had I bought these? Shaking my head, I tossed them on to the pile accumulating on the floor. I lifted out a pair of grey pumps—these could actually be worn to work. They'd been lost in the abyss of the chest. Taking the box, I headed towards the closet and got on my tiptoes, trying to push it into an empty space, but it kept falling forward. There was something back there. With my free hand, I yanked down the item of clothing that was preventing the box from fitting and stopped. It was Jack's sweater. I resisted the urge to pull it towards my face and smell the faint scent of his cologne and, without a second thought, I threw it on top of the pile of shoes.

The buzzing of the intercom startled me awake. I opened my eyes, slightly disoriented, squinting at the bedroom light above me. With a grunt, I moved my leg—it was currently being stabbed by a heel. Shoe boxes and clothes were scattered over my bed. The last thing I remembered was laying my head down just for a moment. I looked at the clock on the nightstand: it was almost two o'clock in the morning. The buzzing continued as I made my way down the stairs. There was only one person who would dare show up at this hour…

"Who is it?" I hissed into the intercom.

Jack's voice came booming in. "Who else are you expecting at this bloody time, let me up." I sighed, bending my head down before answering.

"Jack, go home, I was sleeping. I don't want to deal with you right now, and you're probably drunk."

"Jesus, Kate, I am not pissed. Let me up…"

I knew I shouldn't, it wasn't going to make a difference at this point.

"Please." I heard Jack's voice again.

I hesitated, my finger hovering over the button. Taking a deep breath, I pushed it. It seemed like an eternity before the elevator doors opened. I was waiting for him, leaning against the door. Jack stepped out, still in his tux.

"I've been worried about you. I've been calling your mobile, the house, even the office, trying to get hold of you," he said as he stopped in front of me.

"I wasn't in the mood to talk to anyone. You weren't the only one I was ignoring if that makes you feel any better," I said, letting him in.

"Look, I'm here to apologize. I said some stupid things, and it was wrong of me to get into an argument with you on your birthday. I should not have cancelled on you."

His words gave me no comfort.

"Why are you here?" I said. "If you've come for a shag, you can totally forget it."

He passed his hand through his hair. "I am not here for a shag, Kate. Why would you even say that?"

"Because that is all we do!" I half yelled in frustration.

"So you're saying that's entirely my fault?" he said defensively.

"No, I was a willing participant, but that's not the point. Don't you see what's happening with us here?" I asked and passed my hand over my face—I was about to lose it.

"Kate, you're not making any sense." He took hold of my hands but I broke free, not wanting him to touch me.

"Trust me, for the first time in ages, I am making perfect sense." I said. I took a deep breath. "When I started seeing you again, I knew it was madness, but I thought that I could handle it, I thought perhaps you would change. I even thought that I could have you and then leave you and give you a taste of your own medicine," I revealed to him.

"You don't mean that," he said, looking at me, shocked.

"I do. I know that sounds awful. But deep down, I wanted you to see the mistake you made and feel the pain that I felt."

He grabbed my shoulders. "I'm here, aren't I? I chose you. That has to count for something."

"You are, but it's not enough. Don't you see? I don't trust you. No matter what you do, I can't. Every time you walk out that door, I'm wondering if you're with Amanda or someone else. And today,"—I threw my hands up in desperation—"you didn't even bother to consider that I had cancelled all of my plans for *you*. I'm fighting with my friends over our relationship, defending what we have, and you proved them right."

"I told you, I don't care what they think of me, I only care about you and what you think. I made a mistake. I had to attend this event, I explained that to you."

"It will always be work or anything else you deem more

important. All you've given me are scraps, and I settled for it. You broke my heart into little pieces last time, Jack, and I barely have it together. I'm hanging by a thread." I covered my mouth, realizing what I was saying, what I was finally admitting. I wasn't happy, I had been in denial from the moment I had started things with him again.

"I am giving you all that I can," he said, his voice shaking for the first time.

"I know you are, Jack. I think for the first time since I met you, you are actually giving me a big part of you... but... that isn't what I want any more. You don't even know me. The shoes..." I started to explain.

"If this is about the comment I made, I was a jerk," he interrupted, almost pleading with me.

"I can't accept them." I took a deep breath and picked up the bag. "I have never asked you for anything materialistic." I handed it back to him but he didn't take it.

"I don't want it back," he said, refusing to take it when I attempted again. He looked at the bag like it was something that would burn him.

"The thing is," I said. "If you knew me [illegible] really knew me, you would know what shoes I want—and they're a fraction of the price of these. They are beautiful, Jack, but I can't... it's not right."

"Fine. Then we'll go to the store tomorrow and get the shoes you want," he said. "I love you, Kate. Even though you don't believe me, I do." He cupped my chin but I brushed his hand away.

"I love you too, Jack, it isn't that I don't, but loving you comes at a price I'm not willing to pay, not any more. We're not good together, and if you took a step back and analyzed these past few months, you would see that I'm right."

He slowly shook his head. "You're just upset with me, and you have every right to be. But don't write us off because of one incident."

"I'm not even upset with you any more—and it's not just one incident, it's a series of events. I'm just tired, Jack."

"Kate, please, I'm trying to be a better man here. I've made mistakes, and I'm sorry that I didn't tell you about my plans tonight. Don't give up on me… on us." His eyes softened as they looked into mine.

"Have you heard a single thing I've said? You don't get it, do you?"

"Then help me get it." His eyes sought mine but I wouldn't look at him. It was too risky and I didn't want to cave, because however strong I was acting, I knew I was fragile. Months ago, I would have given the world to hear Jack say what he was saying now.

"I'm sorry, Jack, but I can't," I struggled.

"I'll change… I'll do whatever you want me to do," he started. I felt my heart breaking as he spoke and I shook my head. "Let's just take a time out," he said desperately. "We've both been under extreme pressure. In a few days, we can sit down and we can talk rationally about this."

"I won't be calling you, Jack," I said. We stared at each other without saying another word. He lowered his head for a moment and it took all I had not to rush to him or take back what I'd said. I was scared. I was standing on a shaky foundation, not sure if I was doing the right thing. He looked at me and hesitated, and tears began to form in my eyes that I couldn't hold back. He brushed them away with his thumb and slowly caressed my cheek before kissing it. I closed my eyes, hiding from the look of pain that shot across his face. I could feel him hesitating but eventually he let me go and I heard his footsteps fading away. Hearing the door close, I finally dared open my eyes.

Chapter Thirty-one

It had been a week since my birthday, a week since I had said goodbye to Jack, but the one thing that kept running through my mind was Philip's kiss. And today I was going to see him for the first time since that night. To say I was nervous heading to work was an understatement. Would he address it? Or would he pretend it had never happened? I had picked up the phone so many times, wanting to call him, but every time I chickened out. After all, I had made matters worse.

As I entered the conference room, as per usual, Philip was already there going over his documents at the head of the table. I quickly took in his appearance before he realized I was in the room. Gone was the carefree guy from Saturday. His hair was combed back, the gel darkening his light blond hair, and he was wearing his trademark blue tailored suit.

"Good morning, Philip." I said, making my presence known. My heart raced. He looked up and his eyes seemed to light up for a split second—so briefly I almost thought I had imagined it.

"Kate," he said, giving me a cool nod. "Good to see you bright and early. Are we all set for the presentation?" he asked, making my smile disappear. His tone was clear: he wasn't going to mention it. This would be business as usual.

"Yes, I'm all set," I managed, looking down at my bag and taking out my documents. If I avoided eye contact, perhaps I could make it through the rest of the day.

"Before the meeting starts, there's something I want to talk to you about," Philip said. My heart fluttered, a sense of relief hitting my body… he was going to address it after all.

"As I'm sure you know, Jack has left Lewis & Morton…" Philip began.

I felt a knot in the pit of my stomach. So this was about Jack. I reflected on what had happened in the last week. Jack had resigned from the firm—it was the talk of the office. He hadn't left by himself, he had taken others with him to start his own company. Including some of our own. Jack had left me messages about it but only after he had acted. He'd even offered me a job, but I had yet to call him back.

"Philip, I had no knowledge of any of it… not until Saturday night… and I had no idea he was going to poach some of our team and clients…" I said in defence.

"I know. I'm pleased you weren't involved, but my question is… are you staying or leaving?" His face was firm.

His directness startled me. "I'm staying," I answered. He revealed no emotion, just gave me a curt nod. I felt the words bunched up in my throat. I needed to tell him more, needed him to understand.

"I broke up with Jack…"

Philip looked down at the papers. "Your private life is not my concern, but I'm very happy to hear you are remaining at Spencer & Lockhart."

His tone stung. This was worse than before, now we were

acting like complete strangers. I stared at him, unable to move. Philip lifted his head and stared at me, his eyes softening.

"Kate… I—"

"Good morning, you two, always the first ones in," Andrew said as he opened the conference room door. Philip immediately looked away from me.

As the meeting commenced, Philip took over the room and I couldn't help but stare and take in his appearance, his attitude. Had he always looked this way? So composed and confident? There was something almost regal about him. He no longer looked snobbish. He was handsome, and suddenly he looked taller, his eyes looked bluer, and it hit me… I liked him. Even before the kiss.

I held my hand to my throat. I needed air. This wasn't possible. All this time, my contempt for Philip had been down to the fact that I found him attractive! I reached for the water bottle on the table, my hands shaking. Philip gave me a quizzical look as I drank quickly. I felt my cheeks turning red as I avoided his gaze, fearing that the moment he looked at me he would know exactly what was going through my mind.

Thankfully, the meeting wrapped up soon after and I began to quickly gather my things. I needed to get out of here. I needed to be alone and understand what I had just admitted to myself without Philip looming over me, without the memory of his kiss slamming into me. I shoved everything in my bag, not caring that I was creasing my papers, and with one swift move I made my way towards the door.

"Kate, a moment, before you go…" Philip said, making me stop. I turned to face him, forcing a small smile. God, I liked him. It was so obvious. How could I have been so blind? It had been staring me right in the face this whole time.

"Yes?"

He shook hands briefly with one of the directors before

approaching me. "Do you have time to meet for lunch at the end of the week? There's something I'd like to discuss with you."

My stomach dropped, I wasn't sure if I wanted to talk about the kiss, even though that was all I kept thinking about, and I didn't know anything else about Jack's company if that was what he wanted to discuss—at least it gave me a few days to prepare.

"Sure, I'll call your office to set up a time."

He looked at his mobile. "Let's set it up now," he said. "This Friday works."

Put on the spot, I looked through the diary … "Friday it is," I responded without enthusiasm.

"Philip, great presentation, I have a question regarding the shares…" another colleague interrupted.

"Sorry," Philip said, giving me an apologetic smile. "We'll speak then." I hurried off before he could stop me again. Given the way I was feeling, it was possible I would blurt out that I liked him right here in front of everyone.

In a matter of two weeks, my life had been turned upside down. I had gone from getting back the man I thought was the one—my soulmate, my perfect match—to realizing that I had it all wrong. I had allowed my pride and prejudice to cloud my judgement. All the signs had been there that Jack was not Mr Darcy, but I had wanted him to be so badly, I had failed to see the warning signs. It was like finding the perfect shoe and being told the only size left was a 5 and you were a 6. No other shoe mattered, you were blinded by it. You wanted them so badly, you squeezed your foot in, ignoring the throbbing pain. I had forced things with Jack, and in doing so had totally missed Philip.

Later that evening, I met Elizabeth for dinner. She took in my appearance as I sat across from her.

"You look like crap," she said.

"I feel like it too," I answered. I filled her in on what had happened with Jack and Philip.

"Wow. Philip, with a Ducati... That is so Prince William!" she exclaimed. I looked at her, not understanding what she was talking about. "Prince William rides a Ducati," she explained, like that was something everyone should know. I shrugged and she rolled her eyes. "You need to read something other than the *Financial Times*. Live a little, see the world."

"Reading the *Daily Mail* does not count as seeing the world," I pointed out.

"That's the problem with you, Kate. You need to live outside of work a bit. I feel like I'm failing you as a friend if you don't see the similarities."

I didn't say a word. She placed her hands on the table and intertwined her fingers. "So what are you going to do about Jack?" she asked.

"What do you mean?"

"Are you going to take him back? Is there anything you need to do?"

"No. But I'm feeling conflicted about it. Scared, if I'm being honest. I'm afraid I'm going to pick up the phone and take it all back. Why am I feeling like this?" I asked.

"Hope," she answered. I waited patiently for her to continue. "It's one of the strongest things we as human beings possess. You've known since you broke up with him that you were better off without him. But the heart is different from the mind, Kate. You had hope, as tiny as it was, that Jack would change. That's what kept you going back."

I sighed. "So now what?"

"Date, go out. I still can't believe you kissed Philip," she said.

"Neither can I, but that's a lost cause."

"Catherine Seeley, have you learned nothing from me? I keep telling you, take a chance. Tell Philip how you feel. What's the worst that can happen: he says no? Take a risk, girl."

I contemplated her words. I mean, why not take a risk? I walked in four-inch platforms, which was a risk in itself.

"Speaking of risks," Elizabeth said. "What are you going to do about Emma and David?"

"I've left David a few messages, he hasn't returned one. And Emma… I'm still unsure how to handle that. I've contemplated just showing up at their offices but I don't know how they'd react. How are they? Have you spoken to them?"

"Yes. They're both doing well," she said. "David is making his way through the dating scene—I swear that boy is determined to sleep his way through London. Emma…" she hesitated, putting down her fork. "She's been talking to Henry actually," she admitted. "I think he really regrets what he did."

"That's great. Henry isn't a bad guy," I said finally.

"Well, that's for her to discover. She seems happy. But the three of you need to make up. I miss all of us hanging out together."

Promising I would try again, we parted.

Chapter Thirty-two

Thinking back to the conversation I'd had with Elizabeth that evening, I got ready for bed, happy to put the entire day behind me. My mobile rang and I froze—it was probably Jack again. The phone had been ringing earlier with an unrecognized number, which I'd ignored. Did he think he could trick me into speaking to him? Reluctantly, I looked at the screen and saw Emma's name flashing. I smiled. Leave it to Elizabeth to initiate the first step.

"I'm so glad you called…" I began as I sat with my legs crossed on the bed.

"Kate, David's been in an accident." Emma's worried voice came through, making my blood run cold.

"What?! What kind of accident?" I asked. Panicking, I quickly got up.

"We don't know. The hospital's been trying to reach you. Elizabeth and I are on our way to St Thomas'."

"Did they say how he's doing? What happened?" I said as I hurried into the living room, picking up my boots and hopping on one foot, balancing the phone on the crook of my neck.

"They've told us nothing. We'll see you at A&E." She paused briefly. "Be careful getting there. Don't worry, if I hear something before you get there, I'll call you."

"Thank you. Just make sure he's okay, I'm on my way," I said quickly, and began rushing through the apartment for my coat, bag and keys. My heart was racing as I silently prayed that he was all right. I needed him to be okay. Horrible images flashed through my mind as I tried to imagine what kind of accident he could have had. I was upset at myself for not having pushed harder for him to talk to me. How could I have let Jack come between me and David?

Luckily, I managed to hail a taxi straight away and tried to call Emma and Elizabeth. Both their phones were going straight to voicemail. As the cab pulled up to the A&E entrance, I handed the driver some notes and dashed out towards the information desk.

"Excuse me, you have a patient here, David Cunningham…" I said to the receptionist.

"I'm sorry, the name again?" she said calmly. I wanted to jump over the counter and get the information myself.

"David Cunningham," I repeated quickly. I didn't have time for this. She began typing, looking at the screen. "Is he all right?" I asked.

"I'm not at liberty to say, they're treating him on this floor…" Not waiting for her to finish, I ran through the doors. "You can't go in there without identification," I heard her call after me. I spotted Elizabeth talking to Emma, who had her head down, visibly shaking. I held my hands over my mouth, something bad had happened to David. I froze for a moment not wanting to head over to them, not wanting to hear the bad news. The walk toward them seemed to take forever as my feet dragged on the floor. I wasn't ready to hear the bad news.

"How is he?" My mouth felt dry as I found the words.

"He's fine." Elizabeth said, taking my hand. "He'll need surgery, but it's not life-threatening."

"What happened?"

"He was stepping off the train after one of his pub crawls. He was drunk, miscalculated the gap and fell forward on to the platform. I always knew he was going to break it off one day but I thought it would be in the middle of some kinky sex act," Elizabeth said, chuckling.

Emma finally looked up. She wasn't crying, she was trying to stop herself from laughing out loud. I looked at them like they had lost their minds.

"I don't understand. So why does he need surgery? Did he crack his head open? Why are you laughing?" I asked Emma, not believing that at a time like this she was giggling hysterically.

"Honey, he fell on his penis. They don't say 'mind the gap' for nothing," said Elizabeth.

Emma cracked up, unable to hold it in any longer. She was laughing so hard she had to lean against the wall for support.

"He broke it?" I looked at her, horrified.

"He fractured it. He damaged the urethra, hence the surgery. He fell on it while being in, um… let's say an excited state." She lowered her voice as people walked by us.

"Oh my God," was all I could say. Despite my best efforts, I couldn't help giggling as well and placed my hand on my chest. My heart was still beating at a ridiculous pace and my hands were shaking. "So he's okay?"

"They've given him loads of painkillers, he's in there," she said, nodding at the door across from us. I make my way into the room and saw David lying down, looking groggy.

"David? Honey?" I whispered as I stood next to the bed. He slowly turned his head to look at me.

"Uggs? Seriously? I nearly die, and you couldn't even take a moment to put on some decent shoes? Aren't I worth at least that?" he said, his voice sounding weak.

I smiled. "Oh, shut up, you scared me half to death," I said, leaning down and hugging him.

"Oi, watch it," he complained.

"How's the penis?" Elizabeth asked, coming in. David flipped his middle finger at her.

"Are you okay?" Emma followed.

"I'm on morphine: I'm great, I don't feel a thing. I feel like I'm floating." He closed his eyes again.

"What were you thinking? Actually, scratch that, we know what you were thinking. How did you manage to fall like that?" I asked.

"I'm an idiot." He looked at me and placed his hand over his forehead. "Oooh, you have two heads, did you know that?" he said to me, covering one eye, then the other. "Don't cry for me, Argentina…" He started to hum, losing focus.

The three of us looked at each other, muffling our laughter. "I need to be on whatever he's on," Elizabeth said, taking a look at his chart.

"Sorry, ladies, but you can't all be here," said the nurse, taking the chart away from Elizabeth. "He's going to be moved to a room as soon as one is available, you can all come back during visiting hours."

"Babes, we'll see you later, okay?" I said, giving him a quick kiss.

He waved us off, still humming. We began to laugh again. "I'm glad he's okay," Elizabeth said, giving him another look.

"Why don't we head back to my house, I can cook us breakfast," Emma offered. I smiled at her. I knew this was her way of making a peace offering and I gladly accepted it.

"I'm sorry," I said.

"So am I." We all hugged outside the room like we were in some cheesy movie.

"Go home and change, all of you. It's seriously embarrassing," David called out.

"Not as embarrassing as breaking your d—"

"Elizabeth!" I covered her mouth. Some things never changed, thank God for that.

Chapter Thirty-three

By the time I made it back to the hospital again, David had had his surgery, and thankfully everything was fine. I couldn't say it would be the same for his sex life for the next couple of months but, as the girls had pointed out, perhaps that would be good for him—at least for a while. I held the bag containing the infamous shoes. No matter how many excuses I made to myself to keep them, I knew I couldn't. I had sent them to his office but he had sent them back. So now I had them in tow, having decided to drop them off at Jack's apartment after visiting David. This time, I was going to leave them in person, with a note asking him to respect my wishes and not give them back to me.

As I approached David's room, a hot doctor was walking out and gave me a friendly smile. I turned my head, giving him a second look—he looked like one of those doctors found in a soap opera. "Was that your doctor?" I asked David, taking in his appearance. He had a five o'clock shadow, a rare sight. Only David would look this good after surgery.

He grinned from ear to ear. "Yes, isn't he gorgeous? He's been taking care of me, giving me extra pain medication."

"Why I am even surprised? What is up with the beard?" I said, putting the flowers I'd brought down on the table.

"Thank you, darling. I was going to shave but Dr Stevens commented on how good it looks. I think I may leave it," he said, touching his jaw.

"How is it possible that, even in a hospital bed, you manage to find a man?"

"He's seen the goods," David smiled mischievously. I rolled my eyes at him.

"You even manage to pull with damaged goods?" I snickered.

"Why must you be so evil? He knows there isn't much swelling there," he began.

"Oh, for God's sake, can't we go five minutes without the obvious innuendos?" I said.

"You started it," he said. "Come on, help me sit up, I can't manage on my own."

An older nurse walked in—her dark blue uniform looked more fitted than those of the other nurses I had seen. "David, I told you to buzz for me if you needed to get up. We don't want you ruining the great work the doctor has done, do we?" she said, helping him sit up slowly. David groaned.

"You're so good to me," he said with a smile. "Kate, this is Sandra," he said to me. "She's an angel."

Sandra chuckled, checking his IV bag. "Charm will get you everywhere, dear," she said to him. She smiled. Her hair was in an elegant bun and her makeup was perfect.

"Sandra, this is Kate, my former but now resumed best friend." He gave me a wink and I gave him a dirty look. "Oh, don't give me that look, she knows all about our little fight, don't you?" David said.

"Yes, I've heard all about it. I am glad you've made up, dear, friends must be cherished. I'll be back later. Nice meeting you," she said.

"Cheers," David called out as she left. "I love her. She's working extra hours to buy an outfit for her granddaughter's wedding," he revealed. "I think it's the sweetest thing. Tell me, would my mother do something like that?" He looked at the bag. "Is that for me?" I took out the shoe box. "You really shouldn't have," he said.

"Jack bought me them for my birthday but…"

"Let me see." He lifted the box from my hands. I was about to say no when Olivia, Emma and Elizabeth walked in.

"Ladies, you sure know how to make me feel loved!" David exclaimed, excited at the flowers and baskets of goodies they were carrying.

"How are you feeling, babes?" Olivia asked, looking at the table full of flowers. "Wow, many admirers, I see." She quickly looked over the cards.

"One of them is from Richard, he stopped by earlier," he said almost shyly—one of the many traits not possessed by David. The accident must have knocked him out harder than I had thought.

"So are you two seeing each other or what?" Elizabeth asked, sitting at the foot of the bed. She glanced down at the shoe box, giving him a quizzical look.

"They're not mine," he said, and all eyes turned to me.

"You didn't!" Elizabeth said. Taking the box from David's hand, she opened it and gasped.

"Let me see," Olivia stood next to her and took out one of the shoes. "These are perfection. What possessed you?" she said.

I took a deep breath. "I didn't. Jack did. I tried to make him take them back but he wouldn't. Actually, I'm going to drop them off with his doorman on the way home."

There was a brief moment of silence, then the room erupted, everyone talking at once.

"Are you crazy?!" Olivia exclaimed.

"I can't keep them," I protested.

"Why not?" she said. "You deserve these. This is probably the only good thing he's ever done."

"I agree with Kate, she should return them," said Emma. She gave me a smile. It was nice to have our friendship back. "If she keeps them," she continued, "what message is she giving him?" Emma looked back at me. "Throw them out. I wouldn't even give him the satisfaction of returning them."

David scowled at her and Olivia looked at her, horrified. "Are you out of your mind?!" She grabbed the other shoe from Emma's hand and clutched them protectively against her chest.

"Ladies, calm down," Elizabeth interrupted. "Kate, are you sure? I'm not going to tell you what to do, but they are gorgeous. If I were your size, I'd take them from you, as you know I'm such a caring and giving friend. But you'll know what to do." She smiled at me.

"What the fuck is that supposed to mean?" exclaimed David. At that moment, Sandra walked in, giving us disapproving stares. "Sorry, Sandra. What is wrong with you people? It's a shoe! Kate, keep them and wear them proudly. And every time you take a step, know that you're stepping on his bleeding, cheating heart." He turned to Emma. "And you, I never, ever, want to hear from you the suggestion to throw out a pair of shoes like these again. Atrocious!"

Sandra looked at us. "Ladies, could you lower your voices, and that includes you, David dear. We can hear you at the desk," she said. As she glanced at the shoes, her eyes opened wide. "They're beautiful," she added.

I took a look at her feet. No question they were Collinses but I had a good hunch that Sandra was wearing them because it was part of the uniform. She seemed to me like the kind of woman who appreciated shoes like these. An idea popped into my head. I looked over at David, and it seemed like the same idea must have occurred to him, because he gave me a little nod.

"Sandra, what's your shoe size?" I asked

"Four," she answered, confirming my suspicion—she was my size. I turned to Olivia and extended my hand for the shoes. I could see she had a strong grip on them. Reluctantly, she gave them back to me and I placed them in the box.

"Here," I said, handing her the shoes.

"Oh no, darling, I…" she began to protest.

"I insist, please. Wear them to your granddaughter's wedding and enjoy," I heard myself saying, placing the box in her hands.

"Take them and run, before any of these crazy girls end up cutting them to pieces with scissors or something," said David with a grin.

I gave her an encouraging smile and opened the bag for her to place them in. She did so and slowly took the bag from me.

"Thank you so much," she said, and hugged me tightly. "I know I will find the perfect outfit for them!" She thanked me again and headed out. The girls were still looking at me, shocked. And I had to say I was a little stunned myself.

"That was a very nice thing you just did," Emma said, breaking the silence.

I sat down. "Oh, don't faint on us now," Elizabeth said, taking a piece of paper and fanning me with it.

"I can't believe I did that," I said, exhaling heavily. My hands were shaking.

Olivia looked unhappy. "Me neither. I can't believe you just gave them away like that!"

"Are you okay?" Emma asked me.

"Yeah, I am, actually. I just need a moment." I closed my eyes for a few seconds. It was the right thing to do. Even if I had given Jack the shoes back again, he would only have returned them. It would have turned into an endless cycle until they ended up on my closet shelf, reminding me of what I had left behind or what could have been. When I opened my eyes, I found David's blue eyes peering at me.

"I hope you're not thinking about asking for the shoes back—I won't let you," he warned me.

"I'm not going to ask for them back. It was the right thing to do—she'll appreciate them more than I ever will."

"So, I'm assuming you sang 'hit the road, Jack'," David said, leaning back on the pillow.

I rolled my eyes at him. "Yeah, you could say that."

Olivia had tears streaming down her cheeks. "Stupid hormones," she sniffed.

"I still can't believe you're pregnant," Emma said, then looked at Olivia's feet. She was in full-on stilettos. "Shouldn't you be in flats or something?"

"Why? I'm pregnant, my feet still work. Besides, I'm not even showing yet—and if it's a girl, I want her to love heels. I read that if I wear heels now, the trait will pass on to her."

"Just what the world needs, a mini Olivia. God help us all," David said. Olivia hit his arm. "Oi, watch it, I'm injured here!" he cried.

"I'm proud of you, Kate. That gesture says you're finally closing the chapter on Jack. Now you can move on to that other guy." Elizabeth gave me a wink.

Olivia's head snapped my way. "What other guy?"

"Philip Spencer," David answered.

"Hey, I never said… how do you know about that?" I immediately asked him.

"You kissed him, didn't you?" He eyed me with a knowing look.

I looked at him in disbelief. Sometimes David shocked you with what he knew, it was like he had psychic abilities. "How the hell did you know that?" I asked.

"I know everything about you, Catherine Seeley, remember that. There isn't a move you make that I don't anticipate."

I told them the whole story: my birthday, the kiss… everything.

"I don't know what to tell him. And frankly, what can I

say? 'I think I like you…maybe'?" I scratched my head. "I'm so confused at the moment. This is a guy I thought I hated and he shocked me—not only by kissing me, but by revealing he's liked me since day one."

"There's a thin line between love and hate," Elizabeth said. "The question is, what are you going to do about it?"

"Babe, I think it's time you tried on a different pair of shoes for a change," Emma said. I smiled.

Chapter Thirty-four

Friday finally arrived, and I walked to Philip's office, half expecting to find him with a frown on his face. Only he wasn't there—he had left a message telling me to meet him by the stairs of the National Gallery at noon.

I had contemplated all evening whether or not to bring up the kiss and how I felt about him. I had thought of practically nothing else but what I was going to say to him… and I had decided I was going to do it. He had opened that door and I was going to apologize and say I had no idea how he felt about me… I also needed to say I'd been a blind fool in not recognizing my feelings before.

I headed towards the National Gallery with a knot in my stomach, rehearsing my speech. I spotted Philip standing in the centre of the staircase overlooking Trafalgar Square. As soon as he saw me, he lifted his hand in a frozen wave. I was surprised to see him casually dressed on a workday, and from the looks of it, he was riding his bike again.

"I didn't realize it was casual Friday today," I said with a smile, stopping at the step below him.

"I'm not working today," he said.

"I don't believe it. You, slacking off? What's the world coming to?" I said.

"Even workaholics need a break now and again," he grinned, reminding me of our conversation that day. This was a perfect opportunity to begin what I needed to say. The sun shone on my face and I squinted, avoiding the rays as I looked up at him. Suddenly, I remembered I still had his jacket, which I needed to return to him, but instead of starting with that, I went in full defense mode.

"Well, now that I'm here, what did you want to discuss?" I began, mentally kicking myself.

"How about we take a stroll?" He looked at my shoes. "Or not… I don't want to be responsible for another breakage."

I laughed. "Technically, you weren't to blame for that, the heel was already loose," I admitted.

He grinned. "That's not what you implied last time."

"I'm sorry about that, completely different circumstances," I added. "*But* I can walk in these with no problems."

"Fair enough, but to be safe, allow me…" He extended his arm and I linked mine through it, feeling myself shiver. We walked down the steps and my heart actually fluttered. "I know a little cafe across the street called the Crypt, if you're interested," he said with a cute smile.

"Never heard of it," I teased.

"Hmmm…" was all he said. His mind seemed to wander for a moment and I stopped walking.

"Philip, what is this about?" I asked, not being able to take the suspense any longer.

"Are you sure you don't want to have a cup of tea? I know how you love your tea," he said, and I could see for the first time that he was nervous.

"I'd rather sit out here," I said softly. I looked over at the bench in front of us and took a seat. Right, it was now or never I needed to say it.

"Is this about the Thomson deal, because I can assure you we're ready for the annual meeting. You'll be here, right?" I said instead, cursing myself for chickening out once again. Perhaps this was why he'd chosen to meet here—the Thomson offices were nearby.

"Actually, I won't be here. That's what I wanted to talk to you about," he said, sitting down next to me. I felt disappointed that he wasn't going to bring up our kiss, and at the same time I felt relieved I hadn't said anything since it didn't seem to be on his mind.

"You're heading back to New York?" I asked.

"Yes."

"I hear a 'but' coming…" I said. He turned his head to look at me, his expression changing.

"I've resigned."

I threw my head back and laughed, waiting for him to join me, but he didn't.

"You're serious?" I said, my laughter ceasing.

"Yes, I am. As of this morning, it's official" he said with a sigh of relief.

I stood up quickly. "But you can't, you're a Spencer. Your name is on the stationary, for crying out loud!" This had to be a joke.

He let out a small laugh. "My surname was on the stationary long before I was born, and it will be there long after I'm gone… I hope. However, I think I'll take your reaction to my resignation as a compliment. A few weeks ago, I think you'd have been the one throwing my going away party."

"I can't believe it," I said, sitting back down next to him. "Why?"

"I've been contemplating leaving the firm for a while now. And when you voiced the fact that I've been hiding under my family's wings, it solidified for me that I needed to do something on my own."

I closed my eyes in regret. "Don't listen to me. I talk a lot, I say silly things when I'm upset. You have nothing to prove, Philip… you're brilliant at your job."

"Thank you for saying that… but it's the truth. I'm sure there are plenty of others who would have liked to tell me. But as you say, given that I'm a *Spencer,* they didn't have the nerve."

"So you're opening a firm here in London?" I asked.

"No, New York."

I was speechless. Of all the things I'd expected him to say to me today, that had not been on the list. To think that my mean comments had actually driven Philip to do this made me feel horrible. I had misjudged him and treated him unfairly. I lowered my head in shame.

"Hey," he lifted my chin up. Our eyes locked. "I made this decision, not you. Don't think for a second that your words forced me. You just pointed out what I'd already been struggling with. But there's actually one more piece of news I have to share with you."

"There's more? Are you joining Hell's Angels?"

"Very funny. No, not yet anyway," he laughed. I didn't laugh with him. "I did, however, use the influence of my surname for this next bit."

I didn't ask what. His moving to New York had shocked me. The one thing I'd always counted on with Philip was that when he headed to the Big Apple, he always came back.

"Don't you want to know what it is?" he prodded.

He was going to tell me whether I wanted to hear it or not. Perhaps he was going to announce he was getting married. I straightened up as panic set in.

"Let me be the first to say I'm looking at Spencer & Lockhart's new Senior Vice

President." He grinned as he waited for the news to sink in.

"I don't understand..."

"You've said that you have worked hard and can do more ...well, here's your chance to prove it."

"What?" I asked in disbelief as his words finally sank in. "No, Philip, that is ludicrous. I can't take your job."

"Yes, you can. It's a done deal. You've earned it."

"But..."

"No buts. You've been, and *are,* an extremely valuable asset. I merely pointed out to the board that if we didn't promote you, we would lose you to another firm. Jackson may be many things, but he was right in trying to take you... he knew what an asset we had with you. And besides, I like my money, and I know you'll look after it," he tried to joke.

My head was spinning. "I don't know what to say," I admitted.

"I was expecting you to run off to the shoe shop and –"

I cut him off, hitting his shoulder lightly. "Punk," I said. We both laughed.

"I'm going to miss you, Catherine. Everything about you... your quirky ways, your sharp tongue and... just you really," he admitted, getting serious.

How could I not have noticed that he wasn't who I'd imagined him to be? *Tell him*, my inner voice said to me. *Just admit that you made a mistake and that his kiss is still on your mind as vividly as if it had happened only moments ago.* His blue eyes stared at me, waiting for me to say something. But now it wouldn't seem genuine. He believed in me, had vouched for me, and had trusted that when he nominated me for the position, I would get the job done. Timing was everything, and somehow the time just didn't feel right. As much as I wanted to tell him I felt something for him, that perhaps in another time and place we would have had a shot at dating, I couldn't do that now. He was moving, and who knew if in the end we were even compatible. I knew there was only one thing to say.

"Thank you, Philip, for everything." I extended my hand and he took it. But instead of shaking it, he leaned down and kissed it. "First and foremost a gentleman, aren't you?" I asked.

"For you… always."

Closing my eyes, I pulled him in, hugging him tightly.

Chapter Thirty-five

Three months had passed since Philip's departure. I kept in touch with him with the occasional email. And for now, the regret of not confessing to him was gone. I was busy with all the changes in my life and, at the moment, that was enough for me.

Today, however, I was going to take a gigantic step. It was time. I still believed in my four types of shoe, but perhaps now the expectations were different. Sometimes one needed to look outside the box, look beyond the shoes. Because, let's face it, our style and type were always changing. And thank goodness for that—imagine how boring life would be if they didn't. I was a work in progress and I was happy with that definition of myself. I'd learned many lessons in the past year.

I opened my umbrella as I headed out the door: nothing new… a typical London rainy day, but today that wasn't going to get me down. I looked down at my feet and at my Jimmy

Choo Hunter rain boots the gang had bought for me for my birthday. The note had simply read, "If you must wear them... wear them in style." I smiled as I recalled it.

My mobile rang and I answered without looking at the screen—only one person would call me this early on a Saturday.

"Yes, David, I am on my way."

"Are you sure you don't want me to go with you? I feel like this is a monumental moment and it should at least be photographed or something."

"We decided that it was best if I went alone, remember?" Now that I'd said it, I doubted my decision. Perhaps I should have let him come with me. If there was anyone who would make sure I followed through, it was David.

"What are you doing?" I asked him quickly, about to beg him to meet me after all. There was nothing David liked better than being told he was right.

"Waiting for Richard to get out of the shower," he sighed into the phone. "He takes forever. But on a positive note, I tested it, and it's working," I could hear him grinning.

"Tested what?" Immediately, my eyes opened in realisation. "Never mind!" I said, stopping him before he could tell me all the details.

He laughed. "Let's just say Richard is very happy."

"I haven't even had a cup of tea yet. Too much info—remember what we talked about?" I reminded him of the pact we'd made, which he always seemed to conveniently forget when he wanted to shock me... which was almost all the time these days. Secretly, I hoped he never changed, but I would never tell him that. I thought of what had happened to him since the accident. Despite his protests, he'd found that his classic look 'could co-exist with a funky style' and was giving Richard a chance... until he got over his newfound discovery, that is.

"Why haven't you eaten?" he asked.

"I'm too nervous. This is a big deal for me. Let's talk about something else. Like are you bringing Richard to the engagement dinner?"

I still couldn't believe Emma and Henry had got engaged. She was the happiest I had ever seen her. She stood up for herself and she knew what she wanted, even though it took us time to understand that what she wanted was Henry. But that was the truth about friends: sometimes we didn't give the best advice. What we wanted for someone else might not be what's best for them, and Emma had proven that.

"But of course! Speaking of engagements, Sandra sent me a picture of herself at the wedding. She looked amazing. Wait until you see her in the shoes. There's a picture here for you as well."

I smiled. "They certainly belong to her. I'm glad she was able to enjoy them."

"You did good, darling. I'll see you later, okay?"

"Okay."

I hung up, thinking of those shoes. Jack was still in the process of starting his new business and was doing quite well. I hadn't talked to him because, frankly, there was nothing left to say. And I needed time to break away completely and find myself. Olivia was starting to look pregnant, though she was still wearing towering heels, and Elizabeth was back at Oxford. Everything was back to normal—and I liked it.

Not too long later, I found myself staring at my destination: Christian Louboutin. My knees felt wobbly as I opened the door to the store.

The salesman greeted me. "May I help you?"

"She'll take the simple pumps, patent-leather, black, size 37, four-inch heel," I heard a familiar voice say behind me.

I spun around. David was standing there, smiling at me. I threw myself at him, squealing.

"I can't believe you're here!"

"How could you think I'd miss this?"

"I don't know, I'm just happy you're here," I admitted.

"I know you better than you know yourself—which is something you can't say about me. I knew you would call me to come so I saved you the trouble. I feel like this is your rebirth."

"I don't like you, you know that," I joked.

"Please, you can't live without me. Imagine how boring your life would be if I weren't in it," he said, and pushed my hair to the side. I smacked his hand away. He never failed.

"I suppose that's true. Who else could make me feel so inadequately dressed most days?" I said.

"Well, if it wasn't for me, you'd still be wearing those boring outfits."

"You were doing so good by being here, don't ruin it." I batted my eyelashes at him.

"Point taken."

He crossed his arms, waiting for me to try on the shoes. I'd been waiting for this moment for ages. It was time I took the plunge and got the shoes I'd been comparing every other to. They were shiny, classic and beautiful, and from the moment I stepped into them, I couldn't stop smiling. I stood up, looking in the mirror.

"If I was capable of emotion, I think I'd maybe cry," David teased. "How do they feel?"

"Amazing!" I walked around the store, feeling like a model. I could feel the attitude setting in as I walked back towards David. "They're perfect, they are absolutely perfect." I walked around a bit more, feeling much taller than I was, feeling like I was walking on air.

I looked at the price and David took the credit card out of my hands.

"Charge it, quickly," he said flirtatiously to the salesman. Like I said, some things never changed.

I looked down at my feet, taking in the moment. I'd found the perfect Darcys and had learned a very valuable lesson. A true stiletto-lover knows that it's not the shoe that causes you pain; it's down to the wearer to learn when to take them off.

The End

About the Author

E.V. Hewitt works in the financial sector, lives in New York City, and visits London frequently. E.V. loves *Pride and Prejudice* and, of course, shoes…on sale, steeply discounted. To get more information on the book and the upcoming sequel connect now at: www.evhewitt.com

Printed in Great Britain
by Amazon